DO NOT REMOVE
CARDS FROM POCKET

STRANGE FELONY

STRANGE FELONY

ELIZABETH LININGTON

PUBLISHED FOR THE CRIME CLUB BY
DOUBLEDAY & COMPANY, INC.
GARDEN CITY, NEW YORK
1986

All of the characters in this book
are fictitious, and any resemblance
to actual persons, living or dead,
is purely coincidental.

Library of Congress Cataloging-in-Publication Data
Linington, Elizabeth.
    Strange felony.
    I. Title.
PS3562.I515S83   1986   813'.54   85-20590
ISBN 0-385-23265-9

This one is for my faithful typist
Dottie Ritt
with many thanks

To expect the unexpected shows a thoroughly
modern intellect.
—*Oscar Wilde*

Everyone's queer but me and thee, and sometimes
I think thee is a little queer.
—*Quaker proverb*

STRANGE FELONY

CHAPTER ONE

Maddox had been out on the legwork most of this Friday, and came back to the Hollywood division station about three o'clock. D'Arcy had just turned into the parking lot ahead of him. Maddox looked into Ellis' office as he came down the hall; it was empty, but there were a couple of manila envelopes on Ellis' desk. He collected them and went on down to the communal detective office. D'Arcy was just settling down to his typewriter, looking gloomy.

"George hasn't been in."

"So I deduce," said Maddox.

D'Arcy leaned back and stretched his long lank form in the desk chair. "You know," he said seriously, "I think he's looking worse than just after it happened, Ivor."

Maddox sat down at his desk. "It can't be a thing to get over quick or easy," he said, passing a hand over his jaw, and his tone was somber.

A terrible thing had happened to the Ellises a couple of months ago. Their only child, bright and good-looking twenty-year-old Roy, in his second year at UCLA, on his way home from a date with his girl one Saturday night, had met a drunk driver on the Hollywood freeway. The drunk, of course, had sustained minor cuts and bruises; Roy had died in surgery an hour later. These days, Administration and everybody at Hollywood division was looking the other way and giving Ellis time, not taking official notice of his absences.

Maddox thought about his very new son, John Ivor, at home, and said sadly, "Not an easy thing, D'Arcy." Bad enough to lose a baby, a child, but a son you had raised—the memories of babyhood, of childhood—a grown son on the verge of adulthood and an adult career—He said heavily, "I don't suppose you got anything."

"Need you ask?" said D'Arcy. "Not one damn thing."

"It'll go into Pending. We'll never get anything on it."

It was César Rodriguez's day off. The other detectives were all apparently out on other things; they had the usual heists to work, the burglaries, and this new homicide, which wasn't going to come to anything.

"This'll be the last report on Burton," said D'Arcy dispiritedly. "It's a dead end." He rolled the triplicate forms into the typewriter and contemplated them without starting the report immediately.

That rather messy homicide had showed up on Monday, the corpse of a young woman in a cheap apartment on Oakwood Avenue. The manager had noticed the apartment door was open halfway, hadn't thought much about it for a couple of days, finally investigated and found the woman dead. He didn't know anything about her. She had rented the apartment two weeks previously, paid him in cash, and given the name of Rose Burton. She looked to be about twenty-five, dark-haired, Caucasian, a nice figure, and he said pretty good-looking; that, you couldn't judge now; she'd been strangled and beaten. And there'd been nothing in the place to give them any leads at all. Anonymous clothes, costume jewelry, no identification at all, no Social Security card, no record of a bank account, credit cards, no address book. She had told the manager she had just come to California from Ohio. There were a lot of towns in Ohio. N.C.I.C. hadn't any record of a Rose Burton reported missing from Ohio or anywhere else. And, they had learned just this morning, nobody knew her fingerprints, the FBI didn't have them. If she'd had a criminal record anywhere, ever served in the armed services, ever had a security clearance, the Feds would have had her prints. But there were millions of citizens still who had never been printed, living humdrum respectable lives. Her name might have been Rose Burton or it might not have been. Among the few possessions in the cheap apartment had been no letters, no personal items at all.

"It's a dead end," repeated D'Arcy, lighting a cigarette. "I talked to all those tenants again, and it was a waste of time."

"Yes," said Maddox. "It'll go into Pending, we'll never get any further on it." They didn't know anything about the woman and never would. The absence of a Social Security card made it look as if she could have been a hooker; it could have been the casual pickup who'd killed her; but there was really nothing to back that up either. It could have been a personal motive, the killer removing all her identification. It was all up in the air.

D'Arcy started to type the report, which would probably be the final one, and Sergeant Feinman came in looking disgruntled; he slouched into his desk chair. Maddox asked disinterestedly, "The same ring? It sounded that way."

"Oh, say it in spades," said Feinman grouchily. "And no leads at all." His lean dark intellectual face wore a morose expression.

"The mysteries," said Maddox, and yawned. The only mysteries they generally had—contrary to the tenets of popular fiction—were like that one: just the blank crimes with no leads from the lab or street informants, nothing complex. The burglary ring Feinman had been working on for three months was one like that, and frustrating.

"They knocked out the electricity again. It was an appliance store down on Vermont. They got away with a couple of air conditioners, some calculators, and tape recorders and radios. I left Garcia dusting for prints but you know he'll get damn all."

The burglaries, of course, went on forever, but this ring was a little different from the general run of burglars. The consensus was that there were two or three of them, considering the size of the stolen merchandise. Comparing the M.O. with other divisions, Hollywood had come to the conclusion that their first hits had been out in Valley division back in March, where they had hit a garden supply store for lawn mowers, and then a big hardware store for air conditioners and small appliances. Since then they'd been operating in central Hollywood. The M.O. tied all the jobs to the same ring, and it was a fairly smart operation. Burglars tended to be rather simpleminded, but these operators were halfway smart. A good many businesses these days had burglar alarms connected to the local police divisions, and all but one of the places hit had had those. But where many newer buildings had all the electric connections, the box of circuit breakers, inside the premises, a good many older buildings still had those outside, at the rear of the building. The burglars had simply tripped all the circuit breakers, knocking out the alarm systems, and jimmied the rear doors at their leisure.

It was another blank, where they would probably never come up with any useful lead, and Feinman, who had an orderly mind, was feeling annoyed about it.

"Well, just one of those things," said Maddox. He sat up and looked at the two manila envelopes from Ellis' desk. Somebody ought to look at the mail.

"George hasn't been in?" said Feinman. "A hell of a thing—he's looking worse than just after it happened."

"Yes. Not a thing to get over quick or easy." Maddox slit open the first envelope, and it contained the autopsy report on Rose Burton. He looked it over and said without emphasis, "Hell. Nothing." He handed it to D'Arcy.

The coroner gave them a handful of nothing. She had been in the mid-twenties, she hadn't been a virgin but had never borne a child, healthy young woman with no evidence of drug or alcohol abuse. Cause of death manual strangulation, evidence of beating before death, not by any weapon but probably male fists. There had been no prior sexual intercourse. Estimated time of death between six and midnight last Saturday. All of which was not much help. Nobody in the apartment house had known her, and the chances were they would never find out anything else about her.

Feinman started reluctantly to type a report.

Sergeant Daisy Hoffman drifted into the communal office from the smaller office across the hall and asked, "How's the family?" Trim and blond, she didn't look like the grandmother she was.

"Oh, fine," said Maddox.

"We had another molestation case show up this morning. People. Janitor at a public school. Helen's still out talking to the parents."

Administration had sent them a fill-in for Sue, who was off on maternity leave: Detective Helen Waring. She was a tall thin blonde in her mid-thirties, serene and very efficient, a divorcée with a ten-year-old daughter, and they all liked her. Having got burned once, she wasn't remotely interested in another man, and was all business.

Maddox yawned again and said, "The rate's up. Satan finding work for idle hands."

"And making one hell of a lot of paperwork," said Daisy.

And the weekend approaching, there would probably be a few new heists and assorted mayhem coming up for the detectives to work. Maddox felt tired. As expectable in July, the heat was beginning to build in Southern California, and from now on they could expect the usual foretaste of hell until the middle of October. Cars and buildings were air-conditioned, but in the nature of things there was always the legwork to do on the street. They had four recent heists to work, the remainder of the paperwork on a suicide and an unidentified body, the burglary ring and a few other more anonymous burglaries as well, and inevitably there would be other things coming up.

Daisy drifted back to her own office, complaining about paperwork, and Bill Nolan came in. "We'll never get anywhere on this Burton thing," he said. "I've been talking to some of those other tenants again. Nobody knows a damn thing about her."

"I know, I know," said Maddox. "Dead end." Indolently he slit open the second manila envelope. It had been sent up from the Public Relations office at Central Headquarters downtown. He looked at the contents and said, "Oh, for God's sake. For God's sake."

"Don't tell me something new," said Nolan.

"My God," said Maddox. He read it all over again with slightly more attention. The covering letter from the PR director was rather dry in tone, and brief. Maddox could imagine the polite, brief letter he had sent to this woman, pithily thanking her for her intended help. Conceivably he had passed on copies of her letter to Hollywood and Hollenbeck divisions to give everybody a little laugh. There wasn't, of course, anything they could do about it.

The first Xerox was a flyer issued by the sheriff of Jefferson County, Montana. It had been issued last February, and it was about a missing juvenile: Alice Robard, fourteen, presumed abducted on the way home from school. She lived on a farm outside Centerville, and had about a mile to walk from the school bus stop. At that time of winter her father or older brother would usually meet her there to drive her home, but on February 3 the farm pickup truck had broken down and her father had been about thirty minutes late meeting her. There had been no sign of her since. She was not presumed to be a runaway, a sensible family-oriented girl of religious bent, involved with the 4-H program, not yet dating any boys. Presumably it was fairly empty country around there; no one had seen her, no one knew what had happened to her, no body had been found.

The second Xerox was a letter to the Chief from a Mrs. Doris Ratcliff in Wakefield, Massachusetts. It was a very literate letter, neatly typed, almost apologetic in tone. "Dear Sir, I do not know whether you are familiar with my name or sympathetic to psychic matters but through my psychic gifts I have been instrumental in assisting a number of police departments in locating missing bodies and persons. I enclose letters from several police officers attesting to this, if it should be of interest to you." The letters were from various high-ranking of-

ficers in New Jersey, Kansas, Iowa, and Missouri, all warmly praising
the psychic assistance of Mrs. Ratcliff in locating a crashed private
plane, a runaway juvenile, two bodies of a homicide, and a suicide.
"The parents of Alice Robard had heard of my abilities and requested
that I try to pinpoint her whereabouts through psychic means. I have
attempted to do so, and feel quite positive that the girl is still alive. She
was abducted the day she vanished, and is being held captive, subjected
to sexual abuse. I have the very strong conviction that she is in the Los
Angeles area, somewhere in the city of Hollywood. I hope that this may
be of assistance to the Los Angeles police in searching for her."

"For the love of God!" said Maddox, passing all that over to Nolan.

Nolan looked it over and grunted disgustedly. "A psychic, for God's
sake. Why in hell the PR office bothered to send it on—"

"Oh, don't knock the psychic bit, Bill," said Maddox seriously.
"These people do sometimes get things, all right. In fact, I've heard of
this woman—I think somebody wrote a book about her—she's helped
some departments in locating people, as she says. But for the Lord's
sweet sake—I don't know how big a town she's living in, but does she
have any conception what's she's talking about, the city of Hollywood?" He thought of the thousands of streets, the backwaters, the
main drags running through this big town, just part of the even vaster
area that was greater Los Angeles. "On top of all our other business,
drop everything to look for this kid—and no way to do that anyway."

There wasn't, of course, anything to do about it at all. The psychic
lady might be right, Alice Robard might be here, but there was no way
—physically or legally—the police could try to find out.

"You don't mean you really buy this psychic bit?" said Nolan.

"Oh, it's there. With some people. But not always reliable, and even
if she's right there's nothing we can do about this."

Nolan shrugged. "I've been going round and round on this heister,
too. The funny one. The latest victim couldn't make any mug shots
downtown. If you ask me, whatever pedigree he's got it's somewhere
else, he's just landed here, and we haven't got enough on him to ask
N.C.I.C."

"That one," said Maddox, not much interested. Sometimes the legwork, and persistence, turned up the heisters: not always. By the
description, this one had hit three times in the last six weeks, and they
had turned up no leads on him at all.

Nolan started typing a report. Feinman was on the phone. It was nearly three-thirty, and nobody seemed to have accomplished a damn thing today, but that was often par for the course. The phone rang on Maddox's desk and he reached for it resignedly.

"Sergeant Maddox."

The dispatcher down in Communications said, "You've got a new homicide. The squad just called in."

"So what's the location?" Maddox reached for a pen.

It was an address out on Wilshire. Maddox stood up and said to D'Arcy, "No rest for the wicked. We've got a new body."

"Oh, hell," said D'Arcy, unfolding his lean long self from the type-writer. "They might have let me finish this damn report."

They took Maddox's Pontiac. It was one of the high-rise office build-ings on that main drag, and there were two black and white squads in a loading zone in front. One of the uniformed men, Dunning, was wait-ing for them, a stocky, fair, serious-faced young fellow. "It's the ninth floor, sir," he said to Maddox. "A lawyer—a Leonard Coldfield. By what we heard—Gonzales and I got chased out here about half an hour ago—some woman just came into the office and shot him. There are a couple of secretaries, they're both in a tizzy and couldn't tell us much. Gonzales is up there trying to preserve the scene for you."

"All right, thanks," said Maddox, "we'll take it from here, you can get back on tour." But the Traffic shift was just about to change at four o'clock, and the two uniformed men would be heading back to the station to go off duty.

They rode the elevator up to the ninth floor and found a little crowd being held at bay, efficiently, by Gonzales. Most of the tenants in a building like this would be professional people. The shots had brought them out to the hall and there were fifteen or twenty people there asking questions and excitedly comparing notes, both sexes and all ages.

Gonzales was looking a little harassed. "I've kept everybody out," he told Maddox and D'Arcy, "but the secretaries are still in there. I haven't started to get any names—Don and I only got here about twenty minutes ago."

"And you're coming to end of shift," said Maddox. "All right, leave it—we'll get the names."

Offices here would run to some money; all these tenants would be successful professional people. This door bore the gold-painted identifi-cation Leonard Coldfield, Attorney at Law. Maddox raised his voice to the little crowd. "We'd be obliged if you'd all go back to your own offices, we'll want to talk to you eventually but not right now." They began to disperse reluctantly. The outer office door was half open and he asked Gonzales, "Was it like that when you landed here?"

"That's right."

"Well, you'd better call the lab from the squad, there just might be some prints." He and D'Arcy went in, to find themselves in a square anteroom rather elegantly furnished, with a small reception desk, a love seat and two upholstered chairs, a cheerful landscape painting above the love seat. Two women were huddled together on the love seat. One was plump and dark, about forty, the other one younger and blond. Both had been crying, and they both looked shocked and scared.

"All right, we're detectives," said Maddox. "May we have your names, please? What can you tell us about what happened?"

The older one said, "I'm Marion Haskell. I'm Mr. Coldfield's secretary. This is Harriet Fowler, she's the receptionist. But she just walked in and *shot* him! She just came in—a perfectly strange woman—and Harriet tried to stop her—"

"She didn't say a word!" said the younger woman. "I couldn't believe it—she came in, and I started to say good afternoon and did she want an appointment and—you know, the usual things— And she barged right by me and started for Mr. Coldfield's office—he was dictating to Marion—and I said, excuse me, but you can't see Mr. Coldfield now—and she said, just like that she said, you go to hell, and she opened the door and barged right in, and the next thing, just the next second, there were all the shots—"

"He was dictating Mrs. Albrand's will, and all of a sudden this woman came in, and she wasn't more than inside the door when there were all these shots—I didn't believe what was happening—and Mr. Coldfield fell out of his chair and I saw she had a gun in her hand—I didn't believe it—and then she ran right out—and Harriet started to scream and I went to see if Mr. Coldfield was hurt—and he's dead! He's dead! I couldn't believe it—" She began to sob. "I'd worked for him for fifteen years, such a fine man, a good man—"

Maddox and D'Arcy went into the inner office. It was handsomely appointed with a big flat-topped mahogany desk, a couple of upholstered chairs for clients, the large window presenting a view over the city and the Hollywood hills to the north, brown and dry-looking at this time of year. There was a little sheaf of papers on the desk blotter, and the secretary had dropped her notebook and pen on the other side of the desk. The dead man was lying crumpled at one side of his desk chair; he had fallen from that and died flat on his back on the thick carpet. He was a man in late middle age, rather a good-looking man with a thick crop of silver-gray hair, regular features. His glasses had fallen off and lay unbroken beside him. He was wearing a tailored gray suit, white shirt, and dark tie. The suit jacket was heavily stained with blood.

They looked at him and D'Arcy said, "Fairly heavy caliber. Two or three body shots, maybe more. Needn't have been a marksman at that range and with a big gun."

"See what the lab says."

They went out to the anteroom again. "Had either of you ever seen the woman before?" asked Maddox.

They shook their heads at him numbly. "Neither of us had ever laid eyes on her. She wasn't a client, nobody who'd ever been to the office."

"Could you describe her?"

"It all went so fast," said Harriet Fowler agitatedly. "It just happened—all in about a minute—all I can say is, she wasn't a young woman, maybe in the late forties, around there— But I don't really know— She had on a pink dress, sort of light pink, and her hair was blond—that's all I can say, I'm sure I'd never seen her anywhere before —I never saw the gun, she must have been getting it out of her purse when she went past me—"

"I saw it, just about for two seconds," said Marion Haskell. She had a handkerchief out, wiping her eyes. "She came in, and I looked up, and then there were all the shots—I don't know how many, I was so startled and scared—and I saw the gun—I don't know anything about guns, but it looked awfully big and black—and then she turned and ran out—"

"And we were both thinking about Mr. Coldfield, I ran in there and Marion said, he's dead, and neither of us believed it—and Marion said we had to call the police, and we both went out to the corridor but there wasn't a sign of her, she'd gone, she'd got away—so then I called the police—"

"Did the woman say anything to Coldfield?" asked D'Arcy.

"No, she didn't say anything, she just came in and *shot* him—I can't understand it—he was such a fine man—I worked for him fifteen years, such a good kind man—he was so well thought of—and such a good practice, it's just not possible that anyone would have a reason to murder him—"

They both said it all over again. Maddox told them they would want statements, and both the women agreed to come to the station tomorrow for that. Garcia arrived with all the bulky lab equipment and started to take photographs. It was unlikely there would be any useful prints; Mrs. Haskell said the woman hadn't approached the desk, just blazed away from inside the door. By what both women said, the woman was out to the corridor and not in sight by the time the other nearby office people had come out, alerted by the shots, so it probably wouldn't be any use to question them, but it would have to be tried, of course.

But on the face of it, whoever had shot respectable, highly-thought-of Leonard Coldfield had probably had a personal motive of some kind. Maddox asked about relatives. "Oh yes, he was married and there's a son and daughter," said Mrs. Haskell. "Such a terrible thing—his poor wife—oh, the house is on Elevado Avenue in West Hollywood—"

Maddox left D'Arcy talking to the people in the next office, a firm of architects, and found a public phone in the lobby. He called the station and got hold of Daisy, explained the situation. "You want a female to help break the news," said Daisy, "but what a funny thing, Ivor. Just walking in and shooting the man. All right, what's the address? I'll meet you there."

Maddox called Sue at home and told her he would be a little late. "Explain when I see you. Rather a funny one just broke."

"Well, it's just beef stew and salad, it'll keep," said Sue. "We'll expect you when we see you, darling."

The address on Elevado Avenue matched the handsome office of Leonard Coldfield; it was a big Spanish stucco with a red-tiled roof, a neatly manicured lawn in front. Daisy was waiting for Maddox in her car at the curb. One of the dirty jobs the police came in for was breaking the bad news to the relatives. They walked up the curving brick walk and Maddox pushed the doorbell.

In a few moments the front door opened and they faced a middle-aged woman. She had a rather thin haggard face, but was well dressed in a navy pantsuit, with discreet makeup and costume jewelry. "Yes?"

"Mrs. Coldfield?" Maddox showed her the badge. "I'm Sergeant Maddox and this is Sergeant Hoffman. I'm afraid we have some bad news for you."

Her pale blue eyes widened at them. "Police—oh, you'd better come in," she said. And fearfully, "What—what is it?"

Daisy told her gently, and it was a few minutes before shock gave way to grief. She sat huddled on the couch in an expensively furnished living room and sobbed a little into a handkerchief. They gave her time, and when she stopped crying and sat up straighter Maddox asked her, "We don't like to bother you at a time like this, Mrs. Coldfield, but would you have any idea at all who might have had a reason to want to kill your husband?"

She broke down again, and after a while she said in a low voice, "I don't know any names. Oh, I don't like to say it—I'm so ashamed to say it—and I don't know anything at all, any names or anything."

"But you think there may have been someone with some reason to kill him?"

She shook her head blindly; her eyes were closed. She raised the handkerchief again and said brokenly, "I'm so ashamed. To say it. But I suppose I'll have to tell the police. And I don't know any names—because—because—there were different ones. I never knew their names, you see."

"Whose names, Mrs. Coldfield?" asked Daisy.

"Oh, dear," she said. "Oh, dear, it's all so terrible—having to come out—and tell about it. But I—you see—you see, he was always—all our married life—there were always other women. I've got to say it, got to tell you—after this. He was always after other women. I—I began to suspect it—right after we were married. We were married thirty years, but it always went on like that. I knew about it, he even admitted it—a lot of times—but he was my husband, and there were the children, you see. I never did anything about it."

"I see," said Daisy. "You think he'd been seeing some woman lately?"

"Probably," she said forlornly. "I don't know who. Or where, or anything about it. If he'd been—giving her money, anything like that, I'd know because we have a joint bank account. I suppose he'd have given her cash, or just presents. Whoever the latest one was." She blew her nose. "All so terrible—to have to tell you—and Leonard dead—"

They would need a statement from her too, about that. There wasn't any hurry about it; she was upset enough right now. And not withstanding the joint bank account, there might be some record to be found in papers at his office to identify the latest mistress; they'd be looking, and asking around among his friends. When the wife had known about the extracurricular women, even not knowing names, a couple of his male friends may have known a bit more.

"What a thing," said Daisy at the curb, getting out her car keys. "But men—"

"Well," said Maddox reasonably, "you can't lump us all together. We come all shapes and sizes like everybody else. I will say, he was a good-looking fellow, if you could say a corpse is good-looking. Evidently just the born philanderer. And getting tired of the women quick, maybe."

"So he got rid of one of the latest women and she was annoyed about it," said Daisy. "Open and shut. Now you just have to find her. I should think the secretaries would recognize her if you do."

"And I wonder about that. As they both said, it all happened so fast —" Maddox sighed. "Well, the lab will give us something on the gun, for what it's worth. See what shows up. And no damn leads on any of the heisters, and we'll never get anywhere on Burton. She could have been hustling and picked up the wrong john. There's no indication that she had a job anywhere, and when there wasn't a Social Security card—"

"Yes," said Daisy. "On the other hand, she may have been in the process of voluntarily disappearing. From a husband, a boyfriend, a criminal charge."

"Nobody had her prints."

"Says nothing. Ohio. She could be Jane Smith from Manhattan, making a fresh start out here. For whatever reason. And picked up somebody at a bar."

"If she did, we'll never find out who," said Maddox. "The only prints the lab picked up there were hers, there's just nowhere to look on it."

"Well, we can't win 'em all," said Daisy philosophically. "See you." She got into her car and started the engine.

It was six-thirty. Maddox started for home, and of course the rush hour traffic hadn't begun to clear yet; the freeway was crowded. It was forty minutes before he got off into Glendale and up into Verdugo Woodlands, thankfully turned onto Starview Terrace and into the drive of the big old two-story house on that dead-end street.

When he walked in the back door, Sue's mother, Margaret Carstairs, was busy at the stove. He kissed her cheek. "I've kept everything hot for you. You'll want to relax over a drink first." In about twenty years' time Sue was going to look a lot like Margaret, which was fine with Maddox. He built himself a scotch and soda and carried it down to the living room.

There had, of course, been no politely welcoming woof from Tama, the big brindle Akita, as he came in, and he knew why.

The baby had decided to arrive a couple of weeks early, and had entered the world as a patriotic citizen on the Fourth of July. Sue was still in the hospital when Maddox had been tagged to fly to New York and escort an extradited prisoner home for trial. So it had been Margaret who had brought Sue and John Ivor home from the hospital on the following day.

Tama was moderately fond of both the Maddoxes, but as far as he was concerned Margaret was the head of the household. It had been Margaret who had carried the baby into the house for the first time, and Tama had leaped to the simple conclusion that the baby was an adjunct of Margaret, and thus a new and heavy responsibility for a conscientious dog.

It had taken Margaret nearly an hour to persuade him that it was safe to allow Sue to hold and nurse the baby. The fourth time that Maddox had approached the crib to admire his new son only to be confronted by Tama with hackles raised and lip lifted in a menacing growl, he had said plaintively that enough was enough. "I'm very glad to know you're such a zealous watchdog, boy, but after all he's my baby too. Margaret, can't you get it across to the monster that the offspring's quite safe with me?"

Convulsed with laughter, Margaret had succeeded in reassuring Tama, and these days Maddox was allowed to hold the baby. But the reassurances did not extend, in Tama's world, to anybody else. Various people had called to admire the baby, who was a good placid baby with a lot of black hair—Daisy, several policewomen Sue had worked with, Margaret's widowed cousin and her daughter, the elderly Millsoms who lived next door—all to be regarded by Tama with deep suspicion as potential murderers, and not allowed to inspect the baby except from the safety of Sue's or Margaret's arms. Taking his responsibility seriously, he had to be coaxed out to the backyard for his usual exercise, and when he was in stayed beside the baby every waking and sleeping moment.

His solid bulk was curled up now beside Sue's armchair, where she was nursing the baby. Maddox bent to kiss her and gazed fondly at the baby, who was nursing happily and silently.

"Good day, darling?"

"Reasonably," said Maddox, settling into the armchair opposite and sampling his drink. "We'd better shove that Burton homicide into Pending. Another one just showed up, I hope we'll get somewhere on it eventually. And the weekend coming up, no bets that we won't get more new business."

"The rat race," said Sue. "It's nice and peaceful to be out of it for a while." She'd be off on maternity leave until December when she would join the other detectives at the station again, and, of course, they were much luckier than so many other couples with the wife working a regular job—they had Margaret to look after the baby. And Tama.

"That dog," said Sue, looking down at him amusedly. "The plumber finally came to fix that sprinkler in back, and I had Johnny out there on a blanket under the tree, it wasn't so terribly hot today. Mother had to stand guard all the time he was here, Tama was so suspicious."

Maddox laughed. "Well, I said when we got him I'd feel safer with a dangerous-looking monster guarding the family."

"So what's the new homicide?"

He started to tell her about it.

It was Ken Donaldson's night off, but the other detectives on night watch came in, Dick Brougham and Roger Stacey. For once the day men hadn't left them any work; evidently they hadn't turned up any more leads on the various heisters or that homicide. Stacey, that much-married family man, had some new snapshots of his kids. They discussed the Burton homicide desultorily; they had both done some legwork on that, and agreed it was dying a natural death, they would never get anywhere on it. "Little mystery," said Brougham.

"Which we sometimes get," agreed Stacey. "Not in the sense of the implausible detective novels, no?" The shapeless mysteries they got to deal with were just blanks, where no lab evidence or information from street snitches turned up any leads; the only mysteries were the mysteries of human motive and personality.

At nine-thirty they got a call from a dispatcher, a heist at a liquor store on Santa Monica Boulevard. They both rolled on it.

It was a fairly big place, obviously prosperous. The owner had been there alone, just preparing to close up at nine o'clock. His name was

Dillman, and he was understandably annoyed. "Listen," he said, "the crime rate these days—and you can say this is a high-risk business, I know that—I've been held up twice before, the last couple of years—you got one of them, I had to go down to a lineup and I picked out the bastard right off, a black guy about twenty-five, one of your dicks told me he had a rap sheet this long, holdups and assaults and God knows what, and he'd only done a couple of years in, these Goddamned judges and all the plea bargains, he got probation and parole—God damn it, he was still on parole when he heisted me that time—the other one you never caught up with. That one was a Mex, just a kid, he could hardly speak English but he had a big gun—you never caught that one."

"Well, what about this one?" asked Brougham. "Can you give us a description? How much did he get?"

"Well, for God's sake, that's just it," said Dillman, sounding exasperated. "I don't know how much he got, I haven't checked the register yet. But for God's sake, with the crime rate the way it is, you expect the heisters to be the crazy young people. On dope, whatever, you know. You sure as hell don't expect the old people to go pulling the heists! And this one, that's what he was. For God's sake, a guy maybe in his fifties, maybe even older."

"Can you describe him?" asked Stacey patiently.

"Well, kind of. He walks in here—I was just getting ready to close up—and he shows me the gun and says, let's have what's in the register —and I was so damned surprised, like I say he was maybe fifty, fifty-five, ordinary-looking guy— Well, hell, I don't know, he was maybe about my size, five-ten, sort of stocky, he had on ordinary clothes and a cap—not a hat, a cap—yes, he was a white man—but at least in his fifties, or older, and you don't expect—"

Maybe you didn't expect. But it wasn't the first Brougham and Stacey had heard about this one, or the day men either. The rather funny heister, older than you would expect a heister to be. He had hit seven places—all liquor stores—in the last three months, by the descriptions they had got.

Dillman said he didn't think he could spot a mug shot. None of the other victims had thought so either. It was all up in the air—not much to do on it.

CHAPTER TWO

On Saturday morning, with Rodriguez back and Feinman off, the latest victim of the burglary ring came in to make a statement. It had been a big office-supply store on Western, and the haul had been respectable, several expensive electric typewriters, calculators, tape recorders and tape decks, CB radios. When the store owner had signed the statement and gone out, D'Arcy checked with the lab and got Franks, who told him irritably that there were only twenty-four hours in the day. "We only got on it yesterday morning, for God's sake. There were a thousand prints in a public place like that, naturally, we've only just started to process them. But it looked like the same M.O. on all the rest of these jobs, we'll probably come up empty. We'll let you know if anything shows."

There was now the new heist to work, from last night, which would probably amount to the paperwork and nothing else.

Dillman came in to make the formal statement about eleven o'clock, and Maddox talked to him with Nolan listening in. When he had gone out Nolan said, "I told you, it's obviously the same guy by the descriptions we've got. A fat fellow in the fifties, kind of a pasty-white face, ordinary sports clothes. I'll give you odds he's just landed here from somewhere else. The computers don't come up with anything on the description, so he isn't wanted for a job anywhere, N.C.I.C. doesn't know him, but nobody suddenly starts pulling heists at that age, he'll be on record somewhere."

Maddox agreed absently. But that was all up in the air, like the Burton thing.

Rodriguez was amused by the psychic lady's letter. "I don't know why the hell PR bothered to pass it along, there's not one damn thing we can do about it. The hell of it is— Oh, I don't discount the psychic ladies—the woman could be right, that poor kid could be here somewhere, but there's no way to look." He was more interested in the new homicide. He listened to Maddox's description, absently stroking his hairline moustache, and said succinctly, "Somebody'll know about Coldfield's latest woman. The secretaries may be able to tell us who his friends are, or of course the wife."

"Probably," said Maddox. "They'll be in sometime today."

They came in together after lunch, to make the formal statements, and they were calmer now and answered questions more coherently but they hadn't any more information to offer them than they had yesterday. The woman had just barged in and shot him. Neither of them had ever seen her before, and they could only give a vague general description—a woman perhaps forty-five or older, blond, in a pink dress. With a big gun.

Mrs. Haskell said blankly, "His friends? Well, I don't know anything about any social friends they had, Mr. Coldfield wasn't one for talking much about his personal life, but I do know one of his oldest friends was Mr. Goldfarb, that's Goldfarb and Wolfe in Santa Monica, they were in law school together, sometimes they met for lunch and I think they played golf together."

Unfortunately when Maddox checked and found Joseph Goldfarb at an address in Beverly Hills, a housekeeper told him that Mr. and Mrs. Goldfarb were on vacation in Europe and not expected home for a couple of weeks.

He had Coldfield's keys, and he and Rodriguez went out to the office on Wilshire and poked around there but didn't come across anything relevant. There was a bankbook showing a respectable balance, a precisely kept ledger, but nothing of a personal nature at all. "And could we expect it?" said Rodriguez. "He wouldn't have left any love letters around, or rent receipts, when the respectable secretary might have come across them, after all."

"Damn it," said Maddox, "he must have let his hair down to at least a couple of pals about all the pretty ladies, somebody must know something."

He talked to Mrs. Coldfield on the phone and she told him the names of some friends, a Mr. and Mrs. Norwood, a Mr. and Mrs. Corey. "Saturday," said Rodriguez. "Ten to one if we find them, they'll both be there, both couples, and it isn't likely the men would open up about the pretty ladies in front of the wives."

In any event, Maddox got no answer at either number, and they trailed back to the office. There, Maddox called the lab and got Baker. "Did the coroner's office send over the slugs from our latest corpse?"

"Yep," said Baker. "I just had a look at 'em a while ago. It was a Colt .38 revolver. Gun hasn't been used much, whatever vintage it is. If you ever come across it, we can match it to the slugs. Whoever did it wanted to make sure, there were four slugs."

They would get an autopsy report eventually. He passed that on to Rodriguez. "Um, the woman scorned," said Rodriguez. "He probably asked for it, chasing around at his age."

"And look who's talking," said Maddox. "When are you going to settle down with some nice girl?"

Rodriguez grinned. "So I play the field, I've never met a girl worth giving up all the rest for, *amigo*. But if I ever do, I trust I've got enough sense of self-preservation not to double-cross a female. They can be dangerous when they get annoyed. I wonder if D'Arcy's still dating that Spanish teacher, by the way."

"He hasn't mentioned her lately," said Maddox, idly amused. D'Arcy, adding to his useful information, had been going to night school studying Spanish, but that would be over for the summer.

It was a slow unproductive day. A couple of witnesses came in on the heist that had gone down on Wednesday night, and gave statements without much in them but general descriptions.

Again, Ellis hadn't been in all day. And at four-thirty Communications called in a new body. Rodriguez went out with Maddox to look at it, and it was a sad and bad thing that wouldn't make them much work but paperwork. The address was an old California bungalow on Berendo, in the middle of town. The woman was a Mrs. Simms, plump and gray-haired, and she wasn't in a very coherent state but talking compulsively. "I called the police and the ambulance, but it seemed just ages before anybody came, just ages, and then the officer said she's dead—it isn't possible, Ruthy dead—" It would have been just at the change of the Traffic shift, the swing watch just coming on at four o'clock. The ambulance had just been leaving when Maddox and Rodriguez arrived. The Traffic man was still there with the body.

"Ruthy dead, it's not true, it can't be true, she's only fourteen, and I don't know where Doug is, he said he was going bowling but he goes different places, I don't know where, and I was out shopping—we're giving a wedding shower for Linda and I had the decorations to get and all the things at the market for sandwiches and punch—she said she didn't feel good, Ruthy I mean, she might be getting a cold, she was still in bed. I made her some iced tea, she didn't want any lunch. I know she'd been feeling sort of low in her mind but I never thought—well, how would I think—a thing like that—kids that age get to feeling depressed about any little thing—they're kind of up and down, you know. Doug said leave her alone and she'd get over it—and I don't know where Linda is either, she went out with Audrey, that's her best friend, they were going to a movie but I don't know which one—"

The body was in the garage, the body of a slightly overweight teenage girl hanging from one of the open beams. The rope looked like thin tough clothesline, and there was a line missing from the clothesline in the backyard. The body was wearing blue jeans and a sleeveless blouse. There was a ladder standing beside it in the center of the garage. The face was darkly swollen, tongue protruding. The body swayed very slightly, suspended in mid-air.

"You know how kids that age are, little things mean an awful lot to them, they get to brooding. Doug said she'll get over it—it was Linda getting engaged, she's our oldest daughter, she's just got engaged to Jim, they're going to be married in August, she just got out of high school last month. And Ruthy, you know how kids are, she had this acne, not bad, it's not really bad, and she thought she was too fat, she was always saying nobody'd ever want to marry her, she was too ugly—and then Linda got engaged—it was silly, she was using some stuff the doctor gave her for her complexion, and I was going to help her with a diet—I never thought of such an awful thing, she just said she didn't feel good, and I went off to do the shopping—the shower tomorrow night, oh, my God, what are we going to do about that? Oh, my God—and when I came home she wasn't in the house, and I went looking—and the ambulance men said she's dead but it can't be—Ruthy—and I don't know where Doug is—"

That told them the gist of the story, and they could get the necessary statements later. But the law had certain prescribed procedures. There would have to be an inquest. Maddox told the Traffic man to call the lab. Baker came out presently and took some photographs. A couple of curious neighbors showed up. Just before the morgue-wagon arrived the husband came home, and about then it all caught up to the mother and she went into belated hysterics and they had to call an ambulance for both of them. It was to be hoped that when the other daughter showed up the neighbors would let her know what had happened.

Maddox would be late again in getting home, and Rodriguez was grumbling about being late picking up his date.

On Saturday night the full night watch was on. Business usually picked up on weekends, and Traffic might be busy out on the street with the brawls and accidents and muggings, but they didn't get a call until nine-forty when a heist went down, at an all-night pharmacy on Vermont. Donaldson went on it with Stacey. The pharmacist was a thin middle-aged man, and he was still scared and shaken.

"I just agreed to hold down the job at night to oblige Mr. Gorman, he's the owner— I don't like night work, don't like leaving my wife alone, but it meant extra money and I said I'd do it to oblige. Now, I don't know. There's never much business at night anyway, I don't know why Mr. Gorman wants to keep the place open at all hours, just for the piddling business comes in. I only had four customers since six o'clock, and then this wild man comes in waving a gun at me, and it's just not worth risking my life. All these violent punks around, I'm going to tell Mr. Gorman I'm not about to risk my life—"

"Can you give us a description of him?" asked Stacey.

He nodded jerkily. "Certainly I can, he was a big black fellow, maybe in his twenties, young anyway, he was about six feet or bigger, and he was high as a kite on something—"

"Drunk?"

"I don't know, I didn't smell any liquor on him but he was strung out on something, some kind of dope I guess, waving that gun around, my God, he could have shot me without knowing he'd done it! I'll be damned if I stay on the night job any longer, it's just too dangerous, all these violent punks around. Well, I don't know that I'd recognize a picture, he was only in here about three minutes. I'm not sure how much there was in the register, not exactly, but it wasn't much. Mr. Gorman had bagged most of the day's take for the night deposit at the bank, just left me enough to make change, and as I say I'd only had four customers in, two prescriptions and a couple of cigarette and cosmetic sales. I don't think there was fifty dollars in the register."

"We'd like you to come in and make a statement," said Donaldson. "Maybe tomorrow. And we can show you some pictures, maybe you would recognize him."

"I don't think so. He was just a big black punk. All right, where do I come?"

They told him. He said the heister hadn't touched the counter or register, so it wouldn't be any use to get a lab man out to dust for prints. They went back to the office and tossed a coin to see who would write the report, and Stacey lost the throw. They didn't get another call the rest of the shift, but the radio turned low on police frequency muttered of assorted violence going on elsewhere—a pileup on the 210 freeway, Highway Patrol business, and the Traffic men on this beat dealing with the bar brawls, the drunks on the street, a couple of muggings. Other places in the city would be hairier. Hollywood was no longer the relatively peaceful police beat it had once been, but it wasn't as bad as Central beat downtown, or Seventy-seventh Street.

There had been a general rerouting of shifts in the last couple of weeks, and Patrolman Johnny McCrea had just come onto the grave-yard shift from swing watch. He supposed somebody had to ride the graveyard shift, but he wasn't enjoying it much. It was damned lonely, the midnight to eight watch. Even in the big city most people were home in bed then. There were still bars open until 2 A.M., and if traffic was light there was still some up to about the middle of the shift, when most of the partygoers and late workers had gone home.

He cruised the mostly empty streets, listening absently for his call number on the radio, feeling lonely. At least when there was traffic on the streets, people around, you had the illusion that you weren't alone. If Hollywood ran two-man cars he would at least have had somebody to talk to, but they hadn't been doing that in years, since McCrea had been on the job.

Another car was sent to a minor brawl at a bar on Melrose, and fifteen minutes later there was a hit-run called in nearly out at the county line, out of his area. He would almost have welcomed a mug-ging or an accident, anything for a little action. He found himself yawning, and reflected resentfully that he would probably be riding this watch for at least six months before the shifts got changed around again. He and Joyce had planned on getting married next month, but with her working a day job at the bank, it wouldn't be a very good beginning to married life. Well, it couldn't be helped. He liked the job and meant to buck for rank, get into the investigative end of the job, come in for the higher pay and that more interesting work.

He was just thinking of calling in a Code Seven and stopping at a twenty-four-hour coffee shop for a sandwich when he got a call, to an address on Tuxedo Terrace. That was a very quiet, good old residential area above Franklin, and the dispatcher just said, unknown trouble. He didn't expect a domestic fight, anything violent, in that area—probably nothing more than a prowler. When he got there, it was a big sprawling ranch-style house, and the porch light was on. A man opened the door to him, a middle-aged man in pajamas and robe. He was tall and bald and he was looking both angry and oddly amused.

"Come in, officer. This is the damnedest thing—" There was a woman sitting on the couch in the living room, a good-looking dark-haired woman with a nice figure, wearing a belted housecoat over a nightdress. She was looking a little dazed. "The damnedest thing," said the man, running a hand over his bald head. "I'm Dr. James Gordon, this is my wife Esther."

"Yes, sir," said McCrea. "What's the complaint?"

The man began to laugh, checked himself, and said, "Well, sit down and we'll tell you."

Listening to the story, McCrea couldn't help himself and began to laugh helplessly. But there wasn't anything he could do about it at this hour. The night watch detectives would be gone by now and it would have to wait until morning. All he could do was tell them not to touch anything, and call it in to one of the dispatchers to retail to the front office day watch. Most of the dispatchers were female, and if they were trained and tough policewomen McCrea didn't exactly feel they would appreciate the joke; but he got Sergeant Sweeney spelling one of the girls on her coffee break, and gave him all the details, and Sweeney guffawed.

"Talk about the damnedest thing, that is one for the books all right. I'll pass it up to the front office boys, at least it'll give them a little laugh."

McCrea was still chortling over it when he went back on tour; and he didn't get another call all night.

Maddox got in a little early on Sunday morning; he wanted to locate those friends of the Coldfields' sometime today if possible, and people had the annoying habit of wandering off to church or the beaches on Sundays. He glanced over the night report—just the one new heist to work—and passed it on to Rodriguez as he came in. Then he found the Traffic report sent up from Communications and laughed, handed that over.

"We'd better do something about this right away, if there's anything for the lab to get—" He called the lab and got Harry Baker, who had just come in.

Rodriguez, giggling, said he'd like to hear a firsthand account, and rode up to Tuxedo Terrace with Maddox. The mobile lab van was just behind them when Maddox pulled into the curb.

Dr. Gordon and his wife had apparently just finished breakfast. "You'll be the detectives," said the doctor, looking at the badges. "Come in. The officer last night said there'd be someone coming to test for fingerprints."

"That's right." Maddox introduced himself, Rodriguez, and Baker. "We understand your burglar may have picked up some jewelry."

"The other officer said not to touch anything, he might have left fingerprints," said Mrs. Gordon. She was, they were all noticing, a nice-looking woman, with an excellent figure, if not young—probably in her late forties, not looking it. She had a pretty round face with a smooth complexion, very blue eyes, a warm contralto voice. She looked at the three strange men and gave a little laugh. "It's just silly—to feel sort of embarrassed about it—we're all adults after all. Jim and I have been married twenty-eight years, we've got a grown son and daughter. All I can say is, it didn't strike me as funny last night, I can tell you. But now —oh well."

He said, "We'd been out to a party. Nothing fancy, an anniversary party for some old friends. Just dinner and the evening—we played some bridge. And it being Saturday night, we didn't start home until after one o'clock. They live in Pacific Palisades. I suppose it was slightly after two when we got home."

"And we were both tired," she said. "We went right to bed. I didn't notice anything wrong, everything looked just as usual, except that the lid of my jewel case was open and I might have left it that way when I was getting dressed. We got undressed and went to bed—I should say we've got twin beds. And I was nearly asleep when all of a sudden I realized Jim had come and got into bed with me and was, well, starting to make love to me—I was a little surprised because he'd said he was tired—but, well, I—well, naturally—"

"Began to cooperate," he said gravely, and his mouth twitched in a grin.

"And I got one arm around his neck, and then—my God—there was all this thick curly hair—and Jim's bald—my God, it wasn't Jim at all, it was a perfectly strange man! Right there in bed with me—and I just panicked, I heaved myself up to throw him off and I screamed—and he jumped off the bed—and then Jim woke up—"

"Startled the hell out of me," said Gordon. "I'd dropped off right away, I was dead to the world, didn't know where I was for a couple of seconds. Then I said what the hell's the matter or something—"

"And I got the lamp on, and there wasn't a sign of him, but then we heard the back door—the hinges need oiling—and we looked, but he was gone."

"An amorous burglar," said Baker deadpan.

"And then I remembered the jewel case being open and looked, and I could see there were things missing, rings and bracelets. I'd just taken off the few pieces I was wearing and left them on the dressing table—"

"Well, let's have a look," said Maddox.

It was a rambling old house, pleasantly furnished. The Gordons' bedroom was in front, a good-sized room with twin beds, an adjoining bathroom. The jewelry case on the dressing table was walnut, the lid still standing open. "He got out the back door? Could you tell how he got in?"

"Smashed the bathroom window, the other bath off the back hall," said Gordon.

They went to look. It was the smaller second bathroom, and gave directly onto the backyard. There was a low ornamental wall around the yard.

"We haven't got another dog since Laddie died," she said. "And there are good locks, but neither of us ever thought about that window —it's not very big."

"Big enough for an active man," said Maddox, "and not very high off the ground."

At the opposite side of the hall was the kitchen, giving on to an old-fashioned service porch. The inner door to that was standing open. "You'd left this locked?"

"And bolted," said Gordon promptly, "same as the outside door." The door from the service porch to the drive was also half open. Both doors had inside bolts, both had been jimmied open from inside.

Baker eyed them professionally. "Naturally you didn't leave the keys in the locks. He used something like a chisel. He's an old pro. Left himself an escape route, first thing he did after he got in, in case he got interrupted."

"Which he did," said Rodriguez. "When you realized he wasn't your husband, and screamed, he ran for it. And when he didn't leave any mess, drawers dumped and so on, he probably hadn't been here long. Got in, arranged the escape route—that's a typical pro trick—and started poking around for the jewelry first. And then you walked in. Did you come in the front door?"

"Yes, I was going out to play golf this morning, I just left the car in the drive."

Baker brought out his dusting equipment. They went back to the bedroom and he started going over the jewel case. He lifted four reasonably good latents from the lid, and proceeded to roll prints from both the Gordons for comparison. "You can look at it now, give us some idea of what's missing."

She looked, and said, "Both my good diamond rings are gone—and the emerald bracelet—my mother's engagement ring, that's a smaller stone but worth something, I suppose— The gold bangle bracelet, and my father's watch, his partner gave him that when he got elected to the bench. It's got his name engraved on it, Walter J. Chapman, it's a Waltham—" She gave them general descriptions, but except for the watch all the items were fairly anonymous. The burglar being a pro, he would know a fence; none of this would end up in a pawnshop.

"But where the hell was he?" asked Gordon. "You'd think he'd have cut and run when he heard us coming in—not that we made much noise but we were talking when we came down the hall—and we were both in the bathroom and closet, getting undressed—"

There was a generous walk-in closet. "At a guess," said Maddox, "he didn't have time." He looked around the room. There were heavy gold velvet drapes at the one large window, and that was recessed to make a window seat. "Were the drapes pulled?"

"Yes, of course," she said. "They're always closed after dark."

"And you didn't open the window before you went to bed?"

"Well, no. The air conditioning was on."

"So that'll be the answer. He heard you coming down the hall, and he didn't have time to get out of the room, if he was over here rummaging in the jewel case. He'd have been using a flashlight."

"We never saw that, of course. I switched on the light as we came into the bedroom."

"And he'd just have dived behind the drapes," said Rodriguez. "Little shock for him. He'd have figured to wait until you were both asleep,

and then sneak out. But in the meantime"—he grinned under his hand
—"another idea occurred to him."

"Well," she said philosophically, "there's no real harm done. To me,
I mean. But I hope you can get my jewelry back."

They all trailed Baker back to the rear doors, and he started to dust
those. Maddox edged past the outer door and looked around the yard.
There was a gate in the low wall at one side. "You'd better try this too,
Harry." He went to look at it; it didn't have a lock, only a latch. And
then he said, "Well, well. Another little surprise. Come and look at
this, Mrs. Gordon."

She came and looked. "Why, it's Dad's watch." It was a heavy gold
pocket watch, lying in the grass just this side of the gate.

"He'd have had the loot in his pockets likely, and the flashlight too
—this fell out when he was getting away." Baker came and maneu-
vered it into a plastic evidence bag.

"He might very well have left a print on that, we'll see. If he did,
he'll be on record somewhere. We can't tell you there's much chance of
getting your jewelry back, Mrs. Gordon, but we'll hope to pick him
up."

And whatever his record might say, if they did drop on the pro
burglar, this time he would be charged with attempted rape.

When they came back to the station Maddox stopped at the coffee
machine down the hall from the communal office and got a paper cup
of black coffee. As he came past Ellis's office the door was open and he
glanced in. Ellis was there, sitting at his desk with his head in his
hands. Rodriguez would have seen him and passed by. Maddox hesitated. What was there to say to George Ellis? It would be halfway an
insult to say, we know how you're feeling. All of them might imagine
what Ellis was feeling, but they couldn't know; nobody but Ellis could
know that. And maybe his wife. But you couldn't ignore Ellis, and after
a moment Maddox went in. He didn't know what to say, and he said
casually, "Hello, George. Good to see you back."

Ellis looked up slowly. He was a big man, a broad stocky man with
thick shoulders, but in the last two months he seemed to have shrunk
in on himself. He had lost weight, and the gray suit hung on his big
frame. His face looked gray, and his eyes were bloodshot. He looked up
at Maddox without speaking, and Maddox put the cup of coffee down
in front of him. "Give you a little lift," he said.

"Oh—thanks." Ellis picked it up and drank as if he didn't know what he was doing. Maddox wondered suddenly if the Ellises went to any church. It was curious to reflect that he had worked with Ellis ever since he had made rank and been stationed at Hollywood division, and knew practically nothing about his personal life. That kind of thing didn't come into the job. All the men at the station knew each other well, but in a desultory sort of way, from working the job together. In the nature of things, perhaps, men weren't given to talking personal philosophy on the job.

A long time ago, Maddox had been sent to Sunday School. He had got past the formal dogma, which was too narrow to explain the probably vast areas of ultimate truth. Before he knew he was going to say it, he said, "Look, George, the boy's all right. He's still alive somewhere, you know. Somehow. You'll catch up to him someday."

Ellis looked down at the cup of coffee. After a dragging moment he said in a low voice, "I know that, Ivor. I've got to believe that. But thanks."

"It's got to get easier after a while. You've just got to sweat it out."

Ellis hunched his shoulders. He said heavily, "You don't know. You just don't know. I don't think I can talk about it."

And there wasn't anything else to say to him. Maddox went on into the communal office.

Maddox went on trying to get both the Norwoods and Coreys on the phone up to noon, and then gave up and went out to lunch with Rodriguez. But at one-thirty Mrs. Norwood answered the phone and he told her about Leonard Coldfield. "Is your husband at home? We'd like to ask both of you a few questions."

"Why, that's just terrible," she said, sounding distressed. "Leonard dead—and murdered— I can't believe it. But we wouldn't know anything about it, did you say Sergeant? We hadn't seen either Leonard or Freda in quite a while."

"We'd like to ask you about any mutual friends, that's all."

"Well, for goodness' sake, I don't see why. It wouldn't have been a friend murdered him. Did you say he was shot? My heavens, I can't get over it—he's such a quiet sort of man. And I don't know what we could tell you—the Coldfields aren't especially social people and neither are we. Of course we'll tell the police anything you want to know but we hadn't seen either of them in quite a while. I think the last time was when they were here to dinner, we had the Olivers too, and that was sometime in May."

"Well, we'd like to talk to you," said Maddox. "Sometime this afternoon, would that be all right?"

"Why, I guess so. We weren't planning on going anywhere, we just went to church this morning and came right back. We're sort of expecting our son and his family over later, but I don't suppose you'll take long."

"Fine. Somebody'll be over soon."

However, nobody was destined to talk to the Norwoods that afternoon. Maddox had just put the phone down and opened his mouth to alert Rodriguez when the phone shrilled at him. He said, "Hell," and picked it up.

It was, of course, a new call. A wholesale gang rumble at the Pan Pacific Park on Third Street, with six squads sent out, and it took quite a while to sort out. This time, as expectable, it was the Dukes and the Caballeros, rival Hispanic gangs, and it was the usual violent bloody mess. By the time they had rounded up all those they could lay hands on—the Traffic men said there had been twenty or thirty of them mixing it up when they landed there, but with the arrival of the squads a good many of them had lit out and vanished into the jungle—there was one dead body, four seriously enough hurt to be carted off to Emergency, and six of the rest in cuffs. They all looked to be in their teens.

Maddox and Rodriguez started trying to get the body identified first. Finally one of those in cuffs said sullenly, "It's Carlo Mendez. He was my best buddy, man. We was just tryin' to pertect ourselves from those Goddamned Dukes, they been comin' into our *barrio* and messin' with our chicks." He was a tall thin kid with shoulder-length hair. He had a knife cut on one arm, nothing serious. He supplied an address for Mendez, on Fortieth Street. "I guess his mama better hear he's dead."

"I done it!" said one of the others triumphantly. "I'm the one shot that dude," and he was boasting about it in a loud voice. "I guess nobody can't say I'm a no-good kid not old enough to be in the Dukes, not when I killed that dude!"

One of the Traffic men handed over a gun. "I'm sorry if my prints are all over it, I had to wrestle him down to get it away from him."

"Can't be helped," said Rodriguez. They ferried those six up to the jail and stashed them in interrogation rooms while they checked with

Emergency. Only one of those was in serious condition, from stab wounds in the stomach, and there hadn't been any identification on any of them. The others had parted with a couple of names unwillingly and would be held overnight, transferred to jail in the morning. The charges wouldn't amount to much except for the homicide, and they would all probably get probation. The one who had had the gun was still loudly talkative. He said his name was Alonzo Cordova and he was sixteen. "None of them other damned guys can say I'm too much of a kid to be in the Dukes after this, it'll show 'em I'm the hell of a lot bigger man than anybody thinks, see?" That of course made the homicide a Juvenile matter, and Maddox called their Juvenile office and Mario Vitelli came over to sit in on the questioning. Maddox handed the gun over; it was an ancient Smith and Wesson .32.

"So where'd you get the gun?"

"It was my granddad's. He died last month and my mama she was goin' through his room, sort out stuff to throw away, he had a lot of junk in there. I found it under some old clothes, and it was all loaded and everything, Mama never noticed it. Nobody else in the Dukes packs a gun, they all just carry knives, any serious fightin' come along, see. And Juan and Diego, they always sayin' I'm just a punk kid not big enough for the Dukes, but I guess I showed 'em how big I am, killin' that dude! They never killed nobody." He sounded very happy about it. "It was all them other dudes started it, we was just hangin' around, smoke a little pot, when they jumped us—it was all their fault, they jump us we gotta pertect ourselves, see? And I had the gun on me and I shot that one, he fell right down and I see all the blood."

He parted with an address almost eagerly. "I guess my kid brother'll sure be glad I'm a real big man with the Dukes, man."

"You do get tired," said Vitelli in the hall outside. His thin dark face with its thick moustache wore a cynical expression. "And don't suggest psychiatric evaluation for that one, he's just doing what comes naturally, given the environment. And you know how it'll go."

"Sixteen," said Rodriguez. "Whether he's got other counts on him or not, the worst that could happen to him is getting stashed away with the Youth Authority until he stops being a juvenile, and then he'd get turned loose. You can drop the gun off at the lab. When the coroner's office sends the slugs up, they can match them and file the paperwork."

"Will do," said Vitelli.

Maddox and Rodriguez spent the rest of the afternoon on the background legwork, after talking to the rest of the kids. Only one of them was over eighteen. Then they went to talk to the families, those they could locate. The addresses were all over the place.

Toward the end of shift they went back to the station and Vitelli was waiting for them with a little more information.

"The computers make the job some easier," he said cheerfully. Three of the others, two Dukes and a Caballero respectively, had JD counts of possession and selling pot, and the fourth one had a count of assault. They had all, of course, got probation and never served any time. Four of the parents had shown up in Records Too, one of the mothers with a string of charges of soliciting, two of the fathers with counts of armed robbery and rape. The third father was still in San Quentin doing a five-to-fifteen for Murder two.

There wasn't much chance that any of these louts would ever turn into the useful members of society, but at least when they came of age some attempt might be made to keep them off the streets and off the backs of the honest citizens. And even that was chancy, given the state of the courts these days.

The shift was over and they had wasted most of the day on this senseless thing, but that was the way the job went sometimes. Maddox left a note for Brougham; if the night watch wasn't too busy, hopefully somebody could go and talk to the Norwoods.

Brougham, reading the note, said, "I'm not too clear what Maddox wants out of these people. That lawyer who got shot— I don't know much about it." Neither Stacey nor Donaldson did either.

In any case, they didn't have time to do anything about it. They got a call almost at once, to a hit-run out on Santa Monica with a woman dead, and that took up a good deal of time. At that hour on a main drag there had been a number of witnesses, and they all had to be talked to. Most of them were as useful as eyewitnesses usually were; the detectives got a dozen different descriptions of the car, of the circumstances. They sorted out three men who seemed to know more about it than the others, asked them to come in to make statements tomorrow. At least there had been I.D. on the body; she had been a middle-aged woman named Sampson, and her billfold contained a card, notify in case of emergency. That turned out to be a daughter in Pasadena. She sounded like a level-headed woman. Donaldson told her about the necessity to get formal identification, of an autopsy.

The woman had been a widow, living alone and working at a department store in Central Hollywood. She had probably stayed downtown to shop after work; they had found her car in a public lot.

Donaldson reluctantly started to type a report on it. When they had got back to the station Stacey had gone out on something. He came back about ten-thirty and said it was another handful of nothing, a new heist and nothing helpful on it at all. It had been at a small market on Western, with two witnesses, and all they could say was that the heister looked like just a teenager, and he hadn't touched anything. So even if he had left prints, which was unlikely, it wouldn't be of any use; if he was a juvenile he wouldn't be in Records. They spent a while grousing about the never-ending thankless job, as the best detectives frequently did, and finally Stacey got around to starting a report.

He had just finished that and ripped the triplicate form out of the typewriter, at a quarter to midnight, when the phone rang on his desk and he picked it up, expecting to hear a new call from one of the dispatchers. Instead, unprecedentedly, it was the swing watch commander downstairs, Lieutenant Starke. "Listen," he said, "we've got something a little offbeat. Of course it may be nothing at all, but it's funny and I just thought I'd alert you to pass it on to the day watch in case it turns serious. We seem to have a patrolman missing."

"How come?" asked Stacey.

"Well, I know the man, he was riding swing watch up to six months ago when he got transferred to day watch. His name's Dunning, Don Dunning. He's been with the department for five years, and he's one of the best men we've got. A very steady reliable guy, he took top place in his class at the Academy. He's something of a physical fitness nut. He's twenty-six. Somebody told me he's engaged to be married, but he still lives with his mother. It's an address on Romaine. She called me about forty minutes ago to report him missing—she can't understand it and neither can I. He's due in for day watch at 8 A.M., of course. It was his day off, he was out with his girl, got home about seven, seemed just his usual self. He left again about eight, told her he was going out to pick up a six-pack of beer, and he hasn't come home. Normally he'd have been back in half an hour or so, and of course on day watch he'd generally go to bed by ten-thirty, around there. She called the girl, a couple of his friends, and nobody's seen him or heard from him. Look, he's the kind you can set your watch by, as I say a very steady guy. Absolutely clean record with us. The kind who didn't want to go on riding a squad all his life, wanted to make rank—a real career cop. She's worried, and she knew we could check the indicated places quicker. Well, I have. He hasn't been involved in an accident, he's not in any hospital, he's nowhere. It's weird, because he's just not the kind to all of a sudden go off on a toot, out of his normal routine anyway. Like I say he's a physical fitness nut, he never drinks anything stronger than beer. The mother says the girl says he was just his usual self, they didn't have a fight or anything. What the hell's happened to him?"

"Now that is a queer one," said Stacey.

"I've put out an A.P.B. on his car—of course she could give me the plate number—but that won't get passed out to all the squads until midnight. I got the dispatchers to pass on the plate number to all the squads on tour now in Central Hollywood. But I tell you, I'm feeling worried about Dunning too, he's a nice guy and one of our best men as I say."

"Offbeat is a word for it," said Stacey. "He wouldn't be a candidate for a mugging, knocked out in some dark alley?"

"Not likely," said Starke dryly. "He's big and young and strong, and he's into judo. And he'd be packing the extra gun."

"Yes," said Stacey. All police officers were required to go armed at all times, on or off duty.

"Besides," said Starke, "he was only going to a market on a main drag, in the middle of the evening, with all the bright lights still on. We'll hope to God he turns up overnight—I suppose there could be some explanation—but I thought you'd better be alerted. I know him well enough that I'm thinking something serious could have happened to him."

"I see what you mean," said Stacey. "We'll pass it on to the day watch. Keep us informed."

"Oh, we'll do that all right," said Starke somberly.

A lot of the day watch patrolmen knew Don Dunning and liked him. When they were briefed by the watch commander, coming on shift at 8 A.M. on Monday morning, they heard about his inexplicable disappearance with concern. They would all be on the watch for his car, a middle-aged two-door Buick.

But there were a lot of cars around in Central Hollywood, and it wasn't until eleven o'clock on Monday morning that Ramon Gonzales, at random checking out the parked cars at a big supermarket lot at the junction of Hollywood and Sunset Boulevards, came across the Buick. It was securely locked and the keys were in the ignition. He called in, and it got towed into the police garage for examination.

CHAPTER THREE

It was D'Arcy's day off. Maddox and Rodriguez had been out to West Hollywood, finally talking to Norwood, who was with a brokerage firm. In the end it had worked out better that they could talk to him alone; as Rodriguez said, any of Coldfield's male friends might be reluctant to open up about his extracurricular girl friends in front of their wives. But Norwood didn't open up about anything at all. He was a short stocky fellow in the mid-fifties, and he looked at them blankly and said, "Leonard, chasing the women? That just sounds crazy. I couldn't believe it when Martha said the police had called and Leonard had been shot, who'd want to kill Leonard, for God's sake? And now you saying about women, that sounds just impossible. He wasn't that kind of man —at least," he added cautiously, "I certainly wouldn't have thought so. The last man to go chasing around, I'd have said. Do you know yet who did it?"

"Not yet," said Maddox. "We had it from Mrs. Coldfield that he had an eye for the women, did some chasing. He never said anything about that to you? You knew him pretty well?"

Norwood looked perplexed, passed a hand over his balding head. "He certainly never did, no. I guess you could say I knew him fairly well, I'd been his father's broker, handled that estate for some time. The old man died a couple of years ago, and I'm still handling it for Leonard. There's a tidy little bundle, a couple of hundred thousand. Well, I'd known him for twenty years, and I certainly never thought he was that kind of man. Freda told you that? I will be damned. I'd never have thought that." He shook his head. "I suppose she'd know. But, hell, when you say did I know him well, do any of us know people that well? Sure, we had them to dinner sometimes, they had us, we socialized some, but you could say it was all on the surface. He wasn't a man to talk much about himself, a quiet fellow all wrapped up in his profession, if you know what I mean. We talked about all the surface things, politics, the news, football. He was a pretty religious fellow, not that he talked much about that either but it sort of emerged. He went to the Episcopal church. I don't think Freda did, I sort of gathered that might have been the only bone of contention between them. I just can't believe he was a chaser. He always struck me as a steady family man. He was devoted to the children, there's a son and daughter, Greg and Mary, they're both grown and married. Greg lives up in Visalia, he's in insurance, he's married with a couple of kids and Leonard was crazy about the grandchildren. Mary just got married last year, her husband's a career Army man stationed in Germany. I just don't get this, Freda telling you—but if that's so, I can see why she wouldn't have talked about it to anybody. You think it was some woman killed him? My God, I'd have said the last man. But I certainly don't know anything to tell you about that." He poked his pen at the desk blotter aimlessly. "I'll have to talk to Freda, of course. I know about his will, he left everything to the family, Freda's part in trust, she'll be all right, there's plenty. I can't get over this. But even if it's so, he wasn't a man to do any talking about it, you know, he wouldn't have confided in me or anybody else. I'm bound to say"—and Norwood looked thoughtfully at the desk blotter—"I never exactly cottoned to Freda, she's a funny sort of woman, all gush and chatter, a silly sort of woman, nothing much to her. But I wouldn't have thought Leonard was the kind to go after other women. This shakes me some. But I couldn't tell you anything about it."

"So," said Rodriguez in the car on the way back to the station, "he wasn't the kind to let his hair down with old friends and talk about the extra ladies. If he was paying the rent for one of them it wouldn't likely have been with checks, with the joint bank account. There might not be a record anywhere to say who the ladies were. And it could have been just the fairly high-class call girls."

"That could be," said Maddox, "but I don't think so, César. One like that wouldn't be enough emotionally involved to use a gun on him. I think it was something cozier than that, a woman he might have been involved with for some time on a more personal basis. We can ask for an order to look at his bank record. The wife needn't have been seeing his canceled checks. There could be some pointers, checks to restaurants, jewelers, something showing up on his credit cards more likely. If he squired the ladies around anywhere—"

"She, they," said Rodriguez, and laughed. "In the big town? You're woolgathering, *amigo*. So he charged restaurant bills, theater tickets, on a credit card, even if he was personally known to a couple of maître d's, all anybody like that could say, yes, he used to come in here with a blonde, nobody could say which blonde. It'd be going through the motions."

"I'm afraid you could be right," said Maddox.

They stopped for lunch on the way back. When they got to the station Feinman told them about Dunning's car being spotted. "He hasn't showed up?" asked Maddox. "That's a queer one."

"I just checked with the garage. The car looks clean. Keys left in it, it was locked all around. Franks went down to look at it, but there doesn't seem to be any reason for a lab examination. We don't know that anything's happened to Dunning at all. The car hadn't been involved in any accident, it was just parked in that market lot."

"But where in hell is he?" asked Maddox reasonably. "By what Starke said last night he's a very reliable man, not apt to have a brainstorm and go off on a binge."

Feinman shrugged. "Who knows? We don't know much about it, he could have had a fight with his girl friend and just taken off somewhere. Oh, I checked with the watch commander, he didn't show up for duty at 8 A.M."

Maddox sat down at his desk and ruminated about the things on hand. He was inclined to agree with Rodriguez that the Coldfield thing would probably stay anonymous. Coldfield evidently not given to talking about his extracurricular ladies, nobody who had known him might have known who any of them had been. Whichever of them had shot him, for whatever reason, wasn't going to show up and admit it. That would probably die a natural death. There were the heisters to look for. The computers had turned up four men from Records who conformed to the general description of the big black fellow who had held up that pharmacy, and Nolan and Dowling were out looking for them. There weren't any leads at all on the other one, the fat fellow in the fifties. There would be inquests coming up to be covered, on that suicide, the gang member, and Coldfield, and more paperwork to do on that, and on the hit-run last night.

Feinman said, scowling, "The damn lab's taking their time processing the latents they got from that office-supply place. Not that I think they'll turn anything up, this damn ring are smart boys, probably pros, and they won't have left any prints there anymore than they did at the other places."

"No," said Maddox absently. He thought about the pro burglar who had had other ideas, watching Mrs. Gordon getting undressed for bed, and grinned to himself.

And then Douglas Simms came in, the father of that suicide, and said in a dull voice, "Is this where I'm supposed to come? The officer said—the other day—I should come in and make some sort of statement—about Ruth. About how it happened. I had to go to the morgue and look at her, say it was her."

"Yes, sir," said Rodriguez, getting up. "It's just a formality, Mr. Simms, it won't take long."

Maddox left that to him. Ellis hadn't come in. Feinman was rereading the reports on those burglaries, looking morose. Presently Simms left, having signed the brief statement Rodriguez had typed. Maddox thought fleetingly of that poor damned mixed-up teenager hanging herself in the garage. Whether it was some kind of a sign of the times or whatever, the teenage suicide rate was up.

Then the day watch commander, Lieutenant Jenner, marched in and plumped himself down in the chair beside Maddox's desk. "Nothing makes any sense about this Goddamned thing," he said forcefully. "Dunning's the last man to go off half cocked any way. He's a damned good man, steady as a rock, reliable. I've had a look at his car, and there doesn't seem to be anything in it to give us a clue. The usual stuff in the glove compartment, the trunk. I've just been talking to his mother, she's worried as hell."

"Understandably," said Maddox. "It's a funny one all right."

"Funny!" said Jenner, and added a couple of ruder words. "It's just crazy, Maddox. The mother says he was just his usual self, nothing out of the ordinary had happened lately, he was out with his girl yesterday afternoon, they're engaged, and he never said a word about having an argument with her, anything like that, and even if he had why should he take off this way? He isn't the kind of man to get all upset about a tiff with a girl or anything else. There's just no sense to it. He's one of the best men we've got, the kind of man we'd like more of in the Department. He's never taken a day of sick leave since he's been on the force, he hasn't got a mark against him, he's a top marksman and absolutely clean personally. Judo expert too. You don't tell me he got jumped by some mugger, it couldn't be and anyway he'd have been found by now. I want that car gone over by the lab."

"It might not be a bad idea," said Maddox. "Has anybody checked the hospitals again? In case he has been picked up anywhere?"

"Yeah, I did that the first thing this morning. He's nowhere. Look, by what the mother says he was just going up to the nearest market to get some beer. That wouldn't be the market where his car was found. The nearest place would be somewhere up on Western. For God's sake, it was the middle of the evening, not much after eight o'clock, lights all over and crowds. He couldn't have been jumped by a mugger in the market lot, it'd have been fairly busy, people all around. And if anybody tried to mug him, for God's sake, he's six-one and hefty, and the judo and all, and he'd have the extra gun on him. It's just not possible, and anyway where is he? There wasn't a damned thing to tell his mother. She's so worried she stayed home from work—she's a legal secretary somewhere downtown— I want the lab to go over that car."

"All right," said Maddox. "I'll set it up. It's a damn peculiar situation all right."

Rodriguez had drifted over to listen. "On the face of it, there doesn't seem to be any reasonable answer, unless he did have a brainstorm of some kind and just took off. But why leave the car?"

"He'd never do such a thing," said Jenner flatly. "The whole thing's impossible. But there just could be something in the car the lab could spot, and I think we'd better have them look."

"Yes," said Maddox.

"And I've got to get back to my own office. But you get on this. I've got a damned uneasy feeling about this thing. Some people do go off the rails and do the unpredictable things, but not the men like Dunning. We want to find out what's happened to him, and damn quick. I'll be in touch, call you if anything shows."

Rodriguez sat down in the chair Jenner vacated and lit a cigarette. "It's funny all right. One like that. I suppose it's just possible he was mugged, if he was taken by surprise from behind he might not have had a chance to fight back, but even so, where the hell is he? The mugger wouldn't have carted him off somewhere. I don't suppose he had much cash on him, not that the mugger would have cared."

Maddox took up the phone and called the lab. He got Garcia and explained. The lab men hadn't, of course, heard anything about Dunning. Surprised, Garcia said, "One of the patrolmen? I'll be damned, that's a queer one. Hell, Maddox, those fellows down at the garage had probably messed up any prints there might have been in the car by now. Well, all right, I'll have a look at it. Oh, just a second, Harry wants to talk to you."

Baker's heavier voice came on. "I've got something for you. On the amorous burglar. Just the way I figured, he left a couple of dandy latents on that gold watch. I just ran them through for you and he showed in Records."

"Oh, very nice," said Maddox. "Who is he?"

Baker laughed. "He's an old pro all right. One Floyd Kearney, he's got three counts of burglary with us, got out of Folsom last year from a three-to-five on the latest charge." The pro burglars might pull a hundred jobs for every one they were picked up on; that said he was an old pro indeed. "He's off parole now, there's an address but it'll probably be out of date. At least you know who he is. Now you just try to find him."

"Thank you so much," said Maddox. He passed that on to Rodriguez. "His latest PA officer might point us in the right direction."

"And maybe not," said Rodriguez.

"Well, we can ask." Maddox got back on the phone, talked to R. and I. downtown, and asked them to send up a copy of Kearney's package. Then the coroner's office called to say that the inquest on Coldfield was scheduled for Wednesday. "Damn," said Maddox, "I forgot to ask the lab whether they've matched the slugs from Mendez with that gun. I trust the morgue sent them up." It wasn't too important; it would get done sometime.

Nolan and Dowling came in towing a suspect to question, a big black hulking fellow with a stupid expression, and herded him down to one of the interrogation rooms.

Maddox got on the phone to Welfare and Rehab downtown. He was shunted around some, finally talked to Kearney's most recent parole officer, a fellow named Novak. "Well, he's been off parole for six months. I can't say it's a big surprise to hear he's pulled a new one. He's the typical pro, he isn't too crazy about working the eight-hour job. Funnily enough he's a damned good mechanic, he could hold down a top job anywhere, but he just doesn't like to work that hard. You know the type. I didn't have any trouble getting him a good job when he came out, he was working at a Cadillac agency on La Cienega, living in an apartment on Fountain, but whether he's still there God knows."

"Has he got any family?" asked Maddox.

"Yeah, he's not married, his wife divorced him after he did his first stretch, but he's got a sister, she seemed pretty close, I met her once when I saw him on my regular inspection. I think she'd tried to keep him straight, she seemed like the honest citizen. Let's see, I'd have to look it up for you in the dead file, but I seem to recall her name's Porter. He had her listed as next of kin, I remember, and I ought to have the address somewhere."

"We'd be obliged," said Maddox. He took down the address on Fountain, which Novak remembered, and the name of the Cadillac agency, handed that to Rodriguez.

On the phone to the Fountain Avenue apartment, he talked to the manager. Kearney had moved four months ago, and left no forwarding address. That figured; as soon as he'd got off parole he would have gone back to his usual routine. Three minutes later Rodriguez put down the phone and said tersely, "He quit the job five months ago. They were sorry to lose him, the head mechanic said he's a wizard with engines. You wonder what makes them tick, the ones like this."

"Just congenital laziness," said Maddox. "The sister may know where he is, if Novak can find her address and she's still at the same one." Novak would call back sometime. Dowling and Nolan came back into the office and the big black fellow shambled out. "No dice?" asked Rodriguez.

Dowling sat down at his desk and began to fill his ancient briar pipe leisurely. "He remembered he had an alibi, when we finally got it across to him what time and day we were asking about. He was in the drunk tank when that heist got pulled."

Rodriguez laughed. "At least the alibi not dependent on similar doubtful characters."

"Oh, we checked it," said Nolan. "There are a couple of other names to look for. And the heat's building again, it must be over ninety out on the street." In the station, of course, the air conditioning was on, would be running steadily the rest of the summer.

The end of the Traffic shift was just coming up toward four o'clock when the phone rang on Rodriguez's desk. Nolan and Dowling had reluctantly started out on the legwork again, and Feinman was talking to somebody over at Valley division presumably about the original burglaries pulled there. "Rodriguez." He listened and his mouth drew to a grim line. "Okay, we're on it. Thanks." He put the phone down and looked at Maddox. "I suppose they've called Jenner. That was one of the dispatchers. They've just found him. Dunning. A P. and R. man called in, and the squad car man knew him, of course. The minute he looked at the body."

"For God's sake," said Maddox quietly. "Where?"

"Under some bushes up in Barnsdall Park. The P. and R. men don't get up there too often. He could have been there for days without getting found, they told the Traffic man."

"For God's sweet sake," said Maddox, and picked up the phone to call the lab. Then he called Sue at home and told her he'd likely be late, told her why.

"Oh, Ivor, I'm so sorry." And neither of them had known Dunning personally, but he'd been a cop, and a good cop, and they tended to feel like one big family, the good cops on the same side of things. And Sue was a cop too.

"I'll pick up dinner somewhere, love. Expect me when you see me."

"Good hunting," said Sue.

They got up there before the lab van. The Traffic man was Jowett and his normally round ruddy face was a little pale; he looked shaken. "The Parks and Recreation men hadn't been up here for a while, they just got here about forty minutes ago, to check on some sprinkler heads. They spotted him right off. It's not far up the hill." He'd been waiting at the bottom of the little narrow path leading up the hill, the squad parked just inside the park from Hollywood Boulevard at the entrance to the park. It wasn't much of a park, Barnsdall. It had been there since Hollywood was a small town, a big square block bounded by Hollywood and Sunset, Edgemont and Vermont. Most of it was the hill, solidly overgrown with bushes and trees. There was an art museum and gallery at the top of the hill, and on the way up a children's playground. It wasn't a very popular park, though it was right in the middle of town, seldom crowded and often entirely deserted. Probably nearby dog owners used it for dog walking, and that was about all.

Maddox and Rodriguez followed Jowett about twenty feet up the little path to where the P. and R. men waited, both middle-aged and stolid-looking. They couldn't very well have missed spotting the body. It was lying partially under a big escallonia bush at the side of the path.

"We'd all heard about it," said Jowett soberly, "Don going off and not coming home last night. But I didn't believe it when I saw it was him. One of the nicest guys I ever knew, and only twenty-six, what the hell could have happened to him?"

They didn't touch him, just looked, waiting for the lab man to take photographs. Don Dunning had been a good-looking young man if not exactly handsome, with blunt regular features, a shock of light brown hair slightly wavy off a high forehead. He'd been a broadly stocky man, and it wouldn't have been an easy job to haul him even this far up that path from the park entrance. The nearest you could bring a car was just in from the boulevard, in this case Hollywood Boulevard. He was wearing brown slacks, a beige sport shirt without a tie, and a light brown jacket. His face wore an oddly peaceful expression. He was flat on his back, arms at his sides.

"I didn't believe it," said Jowett. "Don, he's—you can see—he's been shot. My God."

"We can see," said Rodriguez grimly. The entrance wound was clearly visible in the left temple; it hadn't bled much.

Franks came up behind them with the lab bag, and looked at the body. "The hell of a thing," he said softly. "I don't suppose there's anything around to print. You'll just want pictures."

"That's about it," said Maddox. He told Jowett he'd better get back to the station; it was after four-thirty and the shift had changed. While Franks took photographs they talked to the P. and R. men, got their names; they'd have to take the formal statements from them on finding the body, for the record.

Five minutes later Jenner arrived, and he was both sorrowful and fighting mad. He looked at the body and said, "Hell and damnation, one of our best men, we can't afford to lose men like Dunning. I'm Goddamned mad about this. And Goddamned sorry. And damn it, I had to call his mother and tell her and she broke down like you'd expect—he was an only son, I don't think there were any other children. Damn it, damn it, what the hell could have happened to him anyway? In the middle of the evening, people all around—"

"He wouldn't have been heading for the market down there, where the car was left," said Rodriguez. It was a big chain supermarket, the parking lot fronting on both Hollywood and Vermont.

"No, the nearest one to where they lived, she thought."

"Well, the lab's going over the car," said Maddox. Franks took a last shot and stepped back, and Maddox and Rodriguez pulled the body all the way out to the path. Aside from the bullet wound there didn't seem to be a mark on him, to indicate he'd been in a fight of any kind. Rodriguez pulled back the jacket. There was a regulation shoulder holster strapped under his left armpit, and it was empty. Maddox drew in a breath. "The gun's stolen. Do you know what he carried off duty?"

Jenner said, "I can't say for certain, his mother should know, but 90 percent of the men use a .32 for an extra gun." His regulation sidearm, the Police Positive .38, and his uniform, would be in his locker at the station.

"Pray something useful shows up in the car," said Rodriguez savagely.

There wasn't anything more to do here. Jowett had called for the morgue-wagon before he left, and now it slid silently up from the boulevard into the park entrance. The attendants got out, trundled out the gurney from the rear door. There were people on the street down there, the market lot full of cars, but nobody was paying any attention to the little knot of men up here. Jenner began to swear again, watching the body carted off. "I just hope to hell you can find out what happened, who killed him. That was a damned good man. I never hated a job worse in my life than breaking the news to his mother. I suppose she'll have told the girl by now."

And they would have to see them both. Jenner went back to his car and drove off. Rodriguez said, "Give her a little more time?"

Maddox lit a cigarette with a savage snap of the lighter. "I want," he said, "to talk to some people at that market. Gonzales found the car at about eleven this morning—how long had it been there?"

"We can ask. If anybody knows."

Maddox moved the car down there to the market lot, and they went in and showed the badges. A curious checker told them that the market always closed at nine on Sunday nights. Yes, all the employees used the parking lot, but there hadn't been many cars left there when they all went out after the market closed. "We all came out more or less together like we usually do," said the checker. "Well, no, I didn't take any notice of what cars were there, just all of ours, I guess. But Mr. Delgado stayed later, he's the one who closes up anyway, he's the manager. Maybe he'd remember. Oh, his office is in the back, through the stock room."

They went back there and showed the badges again to a suspicious clerk, went past a door marked Employees Only. Delgado was a stockily built swarthy man about forty-five. He was sitting at a battered old desk in a tiny office at one end of the big stock room with its crowded shelves of cans and packages. He listened to what they had to say, and looked saddened. "A policeman," he said. "That's a damned awful thing. We got a damn good police force here, I know that, but we never get enough good officers. Any way I can help you I will."

"What time did you leave here last night?" asked Maddox.

He thought. "It must have been nearly ten o'clock. Later than usual. I had some orders to put through. Generally I take care of all that in regular hours, but we've been shorthanded this week, two of the check-out girls are on vacation, and then Ed—Ed Becker, he's the assistant manager, he came down with the flu, my God, of all times to get the flu, in the middle of summer, but I guess germs don't read calendars. So I had to fill in for one of the checkers, and we've been busy. A lot of working people do their main shopping on the weekend, naturally. We were busy as hell on Saturday, and we're open till ten on Saturdays. And then yesterday I had all these orders to get out, we were running low on a lot of stuff. I stayed late to make them out, and called them into the warehouse this morning. It didn't really matter because my wife's away, she's at our daughter's in Santa Ana, she just had a baby, our daughter I mean, and the wife's helping out. So I went up to the coffee shop around the corner for dinner, and after I closed up the place I must have been here at least forty-five minutes. It'd have been maybe a quarter of ten when I left. And I can tell you for certain that my car was the only one in the lot then. I'd have noticed if there'd been another one, it'd have stuck out like a sore thumb."

"Well, so that gives us a definite time," said Maddox. "Thanks very much."

"Always glad to help the cops," said Delgado. "I sure hope you catch this killer."

Back in the car, Rodriguez said, "So it was left there after nine forty-five or ten. Did the mother say he'd left about eight? The doctors'll give us an estimated time of death but maybe not so close." He stroked his moustache absently. "Can we say he'd have been home by nine if he hadn't run into some trouble? I think we ask at the other market if anybody remembers seeing him, and when."

"We don't know exactly where he was heading. Evidently the mother thought, just the nearest place he could pick up the six-pack."

Maddox had the address, and rummaged in the glove compartment for a city map. "Romaine. The nearest main drag is Western, and there'd be half a dozen places he might have gone. Possibly she'll know definitely."

It was long after six now. They found a public phone and Maddox called her. She sounded as if she had been crying. She said dully, "Of course I knew you'd want to talk to me. And Debby too. Debby's here now, Don's fiancée. She came right up from work when I called her, after Lieutenant Jenner called me. She hasn't any family here, they live up in Fresno."

"We'll be with you in about an hour," said Maddox gently, and turned from the phone. "Any preference where to have dinner, César?"

"Any place."

They went to the nearest restaurant with a liquor license, up on Los Feliz; being technically off duty they could have a drink before dinner.

The address on Romaine, an old block in Central Hollywood, was an old California bungalow with a detached garage in the rear. They went up to the long front porch, Maddox pushed the bell, and the door opened immediately. She heard their names, asked them in. She was a tall dark woman with a full figure, a fine complexion, big dark eyes. Right now her face was ravaged and her eyelids red, but she had her voice under control. She asked them to sit down. There was a girl sitting on the couch in this pleasantly furnished living room, a girl in her early twenties. Ordinarily she'd have been a pretty girl, a small blonde with a pert tip-tilted nose, a wide friendly mouth, but she'd been crying too and her eyes and nose were red.

"You know we're sorry to bother you at a time like this, Mrs. Dunning," said Maddox. "I don't need to tell you that all of us sympathize with you."

"It's all right, I know you've got to ask questions. Try to find out how it happened. But neither of us can imagine what did happen, you know. There wasn't any reason for anyone to hate Don—enough to kill him."

"There doesn't always have to be a rational reason," said Maddox. He looked at the girl.

"Oh, I'm sorry, this is Debby Moore."

"Miss Moore, you were out with him yesterday?" She nodded. "Where did you go?"

She sat up and blew her nose. "We went to a swap meet," she said huskily. "It sounds so silly now. Neither of us had ever been to one before. You know what they are, it's sort of an in thing now. You're apt to find anything at them. People bring all sorts of things, anything they have to sell. They're held on weekends, I think whoever runs them rents the place and then people with things to sell rent space there. A girl I know picked up a brand-new set of cookware for half price. And I just thought it might be fun to go to one. You know, we were—we were going to be married next month—and living alone I've just got odds and ends, there were things I wanted—for the kitchen. And Don said we'd go wherever I wanted to. And he said maybe he could find a window air conditioner for his mother's room, the one there is kind of old and not too good. I saw the ad at the market, for the swap meet. It was out by Hansen Dam Park in the Valley, not in the park but next to it. So we went. We weren't going to stay long, it was awfully hot out there, it always is in the Valley, and I had to be back early because I was going to a baby shower for one of the girls at work. I work at Columbia Records. Don picked me up about two o'clock, and we got out there a little before three, and we split up to look around."

"Why?" asked Rodriguez.

"Oh well, it was a huge place and all the different things were arranged in—like categories, you know. There were big things like appliances and so on at one end, and arts and crafts and clothes and jewelry and things like that at the other side. And we weren't just browsing, we were both looking for specific things, you see. Don for the air conditioner and me for the kitchenware. And it was so hot, and the place was so big and crowded, a big lot with all these tables, and there were swarms of people, an awful crowd. Don parked on Foothill and we said we'd meet back at the car in an hour. And I went looking for the kitchenware and things like that, but I didn't find anything I wanted. I looked at some of the arts and crafts and the jewelry but I didn't buy anything. And about ten to four I went back to the car, and Don was just coming up from the other end of the place. He said there weren't any air conditioners for sale. And it was so hot. So then we came back to Hollywood and had early dinner at Musso and Frank's. I had a drink before dinner and Don had tomato juice, he never drank hard liquor.

And then Don took me home, and I took another shower and got dressed and went to Gloria's for the baby shower."

"Did he seem his usual self?"

"Oh yes, Don was always the same. You know"—she looked at Mrs. Dunning—"he never did show his feelings much, he might be worried about something or happy about something and you'd never know." She gave a dreary little laugh. "I always said we made a good pair, he wasn't a talker and I guess I talk too much, I'd do the talking for both of us."

Mrs. Dunning said quietly, "He was exactly like his father—John was just the same. Close as an oyster. He had feelings but he couldn't show them easily. You never got anything out of him until he was ready to tell you."

"So you might not have known if he was worried about something," said Maddox.

"Oh, I don't think he was, no. What did he have to be worried about? He was just his usual self. We talked about the wedding—we were going to Yosemite for a honeymoon," and she sobbed dryly.

"What time did he leave you at home?"

"About six o'clock."

Maddox looked at the other woman. "You said he got home about when?"

"No, it would have been about seven, I think."

"Where had he been in the meantime, did he say?"

"Well, I knew he was dropping Debby off early, and he said he might go to the gym for an hour. I expect that's where he was. He always exercised regularly, it was a—sort of thing with him, to keep in top shape. He belonged to a men's gym on Sunset Boulevard. When he came home I was just going in to wash my hair. I guess it was nearly eight when I came out to the kitchen and I was surprised to see he'd put his jacket on again so he was going out. He was just hanging up the phone then, and I asked him was he going out and he said just to pick up a six-pack of beer."

"Who had he been talking to, did he say?"

"Oh, I didn't ask but he said it was a wrong number. But when he wasn't back by ten I began to worry. I can't understand what could have happened. And I called a few people—I thought it was possible he dropped in to see Fred and Ann—that's Fred Kowalsky, he and Don were all through school together, he was Don's oldest friend, and they just live over on Marathon—but they hadn't seen him. I didn't really think he'd have gone to see anybody else at that time of night, a couple of his other close friends live further away, and by the time I thought of Wayne, it was too late to call him."

"Who's that?"

"Wayne Cross, he was about Don's best friend in the Department. They were at the Police Academy together."

"We used to double date sometimes," said Debby, "before Wayne broke up with Paula. He's nice."

"But he got transferred to the night shift a couple of weeks ago, and I knew he'd probably have left for work by then. But it got so late, and I finally called the station—"

"Do you know what kind of gun he carried off duty?"

"Yes, it was a .32 Colt revolver."

"Did he have a record of the serial number?"

"Oh yes, it'll be in his address book." She found it and Maddox copied it down. That would go out to all the police labs in the state, in case that gun ever turned up anywhere.

"Do you have any idea what did happen, sergeant?"

Maddox massaged his jaw. "Not much yet, I'm afraid, Mrs. Dunning. But we won't give up on it. We'd like to know just as much as you would."

"The Department was his whole life. He never wanted to be anything but a police officer. He joined as soon as he was old enough, he was really just marking time those couple of years in college."

"Did he say exactly where he was going after the six-pack?"

"Well, I assumed where he usually went, the liquor store just around the corner on Western—it's Golden State Liquors."

"And he impressed you as being his normal self too?"

"Yes, of course. Absolutely. Don was always a quiet one, he didn't show much, but he seemed just the same as he always was. Nobody had any reason—to want to hurt Don. He didn't quarrel with people, he was always just the same."

The girl said, "Well, I thought of something. That Fernandez man."

"Oh, Debby, he couldn't have had anything to do with it. It was just a—a tempest in a teapot."

"Well, I don't know, Mrs. Dunning. Don was annoyed about it. And it wasn't just once the man called and came back to see him."

"Who's Fernandez?" asked Rodriguez.

Mrs. Dunning said, "It couldn't be, it's just a wild idea. Well, we'd just sold Don's father's car. He—John, my husband, he died six months ago," and her voice shook. "It was a heart attack, he was only fifty-seven. The will's just got through probate. Both Don and I had our own cars, and John's Ford was the oldest one, so Don advertised it in the classified section of the *Times* and this Fernandez came and looked at it and bought it."

"And then," said the girl, sitting up straighter, "he made a big fuss, he came here and he kept calling Don on the phone and wanted him to give him some money back because the car went out on him. He said Don had guaranteed it was in top shape and then it cost him a lot of money to fix up. And that wasn't so; Don knew it needed things done to it but he wasn't going to pay a lot of money to fix it up. He only asked six hundred and fifty for it, and Don— Well, Don was just as honest as the day, he told this Fernandez it needed work and he was selling it as is. And Fernandez needn't have bought it, nobody was high-pressuring him. He drove it before he said he'd buy it. And then he kept calling and saying Don had cheated him and ought to give him back what it cost him for the new radiator and battery."

"And Don was annoyed?"

"Well, he had a right to be! He didn't get mad very often, I don't think he lost his temper once in ten years, but he was annoyed. He finally—and that was just last week—he told Fernandez he didn't want to hear from him again, they'd made the bargain and Fernandez could just make the best of it. He hung up on him, I remember."

Maddox exchanged a glance with Rodriguez. "Fernandez had come here to buy the car?"

"Yes, it's just a two-car garage and Don had the Ford parked in the street. But it was just a silly argument," said Mrs. Dunning, "it wouldn't be a reason for—for killing—"

"Sometimes reasons for murder can be silly," said Maddox.

Quite suddenly she put her hands to her temples. "It's just—all of a sudden everything seems so meaningless. You think there must be some order in life, some reason. That's why you make plans. Looking ahead. And twenty-six years—all of a sudden just gone like that—we'd have liked another couple of children, but I had to have the hysterectomy. And John going to night school to get his degree so he could teach and make better money, save for Don's college education. You plan, and you think it's all for something, to make a better future. It seems just yesterday he was starting school—and going out on his first date—and then he was so proud when he got into the Department." She drew a long painful breath. "Cruel—John dying so young. But I still had Don —we had each other. I was thinking about having grandchildren." The girl began to cry quietly. "All of a sudden nothing means anything. It was just all for nothing—all the planning and work and saving."

And both Maddox and Rodriguez were thinking involuntarily, that was just how George Ellis would be feeling.

"Mrs. Dunning, do you know this Fernandez's first name? Where he lives?"

She looked up vaguely. "I saw the check he gave Don—I think his name was Enrico. I don't know where he lives. I don't suppose Don had his address." She handed over the address book but it wasn't there. "You'll let us know—if you find out anything."

"You know there has to be an autopsy. We'll let you know when you can claim his body."

Her eyes looked blind. "Just all for nothing. I haven't been to church in years, John hadn't any use for orthodox religion. It would seem hypocritical, asking a minister to conduct a funeral—I don't know any ministers."

"The funeral director will," said Rodriguez softly. "You don't have to go to church to believe in God, you know. That God has some reason for things happening even if we don't understand them."

And she looked at him more directly and said simply, "Thank you."

"Very eloquent, César," said Maddox. He slid the key into the ignition, didn't switch it on.

"Just plain truth," said Rodriguez rather gruffly.

"Oh yes. I like Fernandez. It brings a little—just a little—light of day. The irrational motive does so often trigger the impulsive kill."

"I like him," said Rodriguez, "because of the bright lights. The absence of. Look at this block, Ivor. A streetlight half a block away. That driveway's damn dark. I'd like very much to know whether there was a six-pack of beer in Dunning's car."

"Oh yes."

"He could have done just what he said he was going to. Gone and got the beer, and come home. People and lights up on Western, it's hard to see how he could have been jumped by the mugger there. But here—well, think it out. Fernandez—we all know these hot-tempered

Latins—is mad at him over the Ford. Dunning told him off, told him
to quit bothering him, but that wouldn't have reached Fernandez
maybe. He came here to complain some more, demand the rebate, and
maybe he'd just got here when Dunning came home. He tackled him,
say in the drive as Dunning got out of his car, and they had another
argument. And he started a fight. No, I know what you're going to say,
Dunning the hefty physical fitness nut, the judo expert, and we don't
know what size Fernandez is. But by all we've heard, Dunning was the
kind who wouldn't get into the loud argument, just stay calm and say
get lost, and that might be fuel to the flame for the hot-tempered
Latin. Say Dunning just turned his back and started up to the house,
and Fernandez attacked him from behind. Dunning wouldn't have
been expecting it. He might have been knocked down against the car,
knocked right out. And Fernandez—wait for it—goes over him, intending to take what cash he had on him, and spots the gun."

"All right," said Maddox. "I might just buy that. But why didn't
anybody hear the shot?"

Rodriguez snuggled back in the passenger seat. "And you a married
man," he said. "Or does Sue waste money on beauty shops? You heard
her say she'd just washed her hair. She'd have been in her bedroom
running the hair dryer. And the neighbors probably watching TV."

"Oh, what pretty deductions you do make. But the only thing I'll
balk on, César—why the hell should he have moved the car and the
body? He must have been driving. Would he leave his car here and go
to all the trouble of moving Dunning's car up there, lug the body into
the park?"

"You're overlooking one thing," and Rodriguez laughed. "The Ford
had gone out on him. It could have been in the shop again, and Fernandez feeling all the more annoyed about that. He came up here on
the bus—and they stop running about nine o'clock. I'll tell you, Ivor,
we'll look for him, and if he lives anywhere in that area, within a few
blocks of Barnsdall Park, that's what happened. He may have had some
idea of concealing the body, who knows? But he took the car to get
home."

"Logical up to a point. And if we find him and he's an undersized
little fellow who couldn't have moved Dunning's body—"

"We'll find out. He could have friends. He needn't be the respectable citizen. Let's look for the name in Records," said Rodriguez, suddenly struck with the idea.

Maddox laughed. "Stranger things have happened. It's a chance. We'll look." He turned the key in the ignition.

On Tuesday morning, Maddox had just got in when he got a call from Garcia in the lab. "I was just about to call you. You went over Dunning's car. Was there a six-pack of beer in it?"

"That's right. Coors light. On the front passenger seat. I wasn't calling you about that, but as long as we're talking about it, the steering wheel was wiped clean—no latents at all—a couple on the door to the glove compartment but they're Dunning's, of course we had his on record. What I'm calling you about, you sent an inquiry down yesterday about some slugs supposed to be sent up from the coroner's office. That gang rumble on Sunday."

"What about them?"

"Well, we never got any. Vitelli dropped off a gun, supposed to be the one used." Garcia uttered a horselaugh. "My God, Maddox. It was in the ark with Noah. Nobody shot anybody with it. It's missing a firing pin and the barrel's crusted with rust. Nobody could fire it, much less kill anybody with it."

"Well, do tell," said Maddox mildly. He thought about Alonzo Cordova boasting so happily about killing that dude. He called the coroner's office and eventually talked to Dr. Farbstein.

"Oh, that one," said Farbstein. "I haven't got to the autopsy yet but I had a look at him. Shot? No, he wasn't shot, he was stabbed. In the stomach. Both intestines perforated, it was something like a seven-inch blade, nothing distinctive about it."

"Thank you so much for nothing," said Maddox.

CHAPTER FOUR

There was an E. Fernandez listed in the phone book at an address on Catalina Avenue. Rodriguez had just turned it up when Maddox put the phone down after talking to Farbstein, and displayed it triumphantly. "There you are, four blocks from Barnsdall Park."

"He won't be the only Fernandez in town," said Maddox, "or the only Enrico." There were a couple of others listed just by initials, just in the central Hollywood book.

"Well, it's a place to start," said Rodriguez. "That's near Barnsdall Park, the general area." They kicked it around a little, and he agreed with Rodriguez. But before they could start to do anything about it Daisy Hoffman looked in and said, "I think one of you had better sit in on something." Maddox raised his brows at her; she was looking grim. "Nobody seems to be in Juvenile, the desk sent them up to me, and it could be a real something, Ivor. Another Barlow thing."

"Oh, my God," said Maddox. "So you can go look for Fernandez, César." He followed Daisy back to the smaller office across the hall. Thank God the Barlow thing hadn't been their business, it had belonged to Long Beach, but it had got a good deal of space in the *Times* a month ago. The day care center with three adults on the staff charged with molesting a number of the children.

In the other office Helen Waring, looking her usual serene self, was sitting with her notebook ready at the desk beside Daisy's, coolly contemplating a man and woman and little girl in the other chairs. Daisy said formally, "I'd like Sergeant Maddox to hear what you've got to tell us, Dr. Remling."

He looked about thirty-five, a wiry middle-sized man with reddish hair and thin nondescript features; and he was obviously in a furious temper. He was formally dressed in a business suit. The woman was around the same age, a pretty ash blonde, and she was dabbing at her eyes with a handkerchief. The little girl was just sitting primly in a chair, looking curiously around the office.

"Let's hear it from the beginning," said Daisy. "We have your name, you're a dentist, you said, and your home and office address." She sat down at her desk. There wasn't another chair; Maddox propped himself against her desk silently.

"I suppose you have to go at it your own way," said Remling in an impatient tone, "but let's get at it so you can arrest that bastard and stash him in jail—close down that damn place."

"We only found out this morning," the woman broke in distractedly. "We knew Brenda didn't like the place but it wasn't until this morning she broke down and told us about it—Martin was just ready to leave for work, and I was getting ready to drive Brenda to school—when she started to cry and told us about it, and oh, my God, if we'd had any idea, but who would have, him calling himself a minister, it's just damnable, and we knew the police ought to hear about it, Martin said we had to tell you right away."

"Minister!" said Remling. "My God."

"It was because she wasn't doing so well in school, I was worried about it. Brenda's ten and she ought to have been reading a lot better and doing fourth grade arithmetic, and everybody says the public schools aren't so good now, and I'd talked to her teacher and she said how about private tutoring, but then I thought about the Hortons. We don't know them so very well, the boy's one of Martin's patients, and I knew Mavis from a bridge club I used to belong to. It was last year sometime she'd been telling me how much better their boy was doing since they'd put him in this private school, so I called her and asked about it and she said it was a marvelous school, the children get individual attention and wonderful teaching, and it was worth whatever it cost, and she told me where it was. Martin and I talked it over and decided to look into it." He was sitting back looking savage, letting her do the talking. "It's a church school, and we don't go to church, but of course it wouldn't do any harm if they preached at the children, it's not as if it's a Catholic school, it's Lutheran, the Grace Lutheran Academy on Highland, right in town, and so we looked into it. He seemed like a nice man, and a minister, the Reverend Mr. Pollard, his wife teaches there, she seemed nice too, and the other teachers— They just have small classes, the children get individual attention, and Mavis said you wouldn't believe the difference in their boy since he'd been going there. And the tuition isn't really terribly high for what they seem to offer. And so we sent Brenda there. This past semester, since January. And she didn't like it much but we thought she'd get to like it in time, the better teaching and all. I took her and brought her home every day. And then when the semester ended last month her teacher talked to us, she's a Mrs. Engel, she said Brenda still needed to catch up on a lot of foundation work, and it might help if she went to the summer session, it's just for six weeks. And so she was going. And I could see she wasn't getting to like it any better but we never dreamed— Oh, it's just too horrible— It wasn't until just this morning she told us why, and of course Martin went right up in the air, that horrible man molesting the little girls, and calling himself a minister, we couldn't believe it but you hear of it going on all over these days. There was that awful case in the papers. And Brenda was just too embarrassed to tell us about it before, weren't you, darling?"

The little girl was scrawny and small for her age, with a thin pale face and light brown hair. She looked at the floor and nodded silently.

"And he's probably done the same thing to the other little girls there, only Brenda doesn't know if he did, but the police ought to know about it. Such a wicked thing."

Daisy shut the flow off. "Let's hear what Brenda has to say, Mrs. Remling." She bent a kind gaze on the child. "You needn't feel embarrassed to tell us about it, Brenda. You know, we're police officers— that's kind of like doctors, we're professional people. We'd like you to tell us exactly what happened, with Mr. Pollard."

She had a reedy thin little voice. She said reluctantly, "Well, he told me to take off my panties."

"Mr. Pollard?"

"Yes, him. He doesn't teach any classes, he comes and says a prayer every morning. And sometimes one of the teachers sends a kid to see him, some special reason. That was when it was, on account I'm not so good at reading, Mrs. Engel told me to go to his office. And he talked to me about the reading. And then he said I was a pretty little girl, and he held me on his lap and I didn't like it and then he told me to take off my panties and I was sort of scared of him so I did, and he—well, he touched me all over. There." She wriggled, looking shy.

Remling snorted and began to swear again. "Perverted old bastard!" he said. "Acting so Goddamned pious."

"You don't know if he'd done that to any of the other girls at school?" asked Daisy.

Brenda shook her head. "I don't know any of the other girls so good. Maybe he had and they were scared to talk about it."

"Did he do that to you more than once?"

She nodded, head down. "A lot of times. Well, maybe six times. When I got sent to see him in his room in the church. He called me names like dear and darling and I had to take off my panties."

Daisy looked at Maddox. "You go and lock that bastard up!" said Remling, "and shut down that damn place. School! God knows what he's done to the other kids."

"It's just horrible," said his wife. "To think of a man like that running a school! He ought to be in jail. And Martin said the police ought to hear about it right away."

"Yes, we're very glad you came in," said Daisy smoothly. "We'll certainly be looking into it."

"You'd better do more than that," said Remling hardly. "You'd better lock that bastard up. Come on, Marlene, we've told them and I don't want Brenda dwelling on this too much, we'd better get her home." He stood up.

"Excuse me," said Maddox, "I think we'd like a medical examination of your daughter, Dr. Remling."

He flushed and then paled. "There's no need for that. The bastard didn't actually rape her, I've examined her myself. Just what's called the fondling, and the next thing that leads to is the actual molestation, we all know that. I'll bet you you'll find he's approached other kids, maybe some of the boys too. Kids that age, they'd be too embarrassed to tell about it. And a good many of the kids there, their parents are church members, they'd never believe the minister would be up to a thing like that, for God's sake. Church school be damned, all the pious talk about individual attention, sure he gave them that, didn't he? You go get him and shut him in jail, close down that place." He took his wife's arm, urged the little girl up from the chair. "Come on, we'll leave it to the police, let's go home."

Maddox watched them march out, sat down in a vacated chair, and lit a cigarette. "Damnable's the word," said Daisy. "And we'll need some help on it. It's Juvenile business."

"Have to talk to the other kids," said Maddox. "Find out if he's interfered with any of the rest of them. Talk to the teachers. And lean on the Reverend Mr. Pollard."

Helen said in her cool voice, "Is there really more of it going on now or do we just hear about it oftener?"

Daisy shrugged, "I wouldn't know. How do we play it, Ivor?"

Maddox contemplated his cigarette. "Summer session, six weeks. This is probably the last week, then. We want to be sure of making a charge stick, on a thing like this. We'll have to rope Juvenile in. I think I'll go and size the man up first, and we'll take it from there. You talk to Juvenile, Daisy. They can go up in a bunch after lunch, start to talk to the kids."

"All right," said Daisy. "At least you might scare him off doing anything else until the class is shut down."

"That had entered my mind," said Maddox mildly. He put out the cigarette and stood up.

"What the hell are you talkin' about?" asked Enrico Fernandez roughly. He stared at Rodriguez and D'Arcy truculently. Rodriguez was liking Fernandez even better than he had before they'd met him. He had turned out not to be the E. Fernandez on Catalina Avenue, but the next one they'd tried out of the phone book. The address was on Avocado Street, and that was in the same general area as Barnsdall Park, a good deal farther away but in the same direction toward it from Romaine. There had been a wife at home, a fat dark woman without much English, but Rodriguez could talk to her. She told them where he worked, at the parking lot of a professional office building downtown. They were talking to him there, outside the little cubicle where he handed out parking cards and collected the validated ones. He was a big man, over six feet and heavy without being fat. He didn't look very intellectual but he was bright enough to know the cops had some reason to question him.

"The car," said Rodriguez.

"Sure," he said, "I bought that damn lousy heap off that guy. Three weeks back. More fool me. It looked like a bargain. The heap I'd been driving died on me, it wasn't worth nothin' but to junk, I had to have transportation. I saw the ad, I called the number, the guy told me where to come. So I bought it, why the hell are the cops interested?"

"And then you didn't think it was such a bargain," said D'Arcy. "It needed some fixing up, and you thought you'd been cheated."

"You're damn right," said Fernandez, and spat. "That guy told me it was running fine. Like hell it was. I'd no more than got it home, the battery went dead. I had to buy a new one, then a week later the radiator springs a leak. My God. He ought to kick back a couple of hundred of that six-fifty, sure I figured I got cheated. I told him so. He just said I'd bought the heap, it wasn't his business if it needed work. Sure I was mad about it. I still don't know why the cops are asking about it, for God's sake."

"He got himself murdered last Sunday night," said Rodriguez. "The guy who sold you the Ford. We just wondered if you were that mad about the deal, Fernandez."

"Murdered!" said Fernandez. "You got to be kidding. I wouldn't kill nobody. That's crazy."

"You'd been arguing with him about it," said D'Arcy in his easy drawl. "More than once. You'd phoned him, you'd gone back to the house complaining about the deal."

"So what if I had? I figured he owed me back some of that six-fifty. But if you think I'd kill somebody over that lousy heap you're crazy." He spat again. "How'd he get killed, anyway? He was just a young guy, that Dunning."

"So he was," said Rodriguez. "He was also a cop, Fernandez, did you know that?"

"Oh, my God," said Fernandez, and lost some color. "No, I didn't know that, for God's sake. Jesus, are you goin' to railroad me on a murder count just because I argued with him about that? Cops, they stick together. Oh, Jesus, I don't know anything about it, but just because I had a fight with him—"

"Did you?" asked Rodriguez.

"Jesus, I just meant the argument, that's all. I never laid a hand on him. I don't know a damn thing about it. The last time I saw the guy was last week, I went there again that night and pestered him, he told me to get lost—he wasn't mad about it, he just told me to forget it. And I called him on the phone one more time but he hung up on me. I never saw him, did you say Sunday? I never saw him again, honest to God."

"Where were you on Sunday night?" asked D'Arcy.

"You asking me for an alibi," said Fernandez. He was looking scared. "Jesus, what can I say? I was just home, my wife wasn't even there, she'd gone to see her sister. I was just home, watching TV, I went to bed early. This damn job, I'm out in the heat all day, I was tired. I went to bed about nine-thirty. Maria, she didn't get home till nearly midnight, I woke up when she came in. But I swear to God I never saw that guy Dunning again. I wouldn't kill nobody."

"I guess that's all for right now," said Rodriguez. "We may be talking to you again."

They went back to his car. "The gun," said D'Arcy. "If he's our X, he'd kept the gun. It's worth something. And it's not quite two days ago. Even if he intended to pawn it he may not have got around to it yet."

"It'll take a little while to get a search warrant."

"Not that long, if we get on it. He's stuck here on the job. He might not think we'd think about a search warrant right off the bat, call his wife to get rid of the gun. If it's at the house."

Rodriguez started the engine. "If it's that open and shut we could pin it down today."

They went back to the station and applied for the search warrant, for both the house and the car.

Feinman told them that somebody had called from Welfare and Rehab and been asking for Maddox. "He had an address you were evidently after. It was a guy named Novak." He handed it over. It was an address for Nancy Porter in South Pasadena.

"That sister of Kearney's," said Rodriguez. "No point in calling her, if she knows where he is she'd just alert him that we're looking for him and he'll vanish into the woodwork. It can wait, we know who he is. But damn it, I don't think Ivor checked with the DMV." There was some time in hand while they waited for the search warrant; he went down to Communications and put through the query. In two minutes the computer up in Sacramento came up with an answer. There was an old Chevy wagon registered to Floyd Kearney, but the address was the one on Fountain Avenue. Rodriguez put out an A.P.B. on it countywide. That might turn him up fairly soon. Tidying things up, he applied for the arrest warrant on Kearney; that would take longer to come through.

Maddox contemplated the Grace Lutheran Church and school. They occupied the same large lot on Highland Avenue. It was a modest-sized church, a square stucco building set back from the street with a patch of lawn in front. There was the usual sign listing the times of services. The school was another square building, beside the church. Its sign was on the building front, Grace Lutheran Academy. He wondered if the minister would be here all day on a weekday, when he didn't teach any classes. He decided to try the school first. He went up to the entrance, found the door open, and walked in. It wasn't a very big building. Nobody seemed to be around. He walked down a hall past several doors on either side, probably to classrooms. The place was silent but he heard children's voices faintly from somewhere. At the end of the hall he came to a door and from a window beside it saw a small playground at the rear of the building. There were about fifteen children there, and a woman in a brown dress evidently supervising them. Individual attention, he thought.

"Can I help you?" asked a pleasant voice behind him. He turned.

"I'm looking for Mr. Pollard."

She was a woman about thirty-five, not pretty but pleasant-faced, with brown hair and gold-framed glasses. She was plainly dressed in a navy skirt and white blouse.

"Oh," she said, "I'm Mrs. Pollard. Was it about an enrollment? The summer session's just ending, we'll be closed until September."

"I'm a police officer, I'd like to see Mr. Pollard on a private matter. Is he here?"

She didn't look alarmed, only surprised. "Well, he's in his office at the church. You can go right in. It's at the rear of the pulpit, just go through the door there." She was curious now.

Maddox thanked her and went over to the church. The double front doors were open. It was a rather bare-looking church, with plain square pews, the pulpit of the same dark wood, holding a big leather-bound Bible on a lectern. He found the door behind that, which led to a short hall. There was a door giving on a small bathroom, a door opposite standing half open. He looked into part of a room furnished as an office, bookshelves on the opposite wall. He rapped sharply on the door and opened it the rest of the way. "Mr. Pollard?"

"Yes, what is it?" The man sitting at the shabby old desk looked up. He was a tall thin bony man with the face of an intellectual; he reminded Maddox oddly of Sergeant Joe Feinman. His dark hair was untidy as if he'd been running fingers through it, his eyes vague behind plastic-framed glasses. He might be around forty. He looked at Maddox inquiringly.

"I'm sorry to interrupt you, sir."

"Oh, it doesn't matter," said Pollard, and gave him an unexpectedly charming smile. "I don't get on with it very quickly, I'm afraid. There are so many interesting bypaths, and it's difficult to know what to put in or leave out." He looked at the blotter, where a page bore a dozen lines of neat small longhand. "I've been working at it for a couple of years—a biography of my father, a most interesting man and he had a most interesting life, at least I think so. But I don't know that anyone will ever publish it, perhaps it's a labor of love." He looked at Maddox with more attention and added doubtfully, "I don't think I've seen you before, have I? What can I do for you?"

Maddox showed him the badge. "I have to inform you that an alleged charge has been made that you've attempted to molest one of the children here, Mr. Pollard. A girl named Brenda Remling."

Pollard stared at him with a blank expression. For a long moment he didn't speak, and then he said, "This must be some kind of joke. Molestation—I don't believe you."

"Dr. and Mrs. Remling brought her to see us this morning and she's quite definite about it." Maddox kept his voice expressionless.

Pollard took off his glasses and his myopic eyes swam out of focus. "Some kind of joke," he repeated. "I can't take this in. Why, it's unthinkable— How could the police think— You are police?" Maddox let him see the badge again.

"Sergeant Maddox, Hollywood division. The little girl's pretty definite, Mr. Pollard. She says you've fondled her private parts on several occasions, made her take off her underwear."

"This is some kind of ghastly mistake," said Pollard. He put his glasses back on and his eyes sharpened. "Why, I've got two daughters of my own, Sergeant. I'm an ordained minister, I hope a man of God. I would as soon commit such a devilish thing as I'd commit murder. I don't understand this."

"She told us that sometimes the children are sent to see you privately, it was on those occasions you had fondled her. I understand you act as what might be called a principal?"

"Yes, you could put it like that, I suppose. We started the school in my father's time, he was the minister here before his death." Pollard was looking merely indignant, not alarmed. "The school has been in operation for about fifteen years. It's quite small, of course, but that way we can give the children more personal attention and counseling. We usually have no more than fifty students. There are four teachers, including my wife. They are all accredited teachers, the other three came to us because of their dissatisfaction with the public schools, were willing to take the lower salaries. I don't even recognize this child's name," he added abruptly.

"You do sometimes see the children privately?"

"Yes, of course. Not that often. If any discipline problem comes up, a teacher may send a student to see me, but that doesn't happen except now and then. Sometimes the children who come to us from public school aren't accustomed to our stricter discipline, and get a little out of hand, but in time they usually conform. Children really welcome discipline, and when their minds are healthily occupied"—he gave a slight smile—"you know the saying about Satan finding work for idle hands. The public schools are too often lax, the children are bored. We try not to bore them."

"Yes, sir," said Maddox. "This little girl just came here last semester. Brenda Remling. She says her teacher sent her to see you because she was slow at reading."

"Oh," said Pollard. "Oh yes, I remember her now. She's in Mrs. Engel's class. Mrs. Engel had spoken to me about her. She's one of those who had a very poor foundation in the basics—perfectly normal intelligence but she was doing work far below her grade level, and didn't seem willing to apply herself at all. Mrs. Engel sent her to me, I suppose you could call it, to give her a pep talk, encourage her to work harder. But as far as I remember I only saw the child once. I think it was just after the beginning of the summer classes." He was looking angry now. "Do you actually mean that this child has come out with this monstrous lie about me? I can't believe it!"

"That's what she told us, and she's pretty young to be doing any deliberate plotting, isn't she? You realize we've got to investigate."

"Investigate what?" asked Pollard blankly. "I absolutely deny any wrongdoing, Sergeant."

"Yes, I realize that, but that's hardly good enough. For the sake of the children, we've got to look into the charge. Our Juvenile officers will want to talk to the teachers, to the children. Find out if any of the other children report the same experiences with you. It's a serious charge. We have to find out whether it's true. If it is, you could be charged with child abuse and end up in jail, and your school would be closed down."

"My dear Lord," said Pollard quietly. "I don't believe this is happening. I don't believe it. It's unreal."

"Well, that's the way it is," said Maddox. "There'll be several Juvenile officers here this afternoon, to begin investigating. I'm afraid your regular classes will be interrupted. And I take it that the children attending the summer classes don't constitute the normal student body."

"No, of course not. This can't be happening. Molestation. I think there are only twelve or fifteen children enrolled in the summer classes."

"I'll want to see the list of the whole student body. We may want to talk to the parents too."

"My dear Lord." Pollard stood up stiffly. "You may look wherever you'd like, Sergeant, you needn't get a search warrant. We certainly have nothing whatever to hide. You'll find the list of all the children enrolled last semester in that file cabinet. Of course we'll cooperate with the police, I can understand that you can't simply take my word or my wife's. Our daughters both attend the school—they're seven and ten— Do you really think, with young children of my own, I could do such a thing?"

"It happens," said Maddox evenly. "You'll remember that recent case—the Barlows have three young children, and everyone who knew them thought they were honest upright citizens, but they've both been charged with a number of counts of abuse and sodomy."

Pollard shut his eyes briefly. "What do you want me to do?"

"You can just leave it to us, or if you like you can explain to your staff here, tell them to expect the other officers. That's up to you."

"I had better do that, to prepare them. At least, thank God, my wife and everyone else will know what a ridiculous lie this is."

Maddox glanced at his watch. "You can expect them around one-thirty, probably. You know, Mr. Pollard, if there isn't anything to this there's nothing to worry about, we'll find that out too. We just have to be sure." He was of two minds about Pollard. The man seemed genuine and straightforward, but he could be the convincing actor putting up a good front.

"All right," said Pollard. "All right. I'd better see everyone now, the classes will be breaking for lunch in five minutes."

Maddox followed him out and watched the tall thin figure striding rapidly toward the school next door.

The search warrant came through just after noon, and Rodriguez and D'Arcy snatched a couple of sandwiches on the way up to the apartment on Avocado Street. Mrs. Fernandez was scared and indignant at the invasion, and Rodriguez had to spell it out for her in Spanish, that the paper signed by the judge let them look wherever they wanted. She lamented and moaned in the background all the while they were looking. It wasn't a big apartment and it didn't take them long. There was just one bedroom and one closet. They were thorough, looking through all the drawers, all the shelves, the kitchen cupboards, the clothes hamper. They didn't find Dunning's extra gun anywhere. There wasn't a garage, just a bare carport.

They both felt disgruntled. Fernandez looked like such a good bet. They drove back downtown to the professional building and showed Fernandez the warrant. "Where's your car?" asked D'Arcy.

"What the hell you want to look in my car for? Jesus, you're gonna railroad me for murder and I don't know a damn thing about it—"

"We don't railroad anybody," said Rodriguez. "We're looking for evidence."

They didn't find it. The old Ford that had caused all the trouble was clean, metaphorically speaking. There were a couple of maps and a flashlight in the glove compartment, nothing in the trunk but the spare tire. They felt Fernandez's eyes on them as they went back to Rodriguez's car.

"Hell," said D'Arcy, "he could already have got rid of it. We never heard about him until last night, and that was twenty-four hours after Dunning was killed. He could have pawned the gun yesterday morning or last night. So he was at work, he'd be off at six."

"Anyway, there's not one damn thing to connect him," said Rodriguez in a dissatisfied tone. "He's a hot bet for it, but we can't pin it on him without evidence. We'll have to forget him. I'm halfway convinced he did it, but there's no way to charge him. He's big enough to have handled Dunning, lugged the body up there."

"You didn't say if Dunning was robbed of anything but the gun. Was his billfold on him?"

Rodriguez flicked his lighter. "Well, it was, but his mother said he wouldn't have had much cash on him. Enough to pay for the beer. There was three dollars and eighty cents in the billfold. Chicken feed.

Fernandez might not have looked beyond the gun. Just took that for what it was worth."

"And because he'd used it to kill Dunning. We can assume he was shot with his own gun, can't we?"

"We haven't got the gun," said Rodriguez morosely. "Fifty percent maybe." The coroner's office had sent the slug from Dunning's body to the lab and the word had come through this morning, it was out of a .32 Colt. In the absence of the gun, that was less than definite.

"We haven't asked Records about Fernandez. I'm thinking about something else."

"What might that be?"

"The phone call." D'Arcy blew a long stream of smoke. "When his mother came into the kitchen he was just hanging up the phone. He said it was a wrong number. But was it?"

Rodriguez said, "Um."

"Both the women told you he was a quiet one. Kind to keep his own counsel like they say. Might be mulling something over and never utter a word about it until he decided to. Could he have had a little trouble with somebody besides Fernandez?"

"What kind of trouble?"

"Who knows? Anything. And whoever was on the phone was calling to say, meet me somewhere and let's talk this over."

Rodriguez sat up a little straighter. "And going to get the beer was just an excuse. It makes a story of a sort, but there's absolutely nothing to back it up."

"Oh, I know, I just thought I'd mention it. And of course, even if Fernandez is in Records with a couple of counts of violence, that's no damned evidence on this thing at all."

"It'd be suggestive." Rodriguez started the engine.

Back at the station he got onto R. and I. downtown, and in three minutes had an answer. Records had a package on Enrico Fernandez. Unfortunately it wasn't one they were interested in. That Fernandez was currently still doing a three-to-five for armed robbery in the San Luis Men's Colony, and he was only five-six, a hundred and thirty pounds.

"Hell," said D'Arcy without emphasis.

The Juvenile officers were waiting with Daisy in the communal office when Maddox got back from lunch, Sergeant Ralston and two policewomen, Sally Henderson and Janet Sumner. He perched a hip on one corner of his desk and told them what he'd made of Pollard.

"He could be, he couldn't be. What we're after is any solid evidence. I'll say this much. He let me look at the list of the student body last semester, and there weren't any dropouts. As an educated guess, not all those kids would be too embarrassed to tell the parents about the fondling—or anything else—and the parents would have snatched them out of the private school."

"And they'd also have come running to tell the tale to us," said Daisy crisply.

Maddox looked at her sardonically. "Oh yes? If the parents were members of his congregation, a little bit in awe of the minister?"

"Don't be stupider than you can help," said Daisy. "Of course they would have, minister or not. Any parent—they'd probably have alerted all the other parents too. But you know, Ivor, it's possible he's just started playing with the kids, never did it before. Never succumbed to temptation before."

"Well, go and ask questions," said Maddox. "See what you can turn up." They started out, and he heard what Rodriguez and D'Arcy had to say about Fernandez. He was halfway inclined to agree with Rodriguez that Fernandez could very well be the X on Dunning, and it was annoying that they couldn't turn up any evidence on him. He heard D'Arcy's idea about the phone call, felt dubious on that one.

"But I'll buy it partly, on account of just what you say, what the women say— Dunning the quiet one. Not a talker. Kept things inside. It's just possible he'd had something on his mind and hadn't mentioned it to either of them. Something that might have had something to do with his murder. And if he had, it's possible that he might have said something to one of his friends. Hell, it's all nebulous, but say it was something he thought might worry the mother and the girl, he'd have kept quiet about it, but might have said something to a friend. They gave us some names, and except for this Kowalsky his closest friends were in the Department. It's just worth asking about."

"Just about worth it," said D'Arcy. "Who are they?"

Maddox got out his notebook. "Ayers, Medina, Sanford, Bertrand. All Traffic men, all around his age. Let's find out about them." He got hold of Jenner on the phone and asked questions. All those men were riding squads on day watch, as Dunning had been. The Traffic shift would change at four o'clock; they'd all be coming back to the station then and D'Arcy and Rodriguez could talk to them. Meantime there were follow-up reports to write. "And this Wayne Cross. They said he was one of Dunning's closest pals. He's just got transferred to the graveyard shift, he ought to be home now. I'll go and see if I can catch him."

"I didn't hear about it until last night," said Wayne Cross. "Don's mother called to tell me. I had to call in—say I was sick, I couldn't report for duty." His hands were shaking and he had to make two attempts to light a cigarette. He looked at it and said vaguely, "I've been trying to kick the habit, but I don't know, it sort of helps, it's something to do." He was about Dunning's age, just as tall but loose-limbed and gangling, fair-haired and handsomer than Dunning, with a straight Greek profile. He sat on the couch in this neat efficiency apartment and stared at the floor. "It's hard to believe Don's gone. We were in college together. But we both always wanted to join the Department, we joined at the same time, we were at the Academy together."

"And he hadn't said anything to you recently about any trouble with anybody?"

"No, I can't remember anything. Only with that nut who'd bought his father's car and was making waves about wanting a rebate. Don didn't have trouble with people, period. He always got along fine with people." Cross was speaking in a flat dull voice, and it was shaking a little too. "Damn," he said lowly, "I'm going to miss him. I'm going to miss him like hell. When we were both on the same shift we used to double-date sometimes, work out at the gym together, stop on the way home for a couple of beers. You know? Hell, I'm all to pieces over it— I never lost anybody—close to me before. I never knew he was missing, I'm on the graveyard watch now, I—"

"When was the last time you saw him?"

"Thursday," said Cross numbly. "Last Thursday. He came by about eight that night, he'd been to the gym. He said he and Debby were going out somewhere on Sunday, if I could get a date we could make it a foursome. But I haven't got a steady girl now, since I broke up with Paula. I've dated one of the dispatchers at the station but she's on day shift so it isn't easy to get together. My God, when I think"—he drove one fist into his other palm—"whatever happened, it was Sunday night —and I checked in as usual and took over the squad— It was a quiet night for once—came home about eight-thirty and went to bed, and all the while—all the while Don was lying there dead." He put out the cigarette. "God. I'll miss him. And I've got to go and see Mrs. Dunning, and there'll be the funeral—"

But he couldn't tell Maddox anything useful, about any worry Dunning had had lately. Maddox left him still staring at the floor, trying to light another cigarette, and headed back for the jail.

"What you mean, I'm off the hook?" asked Alonzo Cordova.

"I mean you didn't kill Mendez, Cordova. You had the gun, but he wasn't shot. He was stabbed. You didn't have a knife. That gun you were so proud of is a piece of junk, it's missing its firing pin and too rusty to use anyway. If it still had its firing pin and you had fired it, it could have blown your hand off."

"I did too shoot that dude! I pulled the trigger and he fell down and I saw the blood—"

"You didn't hear a shot, did you? There wasn't any. You'd all been making the hell of a lot of noise in the general fighting, that's so, isn't it?"

"I guess so," said Cordova. "You mean I didn't kill him, the gun was no good." He looked disappointed about it and Maddox nearly laughed.

"No, you won't be up for homicide this time."

"God damn," said Cordova, "that gun, it made me feel sort of big and smart. And thinkin' I'd wasted one of them damn Caballeros dudes. I thought it was a pretty good gun but I never even held a gun before. I guess I don't know much about guns."

Conceivably, if he went on the way he was headed, he'd find out more in time to come. As it was, Maddox reflected on the way back to the office, they'd never charge anybody with that homicide. Nothing distinctive about the knife, said the doctor. A seven-and-a-half-inch blade. Four of those other louts had been carrying exactly similar knives, and there was no way to pinpoint which of them, in the heat of the moment, had stabbed Mendez to death. He was probably small loss.

At four-thirty Rodriguez and D'Arcy came back to the office and reported a blank. They had talked to those four men, said to be good friends of Dunning, and they had all heard about Fernandez but nothing about any other difficulty Dunning had had recently. "I'm all the

way convinced it was Fernandez took him off," said Rodriguez mood-
ily, "and damn it, there's no way to pin it on him."

They kicked it around a little more, unprofitably, and then Nolan
came in with another heist suspect and Rodriguez went to sit in on the
questioning. The A.P.B. hadn't turned up Floyd Kearney yet. Maddox
wondered what Daisy and the Juvenile officers were getting at the
school. He and D'Arcy were alone in the office, everybody else out on
something. He sat back and lit a new cigarette and saw D'Arcy's eyes
move past him, and turned.

There was a man in the doorway of the office. "The desk sergeant
said to go to the detective office. Is this it? I'd like to talk to whoever
knows something about a murder. Leonard Coldfield."

"Yes, sir," said Maddox. "Come in and sit down. Have you got
something to tell us about that?"

He came in and sat down in the chair beside Maddox's desk. He was
about thirty, a tall and ruggedly handsome man with thick dark hair,
well dressed in a business suit. His mouth was drawn to a bitter line.
"Yes, I have," he said in a harsh voice, "and I don't know what the hell
you're going to think about it. Maybe you'll think I'm seven kinds of a
rat, I don't know what the hell you'll think. I'm Greg Coldfield. He was
my father."

"I see. What have you got to tell us, Mr. Coldfield?"

"He was a good father," said Coldfield. "And whatever you think
about me I'm not going to have his memory insulted. As a man and a
father. I've got to tell you how it was. She—my mother never called me
to tell me he was dead. Murdered. It was Mr. Norwood called me, last
night. It was one hell of a shock, and when I heard what he could tell
me—what you police had told him—I knew how it must have been.
How it had to have been. I live in Visalia, I'm in insurance, I told the
boss how it was and he let me take a week off. I drove down this
morning. I went to the house, and I tackled her right away. Because I
knew."

"Who?" asked Maddox.

"My mother," he said bitterly. "When Norwood said what you'd
told him, I knew. She'd never said that in public before, about Dad
chasing other women. She always kept up the polite social front, nobody but us—my sister and I—knew about it. But as far back as I can
remember she was always saying that, accusing him of having the girl
friends, and it was a damned lie, he never did, he was a good man. A

damned better man than she deserved. The language she'd use on him, the things she said— And he'd given up even talking back to her years ago, it wasn't any use. I don't think she's all the way sane. It's been an obsession with her. She was a little older than he was, but that couldn't be the only reason. I got up the courage once to ask him, years ago, why he didn't divorce her—she never gave him any peace—but he had some straitlaced ideas about marriage, he said, for better, for worse. She's been getting worse the last few years, she was making life hell for him, accusing him of sleeping with every woman he knew, his secretary, his receptionist, all his women clients. I don't think she's been sane for years. I suppose she thought—if she thought about it at all— she'd tell you that and you'd go running off looking for his latest mistress, who was nonexistent. I don't know whether she really believed it or was just so insanely jealous of him that she didn't care if it was true —and I think insanely is the right word. I couldn't get anything out of her but double-talk, but then she went out—she'd got a new dress to wear to the funeral and it had to be altered, she went to get it—and I started looking. I was 90 percent sure it had to be in the house somewhere. I turned everything upside down looking, and I finally found it. It was under a pile of underwear in a dresser drawer." He reached into his jacket pocket and brought out a gun and laid it on the desk. It was a Colt .38 revolver. "I don't know where she got it. But I suppose your ballistics expert can say if it's the gun that killed him."

D'Arcy said softly, "I will be damned."

"She's my mother," said Coldfield, "but he was my father. And she'd made his life hell." Suddenly he bowed his head in his hands. "You go and do what you have to do. I don't seem to care about it any more."

Maddox got home to the house on Starview Terrace at six-thirty. Margaret was just taking a casserole out of the oven, and smiled a welcome; he kissed her cheek. "Dinner in half an hour, you'll want to relax over a drink."

"After the day I've had, too right." He built himself a scotch and soda, carried it down to the living room. Sue was sitting sipping a glass of sherry, and the baby was peacefully slumbering on a blanket in the playpen across the room. Sue returned his kiss enthusiastically and said, "We'd better remember the United Parcel Service in our prayers, darling." Tama was curled up beside the playpen.

"Why the hell?"

"Well, we might have got sued for a lot of money, but he's a very nice man. The UPS driver. You know Mother had ordered that set of cookware for our anniversary, and it came, and the package was heavy. Mother'd gone out to the market and I answered the door. The man was nice and said he'd carry it in for me—and Johnny was in the playpen."

"Oh," said Maddox.

"And he just put the box down, he wasn't in six feet of the baby, but Tama went for him. I just caught his collar almost in time." Sue giggled. "He was awfully nice about it, said he had a couple of kids and he wished he had such a good watchdog. But Tama did bite him on the arm. It didn't amount to much because I got hold of him, but we could have got sued. Did you have a good day?"

"Well, I've got this and that to tell you." Maddox sat down in the opposite armchair.

About two-thirty Johnny McCrea, cruising the lonely night beat, came across a body. It was along the curb on Western. He got out of the squad and looked at it, the nondescript body of a middle-aged man, and concluded that it had probably been a hit-run accident. The body was in the middle of the street. There was identification on it; he had been a Joel Paxton, an address on Forty-first. There wouldn't be any detectives at the office now. He called it in, called the morgue-wagon. The front office boys could take it from there.

CHAPTER FIVE

The inquest on Coldfield was scheduled for ten o'clock on Wednesday morning. Maddox went downtown to cover it, and had a word with the coroner's deputy before it got underway. "We want an open verdict, we may be about ready to make an arrest." The coroner's man was cooperative, conducted the formalities briskly. The jury brought in the open verdict, homicide by persons unknown, and it didn't take an hour. Maddox caught up with the secretary and receptionist as they were leaving.

"Mrs. Haskell, had either of you ever met Mrs. Coldfield?"

"Why, no," she said, "she never came to the office."

And Coldfield wouldn't have had the salon photograph displayed on his desk.

When he got back to the office he heard about the new body from Feinman. "There doesn't seem to be anything to do about it but inform the next of kin, D'Arcy went out on it. Just another hit-run. Somebody from Hollenbeck was asking for you."

"Oh?" said Maddox.

"And there were two more hits last night," said Feinman sourly. "Bill's out looking at the other one, I just got back. Not that ring, thank God, just the ordinary burglars. God damn it, people know the rate's up, and they're just too cheap to install decent locks, real security, and then they scream at us because the burglars are loose on the streets. What the hell do they expect?"

"Don't find fault with the honest citizens, Joe," said Maddox dryly. "They pay our salaries." He took up the phone and called Hollenbeck division. Eventually he was connected with a Sergeant Avila, who said, "Oh, yeah, we thought you'd better hear about it. You remember that funny one that got pulled about a month ago on your beat, the female heisting the gas station? You sent out the regular query on the M.O."

"That's right," said Maddox. "A little something showed. Seventy-seventh Street had a couple like that pulled in their territory, two to three months ago. It was the same general description, a blonde about thirty, all the jobs about the middle of the evening, and nobody ever got anything on it, there was no make on the car."

"Well, she pulled another on our beat last night," said Avila, "out on Washington Boulevard. Same M.O. Same description such as it is. All pretty general, but there can't be more than one female heisting the gas stations, not even in a city this size, no?"

"You wouldn't think so," said Maddox.

"We just thought you'd like to know she's still around," said Avila.

"Interesting but unhelpful," said Maddox.

"Just the paperwork," said Avila.

That one had been a dead-end, there had been nowhere to look for the blonde heisting the gas stations, but there had been some indication that there had been an accomplice. The car had been parked away from the pumps, out of the lights at the station, and two of the attendants had said it had taken off quick enough that probably somebody beside the blond heister had been driving it.

He didn't talk to Avila long, called the lab and got Baker. "Have you had a look at that gun I dropped off yesterday?"

"Garcia checked it," said Baker. "He was just about to call you. It's the gun killed Coldfield all right, the slugs match."

"Thank you so much," said Maddox. Rodriguez came in with a paper cup of black coffee. "The gun checks. It was the one Coldfield found under his mother's underwear. So we bring her in and hear what she's got to say."

"My God," said Rodriguez. He had heard about that at yesterday's end of shift. "Women."

"Jealousy cruel as the grave," said Maddox, "so it says." He stretched. "I can't say I feel much like tackling the woman, but it's got to be done. I'm sorry for that poor devil, the Coldfields's son. What a hell of a thing, César."

"Women," said Rodriguez again, sipping coffee. "Didn't I say they can be dangerous. Do you want to bring her in now?"

"Let's have lunch first," said Maddox. "The inquest on Dunning is scheduled for tomorrow morning, and we haven't had the autopsy report yet."

"I asked priority on it but they're always busy."

D'Arcy came in and said, "There's nothing to do about this Paxton."

"Who the hell is Paxton?" asked Rodriguez.

"The new body. Looks like a hit-run, out on Western. The Traffic man found him in the street about two-thirty. It was more or less in front of a bar there, I suppose he could have been drunk and wandered out into the street in front of a car. Anyway, I checked the address and nobody knew much about him, and evidently he hasn't got any family. It's a cheap apartment, he just moved in a month ago, the manager doesn't know where he worked or anything about him. And there wasn't an address book or anything to say about any relatives. He had about twenty bucks on him and a driver's license with an address in Pacoima, but I called there and it was another apartment, he'd left there six months ago. There's no car registered to him now."

"So the city will have to pay for a funeral," said Rodriguez.

"And I'll have to write a report on it." They all groused about the never-ending paperwork.

Maddox passed on the news about the female heister, and D'Arcy said, "I did some of the legwork on that—funny, the female pulling a heist. There wasn't anywhere to look." He was more interested in Mrs. Coldfield.

Maddox went to see if Daisy was in, but the office across the hall was empty and nobody was in the Juvenile office down the hall. They were all probably still busy talking to the kids and the parents. That wouldn't be a job to get finished in a hurry. He said, "We ought to check that gym. Where Dunning worked out. The mother thought that's where he'd been before he came home, but was he?"

"I'm still thinking Fernandez is the answer," said Rodriguez.

"But there could be another answer," said Maddox. "And before we go to pick up Mrs. Coldfield let's be sure she's home. I wonder if the son's staying at the house. Damnation, I should have asked him, we'll have to get a formal statement from him." But when he called the Coldfield house Greg Coldfield answered the phone.

When he heard Maddox's voice he asked, "Was it the right gun?"

"Yes, Mr. Coldfield, it was the right gun, I'm sorry to tell you."

"I knew it had to be," said Coldfield, sounding tired. "You'll want to talk to her. She's not here. She went out shopping, she said, I don't know when she might come back. Yes, I'm staying at the house. So now I've got to call Mary and break the news. Damn it, damn it, why do things like this have to happen? Should I call to tell you when she comes in?"

"If you would, please."

"All right, I've got to see his lawyer about the will, he had it with Robert Levy, an old friend of his. I don't think there's anything complicated about it, he left everything to the family, but—my God, that just occurred to me this minute, she couldn't get it, could she? I'm not sure how the law reads, but—"

"She wouldn't be allowed to profit by a crime," said Maddox. "There's time enough to think about that, Mr. Coldfield. Please let us know when she comes home."

"All right," said Coldfield.

Maddox shared that news around. "And I'll get to this damned report after lunch," said D'Arcy.

They went out together to a coffee shop up the block on Fountain. They had stashed the file on that Rose Burton in Pending, nobody was ever going to know any more about that and it wasn't worth wasting time on. D'Arcy went back to the office and Maddox and Rodriguez went to look for that gym on Sunset Boulevard. It was called Frank's Gym and Health Spa, and at this hour there weren't many people there. The front anteroom was empty and they went down a short corridor to a big square room at the rear of the building itself. There were weights and punching bags, exercise bicycles, all the appurtenances of physical fitness. There were only three men there. One was a fat man doggedly peddling one of the stationary bicycles, one was doing push-ups on a mat, and the third was supervising that. That one came over to them. "Do something for you?"

"Do you run this place?" asked Maddox. It didn't take second sight to place him; he was a big heavy-shouldered man with ex-pro-fighter all over him like a neon sign, the broken nose and cauliflower ear.

"Yeah, that's right, I'm Frank O'Reilly. You like to sign up for a course?" He looked at wiry thin Maddox with a professional eye. "I could put some muscles on you, you look like you could use some exercise."

"No, thanks," said Maddox, annoyed, "we'd like to ask some questions." He brought out the badge.

O'Reilly was surprised and saddened to hear about Dunning. "By God, that's a damn shame, just a young guy too. Yeah, I knew Don for years, he'd been coming in here since he was in high school. Always kept himself in top shape. How in hell did he get killed?"

"That's what we'd like to find out," said Rodriguez. "Was he in here on Sunday night?"

"Yeah, he was. Not for very long. Lots of times he'd come in nights, or his day off, stay a couple of hours, do some laps in the pool, work out with the weights, but last Sunday he was only here about half an hour, I think. I guess it was about six-thirty he came in. He rode one of the bikes awhile, but he didn't go in the pool. God, I don't know, I had six or seven guys in, and Freddie—he's a young fighter I've been coaching— I didn't notice exactly when Don left but I don't think he was here more than half an hour."

Maddox thanked him. "So," said Rodriguez in the street, "he didn't have time to go anywhere else. He went straight home from here."

"I'm beginning to think," said Maddox, "that Dunning was a little too good to be true. Such a paragon of all virtues. Clean-living upright young cop. Didn't drink hard liquor, didn't smoke, engaged to a virtuous girl. Didn't he ever have any fun, kick up his heels a little?"

"Maybe he never was tempted to. There are some like that. The dedicated career cop. I'm still thinking about Fernandez."

"Waste of time," said Maddox. "We'd never get enough to charge him."

They went back to the office and he called the Coldfield house again but got no answer. Coldfield had probably gone to see the lawyer, and evidently Mrs. Coldfield was still out shopping.

Glen Jowett, cruising his usual beat through central Hollywood since eight this morning, was thinking about Dunning. He hadn't known Dunning well, just as one of his fellow cops on the same shift, but he had liked him and respected him as a good cop, and he'd been shaken, looking at his body. God knew he had seen a lot of bodies on the job, and young ones too, but somehow it had been different, seeing Don Dunning dead. He had been wondering how in hell it could have happened. Of course that was for the detectives to figure out, but he couldn't help wondering. And just yesterday something had occurred to him. It might not amount to anything at all, but he'd been thinking about it and wondering if he ought to tell the detectives. They might think he was just imagining things.

He was a deliberate man, didn't make up his mind in a hurry, but all this shift he'd been thinking about it. It had been a quiet day on the whole, not much business. He'd handed out a couple of moving violation tickets, broken up a fistfight on the street, the rest of the time just cruised, listening for his call on the radio. He called in a Code Seven for lunch at one o'clock. It was murder on the street, up to about ninety-seven. By three o'clock he'd made up his mind to tell the detectives about it, and was anxious to have the shift over. Then at three-thirty he got a call to an address on Mariposa, unknown trouble. He headed down there. When he got to it, he remembered this place, because it had once set him thinking about something else. It was just an old frame house on a shabby residential block. About four months ago there'd been a daylight burglary at that house, and he'd been the one sent to look at it and call the detectives. He remembered the two men who lived here, Peterson and Tinker. You couldn't spot the fags by sight, and they were ordinary-looking fellows, not young, both maybe in their fifties. It had been an amateur burglar and he hadn't got much.

But waiting for the detectives to show, Jowett had talked to some neighbors, asking if they'd seen anything, and the old man living on one side of this house had talked about Peterson and Tinker. He'd been a friendly elderly man, retired from the railroad. "Them two, they're both fags all right, they've lived here together for years, it's Peterson owns the house, he inherited it from his mother. They run a dry cleaners on Vermont. And I never liked them being next door. Only then the Vasquezes' little girl took sick, they live up on the corner, they're nice quiet people. It was this leukemia she had, she wasn't going to get better, going to die. Fact is, she died last month. And she'd always wanted to go to Disneyland. Vasquez, he just works in a store, don't have much money and a raft of kids. And it was Peterson and Tinker went around the block taking up a collection, started it off with twenty-five bucks of their own money. They got enough so the little girl could have a nice day at Disneyland. It was a good thing to do. And it kind of set me thinking. I don't like these damn loudmouthed fags go around braggin' about what they are and marchin' in parades and all, but I got to say these two aren't like that. Quiet neighbors, and they've lived together all these years, kind of peaceful. The Good Book says we shouldn't judge people. I guess that's right. I guess even they come like anybody else, good, bad, and indifferent. Live and let live, hey?"

It had set Jowett thinking too. People did come all shapes and sizes. And that pair were honest citizens, not a mark against either of them. Now he went up to the porch and pushed the doorbell, and it was Peterson who answered the door. He was a tall thin man with a ring of gray hair around a bald spot, and heavy jowls. "You called in a complaint," said Jowett.

"That I did," said Peterson. "We don't like to make trouble for neighbors, officer, but enough's enough and besides it's against the law. It's that camper next door." He pointed.

"Oh," said Jowett. In front of the house next door was a big RV camper looking nearly new.

"You can see it's parked half across our drive. Jerry's got an attack of bronchitis, reason we're home and the store closed, and I couldn't get the car out to go get that prescription filled for him. It's about the sixth time it's happened, we had to ask the guy to move it. He's some relation of the lady there, Mrs. Lopez, I guess a nephew, he showed up in that thing about three weeks back. And it's against the law to park them in the street."

"Yes, it is," said Jowett. "I'll see what I can do about it." He went over to the house next door and rang the doorbell. The man who opened the door was a stocky hairy dark fellow about thirty, with a heavy moustache. "Does that camper belong to you?" asked Jowett.

"That's right."

"Well, it's illegal to park it on the street, sir. I could write you a ticket for it. You'll have to move it. What's your name?"

"Antonio Lopez. Oh hell. Well, I guess my aunt wouldn't mind if I put it in the backyard. Would that be okay?"

"Yes, sir, just so it's off the street. You'd better do it now, the man next door wants to get his car out and you're blocking his drive."

"Oh, all right," said Lopez. He started for the camper. Jowett went back to the squad. It was a quarter of four. He headed back for the station.

When he'd handed over the squad and changed out of uniform he went upstairs to the detective office. Maddox and Rodriguez were there, nobody else. "Can I talk to you about something?" asked Jowett.

"Sure, come in and sit down. What's on your mind?" asked Maddox.

"Well, you might think it's nothing at all," said Jowett. "It's just something I got to thinking about. About Don Dunning."

"What is it?" Maddox offered him a cigarette.

"Thanks, I don't smoke. Well, it's something that happened a couple of weeks ago. It was an accident with a man dead, a fellow named Mike Greene. Don got sent to it first and called for a backup because traffic was getting tangled up, and I got there about ten minutes later.

It didn't look like a big deal except that the guy was dead, but it was his own fault. He was riding a motorcycle and he was drunk. He'd come sailing around the corner of Rosewood onto La Brea and ran smack into a sedan on the main drag and broke his neck. The driver couldn't have stopped in time to avoid him, there were good witnesses. The driver was from out of town, he was in a rented car, he was some kind of electronic expert on business here for his company in Boston, his name was Russell. Man about forty."

"Yes?" said Maddox.

"Well, both Don and I had to show up at the inquest. And this Greene's father, he was there and he made a big scene. He was fighting mad because nothing happened to the driver. Look, it was just stupid. Greene was drunk and he had two counts of DUI, he was driving without a license. It wasn't Russell's fault, it could have happened to anybody. But the father called us all a lot of names and cussed out the coroner for exonerating Russell and said the cops were all crooked and they'd always been down on Mike—he had two counts of Narco possession too—and he'd like to beat us all up for saying it was Mike's fault. And he took a swing at Russell, the bailiff started for him but Don got there first and put an armlock on him."

"Oh," said Rodriguez.

"And he called Don some dirty names and said it was his fault it came out the way it did, swearing Russell wasn't to blame, he'd like to get back at him good, meaning Don, see? The bailiff and Don had a little time with him, and the coroner cited him for disturbing the court, and he got sent up to jail for a couple of hours and had to show up in court next day. We were both there, he just got fined by the judge and was let go. But he was sure as hell mad at Don."

"I see," said Maddox slowly. "You think he might have been mad enough to kill him?"

"It sounds crazy," said Jowett, "a thing like that, but he was an ugly customer. A great big bruiser too, the kind flies off the handle easy. He was mad as hell at Don."

"And everybody else," said Rodriguez. "Russell and the witnesses. And you."

"It was Don gave most of the evidence about the accident, he got there just after it happened. I know it may not sound like much, I just thought you ought to hear about it. In case it does mean anything, about Don. I mean, he did utter threats. And what occurred to me," said Jowett, "is that Don might have been the one he could get at easiest. If you see what I mean. I seem to remember Russell was due to leave town the next day. The three witnesses were all employees at a big office building on that corner, it happened about noon and they were going out to lunch. I don't know where they live."

"And Greene might not have remembered their names, to look them up in the phone book?" said Rodriguez. "True."

And of course Dunning hadn't been in the phone book; all officers were under tight security, not listed anywhere.

"But he knew Don was working out of this division. He knew what he looked like. He could have hung around to spot him coming off duty and followed him home."

"Yes," said Maddox. "He struck you as vindictive? That he might still have been that mad about it a couple of weeks later?"

"I don't know," said Jowett. "Some people get to brooding. I just thought you ought to hear about it."

"You thought right," said Maddox. "Thanks for coming in. We'll keep it in mind." Jowett went out and he raised his brows at Rodriguez. "Comment? We can get his name and address from the court. But could there be anything in it at all? The self-righteous cops always down on Mike. He could have found out where Dunning lived, he could have been waiting for him there when he came home that night. He could have started a fight and knocked him out with a lucky blow. The big bruiser. And then—either he knew Dunning would be armed, or he just discovered the gun on him and shot him."

"But I don't see one like Greene moving the car and the body," objected Rodriguez. "What would be the point?"

"No, neither do I. But we can keep Greene in mind, César. The queer things do happen, people get queer ideas."

They sat in silence for a moment, and then a uniformed messenger came in with a manila envelope. "The lieutenant's not in his office."

"We'll take it," said Maddox. He slit the envelope open and said, "The autopsy report on Dunning." He scanned it rapidly. "Well, it tells us something we didn't know. He had a fractured skull. Right at the back of the head. The doctor says he could have died of it, if he hadn't been shot, if it had gone untreated."

"*Dios,*" said Rodriguez savagely, "just the way we read it—it was Fernandez, God damn it! He was there when Dunning got out of his car, he knocked him down from behind, probably against the car. He's big enough. And then he found the gun."

"But the Ford's running again. Why move the body?"

"We don't know that it was running on Sunday night, for God's sake. It might have still been in the garage. He took the car to get partway home. What's the time of death?"

"Between 9 and 11 P.M."

"Well, there you are. No buses running after nine. He took the car to start home, and he had the bright idea of dumping the body somewhere to delay discovery. Read it!" said Rodriguez. "Maybe he never spotted the gun until he was moving the body. And shot him then. If Dunning was knocked right out, unconscious, he might have been that way awhile before he was shot."

Maddox massaged his jaw, and reached for the phone, got the lab. Baker answered. "What did you come up with on Dunning's car, anything suggestive?"

"Not much," said Baker. "We'll send up a report. I think he was shot in the car. There's just a small bloodstain on the front seat, the top of the front seat, to the left of the passenger's side. It's Dunning's blood type. There were some of Dunning's prints inside and out, but the steering wheel was wiped clean, as we told you."

Maddox relayed that and said, "It's nothing like evidence for the D.A., damn it. But that's probably how it went, whether it was Fernandez or whoever. The steering wheel wiped—anybody would have the sense to do that, leaving the car in that lot." The phone shrilled on his desk and he picked it up and said his name.

"She's just come home," said Greg Coldfield.

"Okay, thanks." Maddox looked at Rodriguez. "We'll be doing more overtime. Mrs. Coldfield's home."

"Well, I haven't got a date anyway."

Maddox called Sue to tell her he'd be late again. "I suppose she'll stay in for a while, we'd better pick up something to eat first." It was just six o'clock; the night watch would be coming in directly.

They picked her up at the Coldfield house. There wasn't a sign of the son; he might be upstairs, shut away. Maddox looked at her with more attention than the only other time he'd seen her. She would once have been a pretty woman, but she hadn't aged well. There were deep wrinkles around her narrow pinched mouth, lines on her forehead. Her bleached blond hair was expensively dressed, her wrinkled claw-like hands manicured with the nails painted blood red, and she was wearing a smart black sheath dress and some chunky costume jewelry, but she looked haggard and her eyes were bitter, shallow pale blue eyes. She looked at the badge in his hand and didn't say anything.

"We'd like you to come in and answer some questions, Mrs. Coldfield."

"It's all Greg's fault," she said in a thin voice. "I never thought my own son would do such a thing to me. But he's just like his father. No feelings at all. He never loved me, nobody's ever loved me." She walked out to the car silently, didn't utter a word on the way to the station. There, they took her into an interrogation room and faced her across the tiny table, and Maddox told her she didn't have to answer any questions without her attorney present. She just shrugged. "It doesn't matter."

"You know we've got the gun, Mrs. Coldfield. We know it was the gun that killed your husband. You might as well tell us about it. You did kill him, didn't you?"

Her eyes slid sideways. "I had good reason to kill that man. The way he treated me all our married life, running around after other women ever since we were married, he was after women all the time." She began to describe in graphic and crude detail what he'd been doing with the other women, her voice going high and shrill.

Maddox cut across the flow of obscenity. "You didn't have any evidence of that, but that's what you believed, so you decided to kill him? Where did you get the gun and when?"

Her mouth went slack and suddenly, shockingly, she giggled. "I bought it. I just bought it. At a place where they sell guns. On Melrose Avenue." They could find the gun shop with a little looking. "I said I lived alone and needed it for protection. The man said I couldn't have it right away."

"Did you give your own name?"

"Oh, of course I did."

Rodriguez shifted and sighed. There was a fifteen-day waiting period while the gun shop would check with the police; when she didn't show up in Records they had let her have the gun. "I got it last Friday," she said.

"And you went right down to his office and shot him."

"Well, yes, I did. He told me never to come to his office again, that was when he was sleeping with that hussy of a secretary and I had a fight with her, a real fight, I pulled her hair and scratched her silly face and told him I knew just what was going on—" The obscenities started again, shrill and ugly, and again Maddox cut her off.

"You knew neither of the women there now would recognize you."

"No, they wouldn't. That hussy quit and he had to get another—he told me never to come to the office again—but of course he was probably sleeping with that new one too, he couldn't keep his hands off the women. And I'd had enough. He deserved to be killed, the way he treated me—he never loved me, nobody's ever loved me. Both the children just ungrateful brats, just like him, no feelings. Greg marrying that stupid girl and I'll bet he cheats on her too, and Mary going off with that conceited fool just on account of the uniform. And Greg turning me into a grandmother— A grandmother—I'm not old enough to be a grandmother! I don't want to be! I don't look old enough to be a grandmother, do I?" Horribly, she simpered at them. "I'll tell you a secret. I'm not really as old as my birth certificate says, they made a mistake on it. I'm really only thirty-one. That's not so very old, is it?"

"Mrs. Coldfield, if we type a statement about what you've told us, would you be willing to sign it?"

She gave them a demure glance. "Well, I guess I would, certainly. You said about a lawyer—the only one I know is Mr. Levy, had I better call him?"

"If you like, Mrs. Coldfield." He left Rodriguez with her, went out and typed the brief confession in triplicate, and brought it back. "Will you please read this over before you sign it?"

Obediently she read, and readily signed all three copies. "So now let's go," said Maddox.

"Oh, where are you going to take me now?"

"To jail, Mrs. Coldfield," said Rodriguez.

Her eyes went blank. "But I told you I did it, I had reason to do it. I'm not going to jail! There's no reason to put me in jail, you bastards, you—" She broke away from Rodriguez's hand and began to scream at the top of her voice. She ran out to the narrow corridor and into the big office and Brougham looked up, startled. Maddox got hold of her and she clawed at his face savagely. Rodriguez snapped, "For God's sake, call an ambulance, Dick!" and grabbed her other arm. She wasn't a tall woman but she was strong, and they had all they could do to hold her until the ambulance attendants arrived. In the end they had to put her in cuffs and she was bundled off still screaming the obscenities. They'd give her a shot at Emergency, and tomorrow the doctors would start looking at her.

"Sue's going to think you've been two-timing her and the girl got mad at you," said Rodriguez. "You're bleeding."

Maddox went and looked at himself in the mirror in the men's room, at two deep bloody scratches on his left cheek, and dabbed at them with a paper towel.

"That was quite a female," said Brougham. "I can hear what the head doctors will say. I don't think she'll end up in Tehachapi." That was the women's prison.

"Atascadero more likely," said Maddox. "My God, that man was a fool. Just because he had straitlaced ideas about the sanctity of marriage. If he'd divorced her years ago, she might not have grown the obsession."

"I wouldn't take a bet," said Rodriguez. "Some other obsession."

"And how right the son was. And I'd better get hold of him," said Maddox. He got him at the house, and told him about it. "She'll need a lawyer. She mentioned a Levy."

"He's not a criminal lawyer," said Coldfield. "I'll see she gets one."

"We'll let you know about any legal proceedings." Tomorrow somebody would be talking to the D.A.'s office about it. It would be out of their hands now. The probability was that there would be a simple sanity hearing and she'd be quietly tucked away.

When Maddox got home Sue and Margaret exclaimed over his wounds and ran for the iodine.

Stacey and Donaldson had missed the excitement. Another heist had gone down at a liquor store on Beverly and they'd been talking to the clerk.

"But, my God," said the clerk, "he looked like somebody's nice fat grandfather!" The clerk was only about twenty-five. "Most of these punks, they're young dudes needing the bread for dope, but he must've been fifty-five at least, I hardly looked at him until he pulled the gun. Then I was so surprised, I couldn't give you a real good description of him. He was sort of old and fat and he had on a cap—well, he was about medium height—" The offbeat fat heister again.

"Do you know how much he got?"

"Well, it was a slow night and a lot of the take was in checks, he just asked for cash. Maybe sixty or seventy bucks." Nobody this one had hit had said they would recognize a mug shot, and they hadn't a good enough description to ask N.C.I.C. if he was known elsewhere. They went back to the station and Brougham told them what they'd missed, and then he and Donaldson started a game of gin while Stacey typed the report.

Thursday, thankfully, was Maddox's day off. He slept late, and Tama let him play with the baby a little while Sue and Margaret went out to the market. He could imagine that D'Arcy was having a session with the D.A.'s office; Rodriguez would have gone to cover the inquest on Dunning. He was also curious as to what was turning up on Pollard. About eleven o'clock he called in, but neither Daisy nor Helen was there and the Juvenile office didn't answer. He got Rodriguez at two o'clock, just back from lunch.

"Well, short and sweet," said Rodriguez. "Of course we hadn't any evidence to offer at all. Just the bare facts, and of course they brought in an open verdict." Murder in the first degree by persons unknown. "I haven't laid eyes on D'Arcy, he's downtown with the D.A., I don't know what's happening, they'll have to wait for the psychiatric evaluation. No, the girls aren't in."

"Well, see you tomorrow."

He had just got in on Friday morning when one of the dispatchers called up from Communications. "That A.P.B. out on Kearney, one of the squads just spotted the car. It's parked in a public lot on Beverly. Do you want the squad to stake it out?"

"We're on the way. Tell him to stay put until we get there. If Kearney shows he can put the collar on him, but we'll be there in twenty minutes. What's the address?"

He took D'Arcy with him. Down there the Traffic man pointed out the old Chevy wagon in the first aisle of the public lot, and got back on tour. Maddox found a slot not far off, and they waited. There was only twenty minutes left on the meter in front of the Chevy, and ten minutes later Floyd Kearney showed up. The amorous burglar. They came up to him as he was unlocking the Chevy.

They had seen a description of him but it hadn't said anything about the general impression he gave. He was a tall thin man about thirty-five with a good deal of thick curly dark hair—remembering Mrs. Gordon's sudden discovery, Maddox grinned to himself—and he had a round boyish face with a mild and amiable expression. He looked at the badge and said, "What do the cops want?"

"You," said D'Arcy. "There's a warrant out on you for that job you pulled up on Tuxedo Terrace on Saturday night."

"For God's sake, how'd you find out about that?" asked Kearney, surprised.

"You left a couple of prints."

"Now that I never did, I'm always damned careful about prints. Where, for God's sake?"

Maddox laughed. "Well, I don't suppose you started to make love to Mrs. Gordon with gloves on. And then you left in a hurry and dropped a piece of the loot."

"Oh hell," said Kearney. "Look, fellows, do me a favor. They'll tow my car away. Let me call my sister so she can come and get it, huh? She's got an extra set of keys."

It was a reasonable request, and they let him make the call from a public phone and drop more coins in the meter.

In an interrogation room at the station, he was quite willing to talk. "It was all kind of accidental, you could say. I'd only just got in that damn place and started to look around when, my God, there they were comin' down the hall, practically in the bedroom—I didn't have a chance even to make the closet. I'd only just got behind the curtains when they come in. I never got caught that way before. I could see through the crack between the curtains, and I see them getting undressed, they were going right to bed. I figured to wait till they were both asleep and slide out— I'd left the back door open, I guess you know that."

"But meanwhile," said D'Arcy, "another idea occurred to you."

Kearney grinned cheerfully. "That it sure as hell did, fellows. She was a nice-lookin' lady, and oh, brother, did she have a beautiful figure, just the kind I like, not too thin but not too curvy, know what I mean? I hadn't had a dame in a while, and she sure looked good to me. And while I was waiting, it just sort of come to me that maybe she'd just think it was her husband, see. I heard him begin to breathe heavy, I knew he was sound asleep, he was in the bed nearest to me. And I just slipped out quiet and went over there. It was dark as hell but I remembered the layout of the place, you've got to do that in my job." He looked rueful. "We was getting on fine, and I'll never know what tipped her off it wasn't the husband, maybe I go at things some different than he does, but anyway she like to scared the hell out of me, when all of a sudden she rears up and starts to scream. I got out in a hurry. I just had on a T-shirt and pants, and all I'd picked up was some odds and ends of jewelry, it was in my pants pocket. I made tracks out of there fast, and damn, I hadn't got to first base with her yet either. I got out the back door, remembering the layout. Where the hell did I leave the prints?" Maddox told him. "Well, that's the way the cookie crumbles," said Kearney philosophically. "They feed you pretty good in the joint. It'll be my fourth burglary rap but I done hundreds of jobs you never found out about."

"A little more than that," said Maddox. "The warrant also says attempted rape."

Kearney leaped up in surprise and indignation. "Rape!" he yelped. "That's a Goddamned lie, I'd never go to rape a woman, I'd never hurt a woman no way! She wasn't fighting me at all."

"At first," said D'Arcy.

"As soon as she did I got out—I'd never rape a woman!"

"Well, it's on the warrant."

"That's a Goddamned bum rap," said Kearney furiously. "Rape! That's a damn awful thing to have on my record! It isn't—it isn't respectable!"

They were still laughing when they started to ferry him over to the jail.

Daisy came back late on Friday afternoon. It was Helen's day off. Daisy sat down beside Maddox's desk and accepted a cigarette absently. "Well, we've all been round and round on this, Ivor, and we're all agreed there's nothing in it. We saw all of the other kids and the parents, except a couple of families away on vacation. Some of the parents were more upset than the kids. Oh, not about the thing itself, but on Pollard's account. About twenty of those families attend his church, and the parents know him very well. All of those practically went up in a sheet of flame at his being accused. He's the best man in the world, a fine minister, it was impossible. His wife impressed us as a very nice sensible woman, and the other teachers. Not that that says anything about Pollard, but they're all intelligent people and they know him. But it was the kids convinced us. All of them we talked to like him a lot, like the school. I know we said that this sort of thing has to

happen for a first time, but it seems queer he'd just try it with the
Brenda girl out of all those available to him. All the kids spoke up loud
and clear, Mr. Pollard's never done anything nasty to any of them, he
wouldn't do a thing like that, he's a nice kind man." She drew on the
cigarette. "And something else, Ivor. We said kids that age are innocent and shy. Don't you believe it. Kids these days can get pretty
streetwise pretty young, in the big city."

"That's true, anyway," said Rodriguez. He'd come over to listen in.

"They all like him, respect him. And most of the parents will have
warned them about that kind of thing, if not in explicit terms."

"Yes," said Maddox. "Naturally. In the big city. Tempest in a tea-
cup?"

"Something more than that," said Daisy. "There's nothing to it, he
struck all of us as absolutely clean, by what the kids said. So that was a
deliberate lie on the Brenda girl's part."

"Why the hell?" asked Rodriguez. "A ten-year-old kid, going to that
trouble— Why should she? She convinced you then."

"She sounded convincing," said Daisy. "She surely did. But I could
have a guess about it. Item, she doesn't like the school. They try to
make her work too hard. Item, she'd been going to a public school and
even kids that age in public school, rubbing elbows with kids from all
kinds of backgrounds, are pretty tough and sophisticated. Brenda would
know all about the nasty old men who ask little girls to take off their
panties. And she'd know if she told that lie to Mama and Papa she
wouldn't be going to that school any longer."

"But, good God, wouldn't she realize what trouble she'd get the man
into?" said Rodriguez.

Daisy laughed sharply and stubbed out her cigarette. "If we're talking about kids that age, they're also completely self-centered. She
wouldn't have given that a second thought. I think she was just making
a bid for freedom, to get back to the public school where they let her
do finger painting and play volley ball and if she can't read they tell her
she just isn't ready for it and not to worry. I'm just glad it came out this
way and there wasn't anything in it."

"So we just drop it quietly," said Maddox.

"Drop it, drop it," said Daisy. "But we ought to spell it out to the
Remlings that there's nothing to it and Brenda told a whopping fat
lie."

"Is that necessary?" asked Maddox.

"Of course it is. They could spread that tale around. That woman's a talker. And besides, they ought to know the truth about their darling daughter. Look, Ivor—the parents who don't know Pollard were understandably upset. Police asking about a molestation charge. We're going to call every one of them back, tell them there's absolutely nothing in it. We can't leave them up in the air suspecting the man. I think that's of prime importance."

"Well," and Maddox fingered the healing scratches on his cheek, "it's your baby."

Oddly enough Saturday was quiet, no new business showing up. There was a new heist on Saturday night, and by what showed on it it was the big black fellow again, and again high as a kite on something, and again nothing but a general description.

At two o'clock on Sunday afternoon Maddox was listening to Feinman complaining bitterly about the lab—they hadn't turned up anything from all the prints on that latest hit by the burglary ring, after taking over a week processing them—when a couple of civilians came wandering in, a man and a woman. The man was short and thin and forceful, and he said, "My name is Edward Forsyth, Red Carpet Realtors, and I have a complaint to make. I want some action taken on this immediately." The woman just stood and looked around vaguely. She was short and fat and dowdy in a cotton dress, flat-heeled shoes.

The phone rang on Maddox's desk. Everybody else was out hunting the heisters.

"Yes, sir, what's it about?" Feinman took the man over to his desk.

"What can we do for you, ma'am?" Maddox asked the woman.

"Well, I don't know," she said indecisively. "The minister said I ought to see you."

"May I have your name?"

"Grace Moriarty."

The phone went off on his desk again and he picked it up. "Listen," said the desk sergeant, sounding distracted, "I've got these two reporters from the *Times*, they're asking all sorts of questions, and I don't know what the hell they're talking about. They want to talk to some detectives—"

CHAPTER SIX

Maddox excused himself from Grace Moriarty and looked into the office across the hall. Daisy was typing a report. "There seem to be some reporters out in front asking for detectives. You'd better go and see what they're after." She looked annoyed but got up and went out. He came back to the other office.

"Will you tell me what it's about, Mrs. Moriarty? Is it Mrs.?"

"That's right," she said. But her voice was drowned by the forceful voice from the next desk.

"The property is on Raleigh Street, it's not a prime area of course but any property in central Hollywood is of some value. It's listed at ninety thousand. The house needs a good deal of work done on it, but the owner is interested in a quick sale. We are listing it for the heir of the deceased owner, he lives in Illinois—we've had it on the market for some time. No one has been interested to look at it in the last couple of months, but I had a prospect just today and took him to see it an hour ago. And the house has been broken into, it looks as if someone has been camping out there, sleeping there, even cooking meals in the fireplace. Disgusting!"

"Has anything been stolen, Mr. Forsyth?" asked Feinman.

"For God's sake, there's nothing there to steal—the house is empty and all the utilities shut off, naturally. But there are some dirty old blankets on the living room floor, and the toilet's been used without being flushed, of course it couldn't be flushed. Disgusting. Whoever broke in smashed a rear bedroom window. I want some police action on it. The property's a good deal run down as it is, and this vandalism just lessens the value. These street people, as they call them, wandering around, dirty tramps vandalizing private property."

"Well, Mr. Forsyth, about all we can do on it is to have the squads check it out on their regular tours. What's the address?" Forsyth supplied it. "I'm afraid we haven't got the manpower to stake it out. You might want to check it yourself. Whoever's camping out there proba-bly is just spending nights there. We'll have the squads watch for them, check it out, and that's about all we can do. I can see it's a little problem for you, sir, but that's all we can do."

"I always understood this is supposed to be a competent police force. If that's the only help you can offer—"

"Well, sir, there are a lot more serious crimes going on after all. We'll have the squads check it out. If you should find out anything more definite you can let us know."

"Oh, very well, thank you," said Forsyth fussily. "It's not a prime piece of property, but this just makes it more difficult to move at all. Oh, very well, thank you." He marched out stiffly. Feinman sighed and took up the phone to call the watch commander.

"My, he was mad, wasn't he?" said Grace Moriarty. Maddox turned back to her. She had sat down in the chair beside his desk comfortably, her knees spread wide and her shabby brown leather handbag on her lap.

"Will you tell me what we can do for you, Mrs. Moriarty?"

"Well, the minister said I ought to tell you about it. He said I'd been fooled. I was telling him about it after church today, and he said I'd been fooled. He's the Reverend Mr. Hall, it's the Methodist church on Fairfax."

"Yes," said Maddox patiently. "Fooled about what?"

She looked about sixty, fat and plain; she had a round foolish face and very blue eyes behind rimless glasses. "Well, I don't know, it sounded all right to me. But I suppose a man might know better. You see, my husband died six months ago. Bill. My, I do miss him some-thing fierce, there was just the two of us, we never had a family. I always depended on Bill, on his advice and all, I'm kind of all at sea without him, you know what I mean. Anyway, there was the insurance money. Ten thousand dollars. I put it in the savings at the bank, but I got to thinking, maybe I should put it some place where it'd earn more interest. Invest it, like. I don't need it to live on, I've got Bill's railroad pension and the Social Security. And when I saw that ad it sounded interesting and I called the number. And she came to see me. This Mrs. Anderson."

"Where did you see the ad, what did it say?"

"Well, it was in one of those shopping papers they give away at the market, people run ads in it and there are savings coupons. It said you could get double your money back for a short-term loan, and I called the number. It was an answering service, so I left my number and she called back the next day and then she come to see me. And when she explained, it sounded sort of interesting. I could see there was the chance of money in it all right. You see, she's the Vice-President's daughter."

"Which Vice-President?" asked Maddox, taken aback.

"Why, of the country, you know. I didn't vote for him," said Mrs. Moriarty, "I mean when he was running with the President, because Bill said we'd better vote for the other ones, but it was them two got elected. She told me just how it was. He'd married her mother years back, before he went into politics, I guess she'd be around forty now, and he deserted her mother before Mrs. Anderson was born. But they were married all right, and her mother never heard of him again, he never paid child support or nothing. And then when he was running for Vice-President her mother told her about it, she was on her death bed then, poor woman. So Mrs. Anderson thought he owes her something, running off and deserting his wife like that, and anyway everybody knows them politicians are all millionaires. And it wouldn't look so good if it all came out about his deserting his wife. You can see that."

Maddox was looking at her, fascinated. "Yes?"

"Well, the only thing was, her mother told her they were married in Chicago and that's where she was born. But she didn't have no papers to show, they'd got lost. So Mrs. Anderson went to see a lawyer and he said it would cost about ten thousand dollars to find all the papers, the marriage ones and the birth certificate and all that. And that would be proof, and they could show them and he'd pay a lot of money, what he should've paid to her mother. Only she didn't have that much money. She said she was trying to raise the money, anybody could lend her anything, and when she got all the money from the Vice-President, she'd pay back double what everybody had loaned her."

Over her shoulder Maddox could see Feinman listening in. His expression was eloquent.

"Well, it sounded like sort of a good deal," said Mrs. Moriarty, "don't you think? Naturally he'd pay a lot or she'd tell how he deserted his wife all that time back—he wouldn't like that. And it wouldn't take long for the lawyer to get the proof, she said maybe in six months I'd get two thousand dollars back for the thousand I loaned her."

Feinman put a hand to his mouth; his shoulders were shaking. "You loaned her a thousand dollars?" asked Maddox. "Did she sign a note?"

"Oh, sure. She was all businesslike. She went to the bank with me and I got a thing they call a cashier's check, and she gave me a piece of paper promising to pay. I got it here." She opened the shabby bag and handed it over. It was the standard form of a promissory note. It was signed Edna Anderson. "My God," said Maddox, looking at it. "Did she give you an address, a phone number?"

"Oh, I had the number, where I called first. Where I could get in touch with her. But she's gone back to Chicago to see the lawyer there and get all the proof. It sounded fine to me, everybody knows these politicians got a lot of money. Do you want the phone number?"

"Please," said Maddox.

She got out a little address book and read it off to him. "But when I told the Reverend Mr. Hall about it he said I'd been fooled and she was a crook and I should tell the police. I don't know, it sounded all right to me. What do you think?"

Maddox pulled himself together and said, "I'm afraid Mr. Hall's right, Mrs. Moriarty. You won't see your thousand dollars again. The woman pulled a con game on you."

"Oh," she said, and her mouth drooped. "You really think so? That's awful. She seemed like such a nice woman."

"But we'd like to find her in case she's fooled other people," said Maddox. "What does she look like?"

"Oh, I don't know," she said vaguely. "She's maybe about forty years old, she's got brown hair and she's thin."

"This is the only number you've got for her, the answering service?"

"That's right."

"Well, thank you for coming in. We'll see if we can locate her."

She stood up. "I feel terrible, losing some of Bill's insurance money," she said mournfully. "If that's so. Maybe you could get it back when she signed that promise to pay."

"Well, we'll see," said Maddox. She waddled out, taking her time.

Feinman said reverently, "My good God in heaven. And people are supposed to be smarter all the time in this progressive modern world."

Maddox finally let himself begin to laugh. "That's a new one on me. My God, the things people will believe. But you still find them falling for the old pigeon drop, Joe. The plausible con artist is always the smooth talker."

"A thousand bucks, for an hour's easy work," said Feinman. "She wouldn't have to give an address to the answering service if she paid in cash and picked up the messages personally. My good God, what a scam."

"Of course only the ones like Mrs. Moriarty would fall for it, but of course there are quite a few of them around." Maddox sat up and wiped his eyes. "And she'll have other tales to tell for other marks. Oh, my. Everybody knows them politicians are all millionaires. Close enough to the truth. I do wonder how many she's taken with that tale."

"We can do some looking. She'll be an old hand at it. Put the M.O. out to N.C.I.C. and see if anybody recognizes it, if she's on record anywhere."

"Oh yes," said Maddox.

Daisy came in, and she was looking cross and belligerent. "Damn all muddled-headed civilians!" she said. She sat down beside Maddox's desk and lit a cigarette. "My God, that Remling!"

"What did the reporters want?"

"That's just it," said Daisy. "That damned dentist and his stupid wife! I called them yesterday, and told them what we thought, about Pollard and about Brenda. They didn't believe a word I said—she was listening in. He used some language nobody should use to a lady, and he said probably we just hadn't bothered to look into it at all, too lazy and slipshod to do our job, and he was going to see the whole damn city heard about it, letting innocent children be victimized by the dangerous perverts, and us calling his daughter a liar. And Pollard belongs in jail and his damn school shut down. Damn the man."

"Don't tell me," said Maddox. "He called the paper."

"That's just what," said Daisy. "He told them his version and these damned reporters wanted ours. I gave it to them straight. But Remling's threatening to sue the city—"

"For what, for God's sake?"

"For not affording proper police protection for citizens, exposing minors to extreme physical danger because the police can't be trusted to do their proper job— Do I know all the legal double-talk?"

"The *Times* isn't going to lay itself open for libel," said Feinman.

"No, but it's a story, and coming just after the Barlow thing, people will be interested. They'll pussyfoot around it, Dr. Remling alleges, Dr. Remling asserts, but I'll bet you they'll run it. Some of these young reporters don't like the cops any more than the street punks. And I'll bet you Remling could find some shyster lawyer to take the case too, ridiculous as it sounds. Oh, damn. Just because that stupid selfish brat told a big fat lie." Daisy put out her cigarette and immediately lit another. "Just because Daddy thinks she's a sweet innocent. Oh, it's a stinking mess, some of the mud's always going to stick to Pollard. I told you we called all the parents back, the ones who don't know him. At least seven or eight of those I talked to were pretty dubious at being reassured it wasn't so. You know, no smoke without fire. He'll probably lose some of his student body next semester."

"And that's a damn shame," said Feinman. "There's a saying about bearing false witness."

"People!" said Daisy. "The *Times* may hide behind the careful words, but if you ask me, if they spread it around Pollard would have a dandy case for a libel suit on Remling. Oh, it's a bloody mess."

"If you could get the kid to admit she lied—"

"Oh, don't be naive, Joe, it's a little late for that, with Daddy shooting off his mouth to the reporters. The truth may never catch up to the lie."

"That could very well be," said Maddox soberly. "You said something about the modern progressive world, Joe. People are still people, quite a lot of them stupid and irrational. Witness Mrs. Moriarty." The phone went off on his desk and he eyed it resignedly, picked it up.

The dispatcher's voice was high and excited. "There's been a kidnapping! At the Hollywood hospital—a baby— They just discovered it was missing and called in! Shall I call the FBI?"

"My good God," said Maddox. "No, not yet. Okay, we'll take it from here." He passed that on. Daisy just shut her eyes for a moment and then put out her latest cigarette and stood up.

The three of them got over there in a hurry. It was an old hospital, the Hollywood Presbyterian, north on Vermont. Even in the lobby there was a furtive air of subtle awareness, something wrong; the grapevine would have carried the news all over the building in minutes. The dispatcher had called the detectives direct without sending a squad. Maddox showed the badge to one of the women at the admitting desk and she said smoothly, "Obstetrics, third floor." They rode up in the elevator. Up there was a more tangible air of concern and alarm. Their arrival precipitated half a dozen nurses in their direction. It was just after visiting hours and only the hospital staff was present. All the nurses started to talk at once, and a couple of interns and an older doctor were coming up to join the crowd. Feinman raised his voice and said, "One at a time, please. Let's have a little order here." They started to calm down some. The one nurse with a R.N. pin on her uniform, an older gray-haired woman, spoke up with authority.

"It's Mrs. Bernstein's baby, her name's Dorothy, she was born last Wednesday. Mrs. Bernstein's due to be released tomorrow. Visiting hours were over at four, and just after the visitors leave we take all the babies to their mothers for feeding. Mrs. Bernstein's nursing the baby. It was Doris who found she was gone— This is Doris Prochek—"

She was a slim dark pretty girl, and she was scared. "At first I thought Betty or Doreen had already taken her to Mrs. Bernstein, it's not always the same ones take the same babies to the mothers, but I checked and the baby wasn't with her, and I told Mrs. Smith and we checked everywhere and she's just gone—such a sweet baby—"

"Are you sure?" asked Daisy reasonably. "You'll have quite a few babies here, and not all the mothers will be nursing them. Some mix-up—"

"That's impossible," said the gray-haired nurse scornfully. "Do you think we can't count? The babies all have name bracelets on, naturally. The Bernstein baby's missing, and nobody seems to have seen anything suspicious. Of course just before we started taking the babies to the mothers the last of the visitors were going out. There's always a certain amount of confusion during visiting hours, I suppose it's just conceivable that one of those could have taken the baby out of the nursery. Of course people come to the nursery to look at the babies, but they're not allowed in. I don't understand how any outsider could have been able to get in without being noticed—and out again with the baby."

Hospitals prided themselves on their efficiency, but they were staffed with human people like other institutions and this sort of thing had happened before at other hospitals. The visitors would have been in the process of getting shooed out, some of the nurses busy at that, others starting to take the babies to the mothers. There would be quite a few nurses on this floor, and while they were all known to each other, they had been busy. A woman in a white uniform walking down the hall would have registered as one of the staff, and even if she was a stranger it would have been assumed that she had come to Obstetrics from some other floor for some reason. It had happened before, the woman wanting a baby managing to steal one from a hospital.

But every one of these people would have to be questioned, their memories probed, the results put together to see if any significant facts emerged to point to anything specific. But all the nurses had their regular duties to do. At least everybody here would be on duty until eleven tonight.

They started trying to bring order out of chaos. They commandeered the waiting room down the hall— Maddox had a fleeting memory of his own session in another waiting room, with Margaret, while John Ivor was getting born. Luckily there weren't any haggard expectant fathers here now. The three of them began to talk to all the staff on a one-to-one basis, occasionally comparing notes. By five o'clock of course the mother had had to be told, and at five-thirty a thin dark young man came rushing in looking wild.

"You're police? The doctor said they'd called the police— Have you found the baby? What's happened to our baby? My God, how could anybody have kidnapped our baby? You got to find her—you've got to do something, call in the FBI—"

Maddox took him across the room and made him sit down. "Calm down, Mr. Bernstein. We're doing all we can, we're trying to find out. We don't know that this is a kidnapping, but we very much doubt it. If a ransom note should turn up, of course the FBI will be called in. But I can tell you, in cases like this it usually turns out to be some woman who just wants a baby, so much that she steals one. She'll be taking good care of the baby, that's simple logic, sir."

"But what are you doing to try to find her? You're just standing around, you've got to do something!"

"We're doing everything we can, Mr. Bernstein. We're trying to find out if any of the nurses remembers anything useful. We've got a description of the baby, and it'll be on the news at six and ten." Of course there wasn't much to describe about a baby. Five-day-old Dorothy Bernstein weighed seven pounds and four ounces, was twenty-two inches long, had dark hair. "Now take it easy. In cases like this most people are eager to help, you know. Anybody who suddenly appears with a baby, people who know her may notice and wonder about it, and we could just get somebody calling in quite soon." He crossed his fingers on that one.

"You keep saying cases like this, it's not just a case like this, it's our baby—our first baby! You've got to find her— Ruth's in a terrible state, the doctor had to give her a shot—"

"I know you can't help worrying, Mr. Bernstein, but we're doing our best."

When the night watch would be on, he called in. Brougham and Stacey came over, leaving Donaldson to mind the store, and helped out on the questioning. By nine o'clock a little something had emerged. Two of the nurses had separately remembered noticing a woman in a white uniform looking into the nursery through the big plate-glass window. At the time neither of them had taken much notice of her. There were still a few visitors there, and they had taken her for a visitor or a nurse from another floor. They couldn't begin to offer any description, they hadn't noticed anything about her. One of them had been hurrying to a patient having a difficult labor, had just seen her in passing. The other one said vaguely that she had the impression she was young. That was all, and of course it needn't have been the woman who had stolen the baby.

When the six o'clock news had come on there had been five minutes devoted to the baby, an earnest plea to the public for citizens to be on the lookout, inform the police of any suspicious circumstance. Bernstein had watched that in the waiting room. He was just sitting with his head in his hands now.

They had done everything they could here for the time being. Neither Maddox nor Daisy nor Feinman had had anything to eat and they were starving. Now they just had to wait and see if the helpful citizens would come through. In a few other cases like this, that had happened, someone calling to say that a neighbor had just acquired a baby and hadn't been pregnant, she said it was her sister's but maybe it was that kidnapped baby on the TV news—and it had turned out to be. It was true enough that a woman who stole a baby just because she wanted one usually took good care of it. But Maddox thought of all those people out there, the casual people, so many transients in the big city, not taking much notice of each other. A woman with a baby, renting an apartment, bringing the baby to an already rented apartment where none of the other tenants knew her, who was going to take notice? And if she left town tonight with the baby, disappeared to some other big city, it was possible that nobody would ever know what had happened to little Dorothy Bernstein. As he started home through the still busy Sunday night streets, his stomach rumbling, he thought about John Ivor at home with the great bulk of Tama beside the crib.

And he had laughed with Sue about the UPS man, but it was comforting to know that Tama was there, fulfilling his new responsibility.

The dispatcher who had called in the first alarm had gone off duty ten minutes later. She told her replacement, June Hobbs, about the baby. "My God, the things that happen," said June. "I hope they'll find it safe. That poor mother must be out of her mind. Some nut stealing a baby out of a hospital, you wonder how it could happen." She sat down at the board and prepared for the usual swing watch business. Sometimes weekends were busy, sometimes quiet.

She got the usual run of business up to eight o'clock. She sent squads to accidents, a fight at a bar, a holdup at a drugstore. She took a coffee break at ten to eight, and visited the restroom, and came back. She wondered if the detectives had found the baby. She wasn't married yet, but she'd like to be, and have babies of her own. She found herself yawning; this could be a boring job when you were used to it, though the civilians thought it must be exciting.

Then it got rather exciting. At eight-five the radio suddenly crackled to life in her ears, the call from a squad. There was usually static in the background, and the voice wasn't identifiable, and she didn't know all the Traffic men personally, but the message was loud and clear. "There's an officer been shot, he's bleeding, it's the corner of Vine and Sunset, this is his police car, send help quick!" Oh, Lord, she thought. Efficiently she called up another squad and an ambulance. Two minutes later another call came through. Robbery in progress, Carl's Bar on Beverly. She sent out another squad. After that it was fast and furious. A call to a dead body on La Brea, a heist at a liquor store, a fight in the street with shots fired, requests for backups, burglary in progress at a pharmacy, another dead body. She began to wonder if a crime wave was getting underway. At the board beside her she could see out of the tail of her eye that Cindy Adelson was being kept just as busy, and Rena Ortiz beside Cindy. There came a little lull, and Cindy said, "What's going on out there? I've had six robberies in progress in the last fifteen minutes, and three dead bodies. The squads must be going crazy." The radio crackled again and she responded. June got another call, to a hit-run, and then another dead body. It was the busiest night she had ever had on the job. Then one of the squads called back, the one she had sent to a robbery in progress. "False alarm, there's nothing going on here." She got a call to a dead body in the street and sent him out on that. Then another squad called back. "That burglary was a false alarm, nothing going on." She sent him back on tour and then there was a call to a five-car pileup on Melrose. She heard Rena say, "For goodness' sake, we've only got so many squads! That's the fourth call I've had about a dead body in ten minutes!" The radio came to life again and crackled in June's ear. "Officer needs help, Beverly and Rossmoor, shots fired!"

Another squad called back. "There's nothing to this heist report, the place is closed."

June said to Cindy, "Are you getting calls about false alarms?"

Cindy was busy, said hastily, "Two so far," and got back on the radio.

Another call, burglary in progress. She contacted a squad. The radio crackled and another Traffic man said, sounding annoyed, "False alarm on that robbery in progress, nothing shows." Rena was talking fast into the mike. The radio crackled. Dead body in street on Beverly. Automatically she dispatched a squad and remembered she'd just sent that one to a 459 call. What, she thought confusedly, was going on out there? She looked at Cindy. "Honestly," said Cindy, ducking out from the headphones, "this is a wild night! That was another false alarm, for heavens' sake."

"There's something funny about it," said June, and took another call to a robbery. She hadn't another squad to send out on it, they'd all been sent to other calls.

Another car called in a false alarm. She hardly had time to think, reacting automatically, contacting the squads, but when she got another false alarm report her mind began to work. "What the hell," said the radio, "dead body be damned, there's no body I can see." The other radio said loudly and excitedly, "Request backup, officer shot, seven hundred block Melrose!"

Belatedly it dawned on June that something was wrong. All these calls were coming from a squad radio. The usual pattern was that the citizens called in on the ordinary phones, a bank of them in front of all the dispatchers, and the dispatchers called the squads. Not infrequently a squad would call in, having spotted something on its regular tour, but this spate of calls wasn't natural. The radio squawked at her again. "False alarm, all quiet at Beverly and Rossmoor, nothing going on."

June said to Cindy, "There's something funny about all this. I'm going to call the watch commander."

Lieutenant Ramirez was on swing watch. He listened to what she had to say and said, "I'll come down." He got there a couple of minutes later and started talking to all the dispatchers one by one as they had a little free time. By the time he got back to June she was listening incredulously to another call. "Robbery in progresh, officer needs ashis —ashis—help. Send backup."

June took off the headphones and said to the lieutenant, "That one sounds drunk, but it's from a squad and that's impossible!"

"Let's have a listen," said Ramirez, and took the headphones. A few minutes later he handed them back and said, "Now that's a damned queer thing. The man's drunk as a skunk, and using a squad radio."

"That can't be," said June. "But I told you, I suddenly realized all these false alarm calls had come from a squad, and that's not natural. Yes, sir, they mostly gave call signs, the squad number, but I wasn't paying attention, I was just relaying the messages."

"Sure," said the lieutenant. "Natural. Everybody else has been getting them too, the squads are going crazy." He ruminated and picked up one of her phones and called the police garage in the basement. "Bert? Ramirez. Say, have we got any squads out of action? Oh. Well, where is it? Okay, thanks." He put the phone down. "Talk about one for the books. There's just one squad out of action. It's in for the regular tune-up, an oil change and brake lining. It's at a Plymouth agency over on Fairfax. Send a couple of men to have a look."

"Yes, sir," said June.

Stoner and Byrd in their respective squads landed at the Plymouth agency about the same time. It was all closed up at this hour, but they got out their flashlights and walked around the building. At the side, up from the used car lot, they could see that the entrance to the garage was open and there was a light in there. They went in. In the middle of the garage, with two or three other cars, a black and white squad was parked, and they could see a man sitting in it. As they came up to it they could see that he was swigging beer out of a can. Stoner laid a hand on the driver's door and opened it. The man had the mike in his other hand and was talking into it.

"Robbery in progresh, Al's bar on Melrose," he was saying, and hiccuped. "Car 159, offisher needs help, shots fired. Car 159, dead body corner of Vine and Beverly."

"What the hell do you think you're doing?" asked Byrd.

The man squinted up at them. "Oh, hello, offishers. Why, I've been havin' the hell of a lot of fun, thash what I been havin'." There were empty beer cans all over the front seat and the floor.

"Come on out," said Stoner, and laid ungentle hands on him and yanked him out of the car. He stood teetering back and forth and gave them a happy smile. "Hell of a lot of fun," he said vaguely.

"Oh, for God's sake," said Stoner disgustedly, "come on, you're going over to the drunk tank."

Nobody had called in with any information about the baby overnight, and there wasn't any more they could do about that now, they'd just have to sweat it out. They all doubted that it was a real kidnapping, but whether a ransom note turned up or not they'd better alert the Feds about it. Eventually, if no leads got turned in, there'd be a nationwide alert out, it would be added to the N.C.I.C. list. Maddox started to call all the radio stations in the county, asking for publicity on it. A lot of people watched the TV news but some didn't who'd listen to the radio.

A disgusted Jenner had been waiting for them when they came in, and told them about the practical joker last night. He'd probably be sobered up by now, and presently Rodriguez went over to the jail to talk to him.

Daisy came in with the morning edition of the *Times*. "Nothing on the baby?"

"Nothing."

"Well, they did it. Have you seen it?" She laid the paper on Maddox's desk, folded back. They hadn't put it on the front page, but it was on page three, and they'd given it two columns. Maddox read it rapidly.

"Very slick," he said. "Very careful. Dr. Remling alleges that. Dr. Remling feels very strongly from what the police told him that there was no investigation. Dr. Remling asserts that the police were negligent in not pursuing the investigation further, that while any suspicion still attaches to Mr. Pollard the city should rescind the school's license to operate. Very slick indeed, very careful."

"You notice also, the *Times* was unable to obtain an interview with Mr. Pollard. He has simply denied all the charges. What else can he say? You notice they don't quote me. I told them in one-syllable words we had investigated thoroughly and reached the conclusion that the charge was false, that the girl had lied for reasons of her own, but that they don't mention."

"And Public Relations is going to be annoyed," said Maddox. "Well, they'll back us up, that's what they're there for."

"Yes, but it's a nasty thing, Ivor. Leaves the bad taste. I'm terribly sorry for Pollard."

Ten minutes later, of course, a call came in from Lieutenant Evans down at Public Relations. "What the hell's all this about?"

Maddox had taken the call, and said, "I'll let you talk to one of the officers who was in on the actual investigation," and he jerked his head at Daisy and mouthed, "PR."

She took the call in her own office, and talked with Evans for quite some time.

It was D'Arcy's day off. And they were all chiefly concerned about the baby but there was some other business going on to work. Feinman asked the phone company for the address of that answering service, to see if they could get a line on the plausible Mrs. Anderson. Maddox had already put out that M.O. to N.C.I.C. Now he got hold of a bailiff at the appropriate court and got that Greene's address. The vindictive father who had threatened Don Dunning. Earl Greene, an address in Atwater. Maddox didn't really think Greene was a very likely suspect for Dunning, but you never knew. Unlikely as it might seem to the detective-novel buff, murders got committed for some very trivial reasons. They'd have a look at Greene anyway.

"Just what the hell gave you that bright idea?" asked Rodriguez.

The man facing him in the interrogation room at the jail was sober enough now. His name was Henry Hatcher, he was thirty-seven years old and he was the head mechanic at that Plymouth agency. He'd never been under arrest before. He gave Rodriguez a rather sheepish smile. "Oh, for God's sake," he said. "I guess it was a damned fool thing to do."

"You can say that for sure." Hatcher was a thin fellow of medium height, with a receding hairline and big ears. "Why did you think of such a thing?"

"Well," said Hatcher simply, "the damned squad car was there. And I was feeling kind of annoyed at the fuzz. I'd just got a ticket, first moving-violation ticket I ever had, and it's gonna cost me a fine. Usually I'm a careful driver, but I was late to work on Saturday and I ran a light, I thought I could get through on the amber. And of course there was a squad car right across the intersection, there would be. Then I had a date with this girl last night and she called it off at the last minute."

"You're not married?"

"I'm divorced. No kids, thank God. I've kind of been going steady with this woman, she's a good kid, but her sister landed in town unexpected and she called off the date. I was kind of at loose ends. And I was just sitting around after I had dinner thinking about that damned ticket, and all of a sudden I thought about that squad car down at the garage. I got a key to the garage, of course, and I had the idea. See, my brother-in-law used to be on the Highway Patrol, and I know something about the language cops use, I mean how they describe things."

"Such as robbery in progress," said Rodriguez. "It amounts to a charge of obstructing the police, Hatcher."

"I know it was a damn fool thing to do," said Hatcher penitently, "it just seemed like a good idea at the time." He grinned. "And it was the hell of a lot of fun, chasing all those squad cars to hell and gone. All for no reason. I picked up some six-packs of beer and went down to the garage and I was getting a kick out of it, I tell you. Chasing the cops all over. I didn't mean to get drunk, but one beer sort of led to another. I'm sorry I did it now. I mean, I like cops all right, I know they've got their jobs to do."

"Well, just don't do it again," said Rodriguez. "You won't be spending any time in for it but you'll be fined to the limit and put on probation."

"That's okay," said Hatcher meekly. "I guess I deserve it."

"Just as we surmised," said Feinman, "the answering service hasn't got an address for Mrs. Anderson. She paid the fee in cash and called in person to collect messages. She'd contact the possible marks by phone, size them up by how they sounded, and go to see the best bets to put over the table. And God, what a tale. I'll just say, it can't be her first time out. When she can make anybody believe that one, she'll have had some practice."

"Oh, probably," said Maddox. Rodriguez came back and they told him about that, about Greene.

"That's far out," said Rodriguez, smoothing his moustache.

Maddox ruminated. "We don't really have anywhere to go on Dunning," he said sadly. There had been a funeral for Dunning on Friday, and quite a few men from the Department would have been there, permission to go off duty, and the Chief would have been there.

"I don't like Greene much," said Rodriguez. "Do you want to go look for him?"

"I think it can wait a little." He hoped all the radio stations were getting the word out about the baby, repeating it. He had contacted all those that broadcast in Spanish too. They talked about it a little; there wasn't much to say.

"My God, the parents must be wild," said Feinman. "My wife was upset about it."

"Oh, so was mine."

After a while they went out for an early lunch. Just after they got back Nolan came in with another heist suspect and Feinman sat in on the questioning. There was no word coming in about the baby. Then a new call went down and Maddox and Rodriguez went out on it.

It had been a piddling little job, a small independent market on a corner of Gower, but the owner had been beaten and stabbed and was in critical condition in Emergency. There was a witness, a scraggly elderly woman who had walked in on it. She was keeping her head. "I just walked up to get some coffee and milk, it's convenient having this place so close, I just live over on Lexington. And I couldn't take it in at first, there were these three black men, well, just boys really, teenagers I guess, beating Mr. Polk, and one of them had a knife—and when they saw me I was scared they'd come after me too but they just grabbed the money from the cash register, that is one of them did, and they ran out— And poor Mr. Polk— It was me called the police—" She couldn't offer any description. "They were just black teenagers, that's all I can say."

They didn't bother to call the lab. Even if the teenagers had JD counts they wouldn't have prints on record, as minors. It was just another anonymous crime, the sort that happened every day in the big city. But there'd be some paperwork to do on it.

On Tuesday about one o'clock—nobody had called in any tips on the baby—Feinman was in the office alone when he got a call directly from a squad car man. It was Gonzales. "We got the briefing to check out this place on Raleigh for possible trespassers. Probably at night. I don't know what the swing watch might have turned up—"

"Nothing," said Feinman.

"Well," said Gonzales, "I rode by yesterday and had a look around. The back door's open and the place is in a mess. It's a ramshackle old house about to fall down. There's a for-sale sign in front. I guess there've been trespassers all right, they left some stuff in the house."

"So thanks," said Feinman, uninterested.

"Well, that isn't what I'm calling in about. I stopped by again just now and this time I had a look around the backyard, and whoever the trespassers were they seem to have left a dead body behind."

"What?" said Feinman.

"That's right. Man about fifty, looks as if he's been stabbed. Looks like a bum, he's dirty as hell and wearing ragged old clothes and he smells of cheap wine. He wasn't there yesterday, that I can say. He's just lying out in the backyard."

"Well, I will be damned," said Feinman. "Any I.D. on him?"

"I didn't look, being trained to preserve the scene for you brainy detectives."

"Okay, somebody'll be out on it."

Jerry Tinker had mostly got over his bout with the bronchitis, but he hadn't gone to work today, let Ed Peterson mind the store alone. In the middle of the afternoon he went out to the backyard and looked at their little garden. They'd both worked hard over that, and it had paid off. The tomatoes and lettuce were doing real well, and the zucchini and green beans. He glanced over the fence at the big RV camper in the backyard next door and his brow wrinkled. There were things neither he nor Ed liked about that camper. He picked a couple of the tomatoes and a head of lettuce and brought them in. By the time Ed got home he had the salad all made, and he'd fed Adelaide the calico cat they both doted on and spoiled.

As they sat down to dinner he said, "I heard it again."

"Oh," said Ed. "That's not right, if it is a dog or cat. Hell of a thing, shut up there in this weather. You don't like to make trouble, and Mrs. Lopez is a nice woman, but it's not right."

"We could call the Humane Society, I suppose," said Tinker. "Maybe we'd better. I don't like to think of it, shut up there."

"It's too late tonight."

"I've got a funny feeling about it, Ed," said Tinker.

The body hadn't any I.D. on it. It had indeed been stabbed, several times. It was the body of a middle-aged man and as Gonzales had said he looked like a bum.

The ramshackle old house was in a mess. There were a couple of ragged blankets in the living room, some clothes. Franks took some pictures, and they sent the body down to the morgue.

"I suppose he could have been the one camping out here," said Rodriguez. "Street people. No way to find out who took him off."

"Well, I don't know. We might stake it out."

"Why the hell? Whoever wasted him won't be back."

"I wonder," said Maddox. "He was about six feet, a hundred and eighty." He cocked his head at the little pile of clothes in one corner of the bare dusty living room. "Look at that jacket, César. It'd fit a fellow half his size."

"For God's sake, you don't think whoever did it might come back here?"

"Street people. The extra clothes are important to them, about all they've got. Not to be abandoned. And it's a homicide. He, whoever, just might come back."

CHAPTER SEVEN

There hadn't been any I.D. on the body. Franks had taken the prints, and the computers did make life easier for the cops these days. Maddox had just got back to the office and finished talking with the watch commander about the stakeout when Franks called him. "We got an I.D. on the body, his prints were in Records. He was a Joseph Chebinski, he had a count of burglary a long while back, there's nothing about a next of kin."

"Well, so at least we know what name to bury him under," said Maddox.

There hadn't been any calls about the baby, nothing had come in about the baby at all.

Ellis had come in today, and he looked as if he had dropped more weight, as if he'd aged ten years in the last couple of months. None of them knew what to say to him, how to talk to him. But naturally he was concerned about the baby too, and just after that he came into the big office, and asked if there was any news. Maddox was there alone; two new heists had gone down last night. "Nothing showing yet. Sit down, George."

Ellis wandered over to look out of the window. "I'm not being much use to you these days, I'm sorry."

"Life's got to go on, George. And I know that's a trite and easy thing to say."

Ellis came back and sat down beside his desk. "Oh, my God, Ivor, I know. It's not the boy. I could get over that, these things happen and you've got to go on somehow. Damn it, it's Frances. She can't get over it. She's turning into a lush, Ivor."

"Oh," said Maddox.

"She'd never take a drink except on special occasions, a glass of wine on birthdays, like that. The first time I found her passed out, I didn't believe it. I suppose she found it dulled the edges, and she's just gone on from there. It's the main reason I've been staying home. I can't trust her. God knows I've tried to talk to her, it's no use. If we had any relatives, if there was somebody to stay with her, give her a shoulder to lean on, but there's nobody. She wants to go out to the cemetery all the time, sit by the grave. And half the time she's not fit to drive."

"Oh, my God," said Maddox.

"I'm keeping the keys to her car, but she went out and got an extra set. She was gone when I got home on Saturday, and I was out of my mind thinking she'd smashed herself up, or killed somebody the way that bastard killed Roy. I knew where she was, if she got there. I went out to the cemetery, and she'd crashed the car right at the entrance. At least it's out of commission for a while."

"Oh, my God, I'm sorry, George."

"You know the routine," said Ellis. "You keep the money away from her so she can't buy it, and she goes out and pawns her jewelry to buy the liquor. She did that last week. I kept thinking she might pull herself together, get over it, but it's nearly two months and she's just getting worse. If we'd had other children— But Roy was all we had, I guess we were both too much wrapped up in him. I saw our doctor yesterday, he's arranging to put her in a sanitorium for a while, see if she can pull out of it."

"That's the hell of a thing. I'm sorry, George."

"He says that maybe counseling will help, but it's had me crazy, worrying about her, you can see. Once I know she's being taken care of, I'll start to pull my weight around here again."

"Don't worry about it, the important thing is to see she's taken care of," said Maddox gently.

"Yes, he's supposed to call me sometime today."

Feinman came in with Dowling and Ellis got up and started back for his own office, not speaking to either of them.

"Nothing on the baby?" asked Feinman.

"Nothing." Maddox told him absently about Chebinski. "We'll stake it out in case the other bum comes back." The phone rang on his desk and he reached for it.

It was Baker in the lab at the other end. He said, "I've got something for you."

"What?"

"Well, scientifically speaking, glass is a very interesting subject. You remember that hit-and-run found in the street, I think the name was

Paxton. There was a good deal of glass in his clothes and hair, and the coroner's office sent it all up to us for analysis in case we could pinpoint the type—glass from the headlights, you know. Different manufacturers use different grades and combinations. Well, it's not glass from a headlight at all, it's glass from a liquor bottle. He wasn't hit by a car, somebody beat him over the head with a bottle."

"Oh no," said Maddox. "I don't think we've had an autopsy report yet. It didn't look like anything to work. He was found outside a bar."

"Well, there you are," said Baker. "He probably had a fight with somebody in the street."

"Thank you," said Maddox. "All up in the air, it could have been anybody hit him over the head. If it was after the bar closed there might not be any witnesses, or if there were we're not going to find them."

"I just thought you'd be interested to know," said Baker.

D'Arcy had just come in; he'd been the one on that and Maddox passed on the news. D'Arcy groaned. "There's nothing to do on it, Ivor. The man seems to have been a drifter, I didn't find anybody who knew anything about him. There's no car registered to him. If he was at that bar and got into a fight outside it later, nobody'll ever find out anything about it."

"I know, I know," said Maddox. "Waste of time to look."

Nobody was calling in about the baby. "There's nothing on it?" asked D'Arcy. "That's one hell of a thing. It could be we'll never find out anything about it, the baby's just gone."

"Don't be a pessimist." But with no ransom note showing—they hadn't expected one, of course—D'Arcy could be right.

Maddox sat worrying about the baby, thinking about what there was on hand to work, thinking about Ellis. That was a bad thing and a sad thing, about Ellis' wife. Maybe the sanitorium and the counseling could straighten her out, but maybe not too.

"Excuse me," said a polite voice and he looked up. A weedy little young man was standing in the doorway.

"Yes, sir?"

"I had to come to see you. The police." He wasn't more than twenty-five, he had thin blond hair and a weakly girlish face. He was dressed in neat sports clothes. "I have to see the police," he said eagerly. "I've got to confess. My conscience has bothered me about it. My name's Jonathan Barber, and I killed Mr. Polk. As soon as Mother told me how he'd been hurt I remembered it was me who did it. He ran the market on the corner, you know about it, don't you? He got stabbed when he was robbed yesterday, and it was me who did it. The queer thing is, I don't recall what I did with the money, but I did that. I do all kinds of terrible things all the time. I think maybe I killed that baby they were talking about on TV, but I haven't remembered about that yet. Maybe if I saw Dr. Koenig again he'll help me to remember. But you'd better put me in jail before I do something else bad."

"Mr. Barber," said D'Arcy quietly, "just take it easy."

"Polk," said Maddox. The witness had been quite definite about the three black teenagers, and Polk wasn't dead. "Where do you live, Mr. Barber?" He rattled off an address glibly, Banner Avenue. "Do you know your phone number?" He knew that too.

"You'd better put me in jail, I do all these bad things. I kill people and rob them all the time. Dr. Koenig understands about it, you know. As soon as Mother told me what happened to Mr. Polk I remembered doing that."

He went on talking to D'Arcy while Maddox got on the phone. Presently a woman answered. "Mrs. Barber?"

"Yes, what is it?"

"Have you a son named Jonathan?"

"Why, yes, he isn't here right now, he said he was going to the library."

"No, he's with us. This is the police. He seems to be a little confused, he's confessing to a crime he couldn't have committed."

"Oh, dear," she said, "is he up to that again? I told the doctor I thought he was getting worse and ought to go back in the hospital. Well, it's the one at Camarillo. Oh, dear, he's not right in the head, you know, hasn't been for years. But when he takes his pills he's nice and quiet, no trouble, and he never tries to hurt anybody, you know. He can take care of himself and get around on the bus. Oh, dear, I'd better come and get him and call the doctor."

"I think you can leave it to us, we'll send him to the local emergency hospital and inform his doctor. What's the doctor's name?"

"It's Dr. William Koenig, his office is on Third Street, he's one of these psychiatrists you know. Oh, dear, but I expect Jonathan'll be better off back up at Camarillo. Well, all right. Will you please tell Dr. Koenig to call me? I'm very sorry if Jonathan's making you any trouble, but he's got up to that before, saying he's done all sorts of crimes."

"Yes, we gathered that," said Maddox. "We'll take care of it, Mrs. Barber." He reached for the phone book to look up the office number.

It was a routine report and to Jack Adams of the Ann Street Humane Shelter just another job. He got around to it about four o'clock that afternoon. Possible cruelty to an animal, the address on Mariposa Street. He couldn't get an answer at the house, but the report had mentioned a camper in the backyard. He went around the house and looked at it. It was big and nearly new, and it seemed funny that somebody had nailed sheets of plywood over all the windows. He tried the rear door and it was locked, but suddenly he heard something inside there. A funny kind of moaning sound. He thought, cat or dog locked inside, in this heat that would constitute cruelty all right. He hadn't any legal right to invade private property, but there wasn't anybody at home at the house, and he liked animals or he wouldn't have been working for the Humane Society. He looked around for something to use, and got a screwdriver from the back of his truck, came back and started to pry off the piece of plywood from the rear window of the camper. It came off with a little screech and he looked inside. He could see something moving in there but it looked too big to be a cat or dog.

All of a sudden the window was pulled open just a crack from inside and a voice said weakly, "Oh, you're not him! You're not him! Oh, get me out, get me out of here, please! I want to go home!"

"My sweet Christ," said Adams in naked astonishment. It was a girl, just a young girl, and she looked terrible. She was wearing a man's old bathrobe and nothing else, and she was thin and pale with light brown hair straggling around her face. "How'd you come to get shut in here, miss?"

"The door's locked, and I can't open it, can you get me out? Please, I want to go home." She was crying weakly. "My name's Alice Robard and I live in Centerville, Montana, I've been locked in here I don't know how long, and I want to go home to Mama and Daddy—"

"Sweet Christ," said Adams, and began to pry the screen off the window.

Rodriguez got to the emergency wing at Cedars-Sinai at six o'clock. Maddox and D'Arcy were poking around at the house, talking to neighbors, waiting for the owner of the camper to show up. Rodriguez talked to a Dr. Unger in the waiting room. Unger was looking shocked and angry.

"I thought I'd seen everything, Mr. Rodriguez, but this is one hell of a thing. It's something of a miracle she's in as good shape as she is. Oh, she'll be all right, physically. She could be in worse shape. She's dehydrated and underweight, and she's been subjected to sexual abuse over a long period. But she's quite rational and eager to talk. The poor kid's so grateful to be rescued, she says she's been in that camper since February."

"*Santa Maria!*" said Rodriguez.

"The hell of a thing," said Unger. "We've got her cleaned up and she's having a meal, you can see her, she's been talking nineteen to the dozen." He took Rodriguez down the hall to a two-bed room; the girl was the only one in it. "Here's a nice policeman to see you, my dear. He wants to hear all about it."

"Oh, are you a policeman?" The girl looked up eagerly. "Oh yes, you've got to arrest him! He ought to be in jail!" She might be a pretty girl when she'd been fed up and got her strength back; she had a small straight nose and a high forehead and a little square chin. Rodriguez had been remembering about this one. The psychic lady's letter, and the sheriff's flyer on Alice Robard, fourteen. "Oh, I want to tell the police all about it. I didn't know where I was, I was so surprised when the nurse said this is Los Angeles. That's a long way from Montana," and she sighed. "I suppose it'll take a while before Mama and Daddy can come to get me and take me home."

Somebody on the night watch would be calling that sheriff, the parents would know about her very soon. "They'll be coming just as soon as they can," said Rodriguez.

"Oh, I hope so. I lost track of time while I was in there, but it was February. We'd had a lot of snow, and when I got off the school bus Daddy wasn't there yet and I was waiting—when he drove up in that camper, and—and—" She'd finished everything on the tray, and now she said wistfully, "Could I have another glass of milk?" Rodriguez got the nurse. "Oh, thank you," and she gave them a blinding bright smile. "It's so lovely to be *out.*" She leaned back on the pillows. "He asked me how to get to Butte, and I went over to tell him, and he got out and grabbed me. He was awful strong and there wasn't anybody around. He put me in the back of the camper and locked me in and I've been there ever since. I tried to fight him sometimes but it wasn't any good, he was too strong. And he—you know, did things to me."

"We know about that."

"There was a toilet and a shower, but the shower didn't always work, I guess only when it was hooked up to some water, the toilet's one of these chemical ones. And he put the boards across the windows so I couldn't see out or anybody else in. We'd drive and drive and then he'd stop and do things to me again. He said to call him Tony. And he never did any cooking on the little stove, he just got me things to eat like hamburgers and hot dogs and malted milks. And it just seemed to go on forever, I thought I'd be shut up there for the rest of my life."

"Do you know how long you've been here?" asked Rodriguez.

"Pretty long, he only moved the camper a little way from where we were before. I guess that was a couple of weeks ago." How right the psychic lady had been, thought Rodriguez. "And sometimes he brought me magazines to look at. He'd go off and be gone a long time and sometimes when he came back he was drunk. That was awful." She shuddered.

"Well, it's all over now," said Rodriguez. "You just get some sleep and your Mama and Daddy will be here soon."

"Oh, I hope so. That was another thing, the beds in the camper didn't have any sheets, just a couple of blankets, and when it was still winter it was so cold, and it seemed just forever I'd been shut up, but then it started to get warmer and I knew it wasn't winter any longer. But just the last while it was even worse because it's been so hot, I couldn't hardly breathe. He brought me a jug of water but it was all gone by yesterday, and I was so thirsty. I'd tried to call for help lots of times in case anybody was around to hear, but I couldn't tell because of the boards over the windows. He had a lantern there like the one we've got for when the electricity goes off, he let me use that sometimes but the rest of the time it was all dark. And it was just forever. I used to cry a lot. But you know one thing that helped, just an awful lot," and she looked at him solemnly. "I tried to pray but it was kind of hard. God seemed awful far away, you know? Even Jesus seemed a long way away. But I kept thinking of what it says about the valley of the shadow of death, it felt like that's where I was, and it says about that, I will fear no evil because God's still there. I guess that sort of encouraged me even when I felt worst. And—and I hope Mama and Daddy'll get here soon."

It would be some satisfaction, thought Rodriguez, to get his hands on Antonio Lopez, but of course they couldn't do that sort of thing in these civilized days.

While they waited for somebody to show at the house, Maddox and D'Arcy talked to Peterson and Tinker next door. They were profoundly shocked.

"I had a funny feeling about it," said Tinker. "I'm sure glad we called somebody and she got found. That poor little girl. Mrs. Lopez is a nice woman but we don't know anything about her nephew."

"I wonder," said Maddox to D'Arcy in the car, "if we do. There's a little bell ringing in my head about that name. Of course it's a common Hispanic name."

About ten minutes later a woman came walking up to the house, unlocked the front door, and went in. They followed her. She let them in when she saw the badge. She was a stout placid-looking dark woman about fifty, and it took her a while to understand what they were telling her. Then she began to babble in Spanish and cross herself and cry. Antonio, she hadn't seen him in ten years, he was the son of her brother back in New York, they wrote letters sometimes, and she knew Antonio had been in a little trouble with the police, which was terrible because they'd always been honest respectable people, but she didn't think anything very bad. He had come with the big truck about three weeks ago, and said he wanted to find a job in California. He had told her family news, how his father was promoted to a better job and his sister had a new baby. She'd been glad to welcome him, family. She hadn't thought much about the big truck, she didn't mind it in the backyard, she didn't have grass or flowers there. He went out there, she thought he had extra clothes in it, sometimes he slept there. She was away all day, she worked at a drugstore uptown. She was a widow and the good God had never given her children, she was alone. She couldn't believe Antonio had done such a terrible thing. She didn't know where he was, he went out most days, looking for the job, she thought. Sometimes he came home late and sometimes early.

In fact today he came home about seven o'clock, and the minute Maddox and D'Arcy laid eyes on him the bells began ringing louder in their heads. He came into the living room through the front door and looked surprised to see them. He was about five-ten, a hundred and seventy, black hair, with a heavy black moustache. "Mr. Lopez," said

Maddox, "you're under arrest. And by God, I don't think we'll even have the satisfaction of hanging onto you. We've seen your ugly face before and if I'm right it was on a flyer from the Feds. You're wanted on a federal count somewhere back East. But there'll also be the charge of kidnapping. The girl got out, Lopez."

D'Arcy brought out the cuffs. Lopez started to swear and rounded on the woman fiercely. "Why the hell did you go messin' with the camper anyway?"

"No, no, I didn't—"

"Then how in hell did the girl get out?"

Maddox laughed without mirth. "The people next door thought you were abusing a dog or cat, and they've got nice soft hearts for animals. They called the Humane Society. Come on, we're taking you in now."

On the ride uptown D'Arcy asked him, "Why in God's name did you keep the girl all this while, Lopez?"

Lopez growled, and then he said in a surly tone, "God damn, so I didn't have to pay out to the Goddamned hookers, they rip you off like hell, charge too much. That way, I always had her handy."

Neither of them could think of anything to say to that one. They stashed him in jail and went back to the office to look up that flyer. There he was as big as life, wanted for a bank job in Elmira, New York. He'd pulled it with two accomplices and they were both on the wanted list too. That had been early in February. "We seem to be missing regular meals lately," said Maddox. His stomach was rumbling again. While D'Arcy told the night men about it he called the local FBI office and talked to somebody called Flores. "He's all yours, the kidnap's a federal charge too, across state lines. You'll find him in our jail. The camper's registered in his own name with New York."

"Good God Almighty," said Flores. "That poor damned kid. Is she all right?"

"Going to be. Somebody here's called the Montana sheriff." He had left a note for the night men about that. Off the phone he asked about it and Stacey said he had done that.

"He couldn't leave off thanking us, he's an old friend of the family and said he'd go right out to let them know the good news. They'll probably be flying in sometime tomorrow."

"That camper," said Maddox. "I don't think the local Feds will have any accommodation for it. We'd better have it towed in to our garage, they can go over it there." He called the garage, and then he started home.

An hour later the night watch got a call to a heist. Stacey listened to the pharmacy clerk and thought that this was getting monotonous. "He was a great big black fellow and he was high as a kite on something, I wasn't about to argue with him, him waving the gun around—"

"Do you remember if he touched anything in here?"

"He sure did, like I say he was staggering all over the place and when I handed him the money from the register he kind of lost his balance and fell against the counter, he put his other hand on it to sort of save himself, right by the register—"

So Stacey called the lab and one of the night men came out to dust the counter. He looked at the results with satisfaction and said, "Nice clear palm print and a couple of good latents. If he's on file anywhere we'll spot him for you."

Feinman had just got in on Wednesday morning when the lab called. "That heist last night," said Garcia. "There were some good latents and a palm print. I just ran them through for you and the guy you want is Samuel Weaver, he's in our files. He's got a string of accounts for about ten years back, possession, selling, assault, armed robbery. He's just out on parole from Folsom on that charge."

"Typical," said Feinman. He was dialing Welfare and Rehab when Maddox came in, and told him about that. He got Weaver's parole agent at that office.

"Oh, Lord God. Of course nobody could expect anything else from that one. He's burned out whatever brain he had with the dope, he's quite unfit to hold a job of any kind. He's living with his mother, she's on welfare, down on Norton Avenue," and he added the address. Feinman passed it on to Maddox.

Nobody had called in any information on the baby. The radio and TV news were still mentioning it, asking for the public's help, but sometimes people waited awhile on one like this; it could still come.

"I suppose somebody had better go and see if Weaver's home," said Feinman.

Maddox got up reluctantly. "I suppose so." Rodriguez had gone out on the legwork, and Maddox and D'Arcy went out together.

The heat had subsided a little but the air conditioning in the car was still welcome. The address on Norton was an ancient apartment house in a run-down block. They found the Weaver apartment on the second floor. The woman who answered the door was very fat and very black. She looked at the badge in D'Arcy's hand and said, "Oh, my, has that boy of mine been up to something again?" Her tone was indulgent. "That Sammy, he's always up to something, can't seem to help himself. Oh, sure, he's here, he's still in bed. He never did like gettin' up early." She pointed out the bedroom door. In the tiny second bedroom, sparsely furnished with a single bed and a three-drawer chest, a man was sprawled prone on the bed, naked and inert. "Weaver!" said Maddox sharply. He didn't stir. Maddox went over and looked at him, felt a naked arm.

"Well," he said dryly, "Sammy won't be getting up to anything ever again."

"DOA?" asked D'Arcy.

"That's just what." They rolled him over and it looked like the typical overdose. There was a stash of heroin and the hypodermic in plain sight on the chest.

"If there's a phone I'll call the morgue-wagon," said D'Arcy. "At least he's out of our hair for good."

Mrs. Elise Camacho got to the hospital at a quarter of two. Visiting hours didn't begin until two, and they were strict about the hours. She couldn't see her husband for fifteen minutes. She sat down on one of the benches in the entrance lobby and panted a little. It had been a hot walk from the bus. Both her sons and their wives were at work or they would have driven her; she didn't drive. But tonight the family would all come together in a car, easier. The hospital was air-conditioned but she fanned herself with a handkerchief until she felt better. At least, thank God, Eduardo was going to be all right after the accident, just the broken leg, and the nurses here were nice and kind. She noticed that someone had left a big paper bag on the bench. That was funny. It was a grocery bag from a Lucky supermarket by the sign on it. Somebody's groceries? she thought. A funny place to leave it.

The clock moved up to two o'clock, and she got up. But her female curiosity got the better of her, and she took hold of the bag. There was something in it all right, a solid weight. She spread open the top and looked, and then she said, "Holy Mother of God!"

A loud healthy wail answered her. Miss Dorothy Bernstein had waked up hungry and wanted her mother.

"Well, thank the good Lord," said the doctor up in Obstetrics, "she's perfectly all right. She's fine. She's even been bathed and changed recently. The damnedest thing I ever saw. Gets spirited away from here on Sunday afternoon and then left down in the lobby on Wednesday. In a paper bag. A paper bag, for God's sake!"

"Where is it?" asked Rodriguez urgently.

"Where's what?"

"The paper bag. You didn't just throw it away, did you?"

"Oh, I suppose it's somewhere around."

"Was the baby wearing the same clothes as when she was taken?"

"Well, if you could call it clothes," said the doctor. "A diaper. Yes, it's hospital issue. Of course, since Sunday—that says it's been washed. She's still got her name bracelet on too." Everybody up here was beaming and relieved and happy. The baby was all right, just fine. Rodriguez hadn't seen the baby; as soon as they'd checked her over she'd been taken right to her mother, and a few minutes ago when Rodriguez arrived, young Mr. Bernstein had rushed past looking dazed and overjoyed.

"The bag," said Rodriguez, "for God's sake find it."

"What on earth do you want with the bag?" asked the doctor in surprise.

"Doctor, the lab can lift prints from nearly any surface. Somebody could have left some prints on that bag. And we'd really like to find out who stole the baby. For one thing, she's probably some kind of nut."

"Oh," said the doctor. "Well, it was Betty Johnson who brought her up. We can ask her."

Betty Johnson said blankly, "The paper bag? Well, I put it in the trash, of course."

"Where?" asked Rodriguez.

She showed him. Tidily trained, she had folded it twice and put it in the plastic-lined wastebasket in an examining room. Rodriguez fished it out, wishing he had an evidence bag. It couldn't be helped. He didn't handle it more than he had to, and dropped it off at the lab at the station.

Everybody here was feeling relieved about the baby too, and Baker had said interestedly that they'd get right on that bag.

Feinman said, "That sheriff called back—the one in Montana. The Robards are getting a plane from Butte sometime this afternoon."

"Good," said Rodriguez. "What a thing. That Lopez—at least the Feds are doing the paperwork."

"I ran into Jenner a while ago, and he's grousing about that camper cluttering up the garage. Says there's been an army of Feds swarming all over it."

"Let them worry about it," said Maddox. "I suppose they'll be taking it away sometime."

Daisy had been out; when she came in ten minutes later and heard the news she said, "Oh, thank God. Thank God. But of all the queer things, bringing the baby back."

"Maybe the nut found out a baby's too much trouble after all," said Feinman with a broad grin. "The diapers and the feeding."

"But she'd washed the diaper," said Rodriguez, and the phone rang on his desk. He picked it up.

"Say," said Garcia, "we've got something for you."

"Already? You pulling off miracles now?"

"No, we haven't found any prints yet. But the damndest thing showed. We were all interested in this bag, we started on it right off. You know the old saying, about not seeing the trees for the wood, or is it the other way around, anyway we used gloves to cut it apart so we could lay it out flat, and it wasn't until a minute ago that Harry noticed there was something on it in ballpoint."

"What?" asked Rodriguez.

"Just a phone number. I'll give it to you." He read it off.

"By God, that may be a break." Rodriguez passed it on to the rest of them.

Maddox sat up with a jerk. "But what a hell of a funny thing. A phone number written on a grocery bag, why would anybody do that?"

"Don't ask, just use it," said Rodriguez. "I could make a deduction. The nut is thrifty and probably a good housekeeper. Some people just throw bags away, but some people keep them for trash or to use as shopping bags or whatever. It was around the house so she used it to put the baby in."

"Very likely," said Maddox. "Give me the number." He called the phone company and explained. Correctly the supervisor called back to verify that he was bona fide police and told him that it might take a while. "As soon as you can get it, please."

"I'll do my best, sir."

They were still sitting there talking about it when a man hesitated in the doorway and said, "Sergeant Maddox."

Maddox looked up. It was Pollard. "I'd just like a word with you."

Maddox got up and took him into the smaller office across the hall, and Daisy followed. Pollard sat down heavily. He looked tired and rather gray. "I really don't know why I'm bothering you, I don't suppose there's anything anyone can do about it. But I'd like to say," and he included Daisy in his glance, "that I quite understood why the police were bound to investigate. With such a terrible allegation, and children involved. Of course you had to look into it to be sure. And Sergeant Hoffman was very kind about it, reassuring me that you were quite certain it wasn't true. But—" He put a hand to his head and ruffled his dark hair. "All these newspaper stories—this Dr. Remling— I'm afraid there must be many people who believe I'm guilty. It's all so circumstantial, but the implications—"

"Yes," said Daisy, "we don't like it either, the implications that we're not doing our job. There are always people willing to believe that cops are all crooked and all ministers secret lechers."

"It's made me feel unclean," said Pollard. "And I'm afraid it's going to have an unfortunate effect on the school. You see, not all of the parents belong to my congregation, know me personally and trust me." His half smile was pallid. "Of course it's summer vacation now, but we generally like to get the enrollment list for September made up early. My wife has been making the routine calls—we are both very distressed about it—thirty-five of the parents have told us the children won't be coming back to the school. That's more than half the student body."

Daisy looked as if she'd liked to swear. "That's a damned shame," said Maddox.

Pollard's eyes were bitter. "As if that wasn't bad enough, I would have thought that the members of the congregation at least, who've known me a long time, wouldn't have paid any attention to this damnable story, but one of our oldest members, Mr. Miller, called me yesterday to say he and his wife would no longer be attending the church. He was rather rude and abrupt. It has really shaken my faith."

"I can understand that," said Maddox. "It's a damned shame. You know, Mr. Pollard, you might have a very good libel case against Dr. Remling."

"And I had even thought of that, sergeant, but only for a fleeting moment. It would be quite against my principles as a Christian. Judge not lest ye be judged. But I have thought, if it were possible to make that child admit her lie— I don't know the child well, but she's had Christian teaching at the school, if I were to see her personally and plead with her—"

"Don't even dream of it," said Daisy earnestly. "It would be fatal. They'd never let you talk to her anyway, and you'd never be able to back her down. We'll just have to hope that in time everybody will forget it."

"Nobody's ever going to forget that I was suspected of such a thing," said Pollard. "People don't forget a thing like that, about a minister of all men. They'll keep on saying and thinking, no smoke without fire. Just as I suppose you'll never change the minds of the people who dislike the police."

"That's about it," said Maddox ruefully.

"All because of that selfish little brat," said Daisy. "I'd like to whale the tar out of her. But there's another saying, Mr. Pollard. You find out who your friends are when you're in trouble. People who really know you won't believe it, and once this fuss dies out of the papers people will forget that your school was connected with it. In time you'll get other parents sending their children there and build up the student body again."

"I'm sure I hope you're right," said Pollard. He got up. "I just wanted to tell you that I bear no malice toward the police, I quite see that it was your duty to investigate."

"That's very good of you, sir," said Maddox. "You might have blamed us as well as Remling."

"No, no," said Pollard. "But it's all very worrying. Well—there's nothing any of us can do about it," and he went out quietly.

"Damn," said Daisy. "And damn that brat." Maddox shrugged and went back to the other office. Helen Waring had come in a few minutes ago and now she looked at Daisy directly.

"It would certainly be fatal for him to approach the kid. But I wonder if you and I could."

"How?" asked Daisy.

The supervisor called Maddox back twenty minutes later. "That number is listed to a Mabel Rouse. I have the address for you." It was Stanley Avenue.

"Thanks very much," said Maddox. "Come on, César."

It was a middle-aged apartment building needing paint. Rouse was listed at a rear apartment on the ground floor. Nobody answered the bell. Maddox was feeling impatient, and tried the next apartment. The woman who opened the door had bleached blond hair and too plump a figure. "We're insurance investigators," said Maddox. "Do you know Mrs. Rouse next door?"

"Well, hardly at all. What you after?"

"Do you know where she works?"

"Oh, yeah, I can tell you that. She's a checker at a Lucky market."

"Which one?"

"I don't know, I think it's somewhere in town but they're all over the place, of course."

"Have you seen her recently?"

"Well, no, I haven't, people don't neighbor much in this place and she's at work all day."

"Do you know what time she usually gets home?"

"I couldn't say. Oh, I can't say if she knows anybody else here."

"All right, thanks." They tried all the apartments on that floor, and found only one other woman at home; she didn't know Mrs. Rouse at all. There was no manager on the premises.

"Hell," said Rodriguez, "are we going to miss dinner again hanging around on a stakeout?"

"It's not really urgent," admitted Maddox. "The baby's all right. We'll find her home sometime. We can find out which market through the personnel department."

"I don't know why you want to talk to Brenda again," said Marlene Remling nervously. She let them in reluctantly. "You talked to her enough already."

Helen said pleasantly, "Just a couple of loose ends, Mrs. Remling."

This was a well-maintained single house in a good neighborhood above Franklin, with a neat front yard. The living room was orderly, well furnished. Brenda Remling, in jeans and T-shirt, was watching TV in one corner. Her mother turned it off and said, "The policewomen want to see you again, darling. Don't be scared, there's nothing to be scared of now."

"I'm not scared," said Brenda, but she looked surly. "What do they want again anyway?"

"The truth," said Daisy. "You've had a good deal of fun out of this, haven't you? Being the center of attention and getting your name in the papers—but I forgot, you can't read, can you?"

"I can when I want to. I told you the truth."

"Well, we know you didn't," said Helen. "You told a lie about Mr. Pollard."

"I never. He did just what I said."

Mrs. Remling looked at them suspiciously. "I won't have you saying such things to Brenda, she's just a little girl, she wouldn't know how to lie."

Daisy laughed. "Oh, you don't know much about your daughter, do you? She's just a stupid little brat but she told a lie that could ruin a man's life, and now your husband's kicking him while he's down, isn't he? It was a silly lie, Brenda, because everybody but your stupid father and mother know it was a lie."

Brenda went an ugly shade of red. Her mother said, "You get out! You can't come here and say such things—"

"Oh, Brenda can say whatever comes into her stupid little head, but we aren't supposed to tell the truth, is that it?" asked Daisy.

"I'm not either stupid," shrilled Brenda.

"I'm going to call my husband this minute and tell him the police are bullying Brenda—" and she flounced out of the room.

"You stop calling me names," said Brenda.

"Well, you are as stupid and silly as you can be," said Helen in a patronizing tone. "You're too stupid even to realize what you've done, but if you did know you wouldn't care because you're also a selfish brat." They could hear Mrs. Remling on the phone in the next room, her voice high. "A very stupid silly little girl," drawled Helen, "thinking everybody would believe what you said. Well, nobody with any sense did believe you, only your stupid parents. And they'll stop believing you when they find out what a silly lie it was."

"You did too believe me!" shouted Brenda. "I knew just what to say and how to say it too, and just the way I planned it out, they said I don't have to go back there again, that crappy dumb school with them preachin' at you all the time. I was smart enough to figure that out!" Behind her Mrs. Remling came back into the room.

"Yes, you hated the school, didn't you?" said Daisy.

Brenda gave them a scornful look. "Sure I did, anybody would, those other kids are crazy, let the dumb old teachers boss them around, and the way they make you work. And talkin' about God all the time— I was smart enough to get out of that, wasn't I? I knew if I told them that about Mr. Pollard I wouldn't have to go there no more." Mrs. Remling let out a squeak, but Brenda was too mad to care that she had given herself away. She turned on her mother. "It was all your fault! Send me to that dumb old school, the teachers give us all that hard homework, we never had homework in the other school—and you got to wear dresses instead of pants, and there's no gym, and I never knew what they was talkin' about, things called phonics, and those books you're supposed to read with funny old pictures, and what's so damned important about readin' anyways? They made you work too hard at that dumb place—"

Daisy smiled brightly at Mrs. Remling. "Is your husband rushing right home to throw us out? Don't worry, we're just leaving. But you'll have something to tell him, won't you?"

Maddox was just in time to talk to the personnel office at the Lucky market chain's main branch. They seemed to be efficient, and within ten minutes he was informed that Mabel Rouse worked at a market on Santa Monica Boulevard, from nine to four three days a week and four to ten the other three days. "I'll be damned if I do any more overtime on this," he said. "Hand it to the night watch." It was one of the days she'd be on until ten. He left a note for Donaldson and left at the end of shift. "Of course the night watch had been concerned about the baby too, especially Stacey with six kids of his own, and he went out to that market right away. It was a big market with eight check-out counters and he approached the first checker without showing the badge. "I'm looking for Mrs. Rouse, do you know her?"

"Oh yes," said the plump young woman. "But she's not here now, she's on vacation, she won't be back until next week."

Stacey felt nonplussed. "Do you know if she was going away anywhere on vacation?"

"Oh, I don't know." There were customers lined up behind him with market baskets. "I'm sorry, sir, I'm busy."

"Where can I find the manager?"

"That's him over there," and she pointed at a fat man talking to one of the box boys. Stacey approached him and showed the badge. The manager was astonished at the questions.

"Mrs. Rouse? Why, she's one of our oldest employees, very reliable. Why are the police asking about her?"

"What can you tell me about her? Is she married, divorced, how old is she?"

"My God, I don't know, maybe forty. I do know she's divorced. But why the police are asking— She's a perfectly respectable honest woman—" He hadn't any idea if she'd gone away somewhere on her vacation.

Defeated, Stacey went back to the station. They didn't get a new call until nearly nine o'clock, and it was a heist at a gas station on Western. The attendant was a young fellow named Castillo, and he was young and very much on the ball. "Of all the Goddamned things, it was a dame! A dame maybe thirty, blond. She had a gun, yeah. She had on a red pantsuit. This car pulls in, and parks over there away from the pumps, she gets out and I think it's just somebody wants to use the restroom. But by God, she walks into the office and pulls the gun. I gave her all the cash out of the register, maybe a hundred bucks, and out she goes. But I got the plate number for you."

"What?" said Brougham.

"Yeah, the car wasn't all the way out of the light, I saw the plate," and he produced a slip of paper. "There was a guy at the wheel. The blonde gets in and he takes off. But I got what they call a photographic memory and I wrote down the number right away."

Sometimes they got the breaks. Brougham asked him to come in and make a statement tomorrow. They went back to the station and sent the query up to Sacramento. The plate was registered to a Sydney Fischer at an address on Norma Place in West Hollywood. "Maybe he went right home," said Brougham.

When they got there, the car with the right plate was sitting in the drive. The man who answered the door was about forty, balding, with a little paunch. He looked surprised at the badges. "You just got home, didn't you, Mr. Fischer?" said Brougham.

"How'd you know that?" He hadn't asked them in. A woman came up behind him and said, "Are they cops? What do they want?" She was about thirty-five, she was blond, and she had on a hot pink pantsuit, but some people were color blind. Sometimes they got the breaks.

CHAPTER EIGHT

"Unfortunately, it wasn't the right blonde," said Rodriguez, passing on the night report to the rest of them. It was Maddox's day off. "She'd been there all evening playing cards with her sister and another couple. They were still there. Fischer was hopping mad to be taken to jail, said he didn't know a damn thing about it. He's the manager of a furniture store on Melrose Avenue. They left him to cool his heels overnight. And then the stakeout at the house on Raleigh Avenue turned up something, that was after the night watch was off, the Traffic man left them for us. They were both on the way to being drunk and they're in the tank. I suppose we'd better talk to all of them. Come on, Joe, you can do some work for a change."

Over at the jail they talked to Fischer first. He was still mad, but he answered questions readily. "I don't know what the hell this is all about, I've never been in any trouble with the police, for God's sake, those officers last night said something about armed robbery, that's just crazy. I don't know anything about a robbery."

"Well, Mr. Fischer," said Feinman, "your car was involved in a robbery last night, at the holdup of a gas station on Western. The victim gave us your plate number. There was about a hundred dollars stolen, and when you were brought in here last night you had a hundred and four dollars in cash on you. It was a woman who committed the actual robbery, you were driving the car. Would you like to tell us who the woman is?"

"My God," said Fischer. "I don't believe this, one of us has to be crazy. That's my own money, or at least half of it is, I've been collecting from the employees at the store, we were taking up a collection for one of the girls who's getting married. Oh, my God— That girl— This is just weird—I don't believe it—"

"What girl?" asked Rodriguez.

Fischer lit a cigarette and sat forward in the small uncomfortable straight chair. "My God, I can't believe it, but I'll tell you just how it happened. Look, I'm a respectable honest man. I've got a clean record, you can look that up. That damned girl—by God, it's the last time I ever go out of my way to be nice and kind to anybody again—I'll tell you just what happened. I stayed late at the store to work on the books. I came out about eight-thirty, a little before, and when I got to my car in the lot there was this girl there. Well, a woman. Of course I thought at first she was a hooker, I was about to tell her to get lost, but she was acting nervous and she said she's scared and would I help her please. She said her car had broken down, and she belonged to the auto club and they'd towed it in, but she was stranded. The buses were about to stop running and she hadn't enough on her to call a cab and she lived way out on Delongpre and she was scared to try to walk home in the dark." He was smoking rapidly. "By then I'd sized her up and she talked like a nice ordinary girl, she was just in a little spot. Hell, look, I've got a sister about her age, I wouldn't like to see her trying to get home along the dark streets. I felt sorry for her and I said sure I'd drive her home. She kept thanking me, she seemed like a nice ordinary girl. We got into the car, and I no sooner turned out to Western when she had another idea. She says she hates to take me out of my way, and her sister just lives up on Fountain only she's not sure if she's back off vacation yet, if I'll stop at a public phone she'll call and find out, there's one at the gas station on the corner. So I pulled in there, and she got out to phone. In about four minutes she comes back and says her sister's home and I should take her there so I drive her up to Fountain and let her off where she said. And she says she'll never forget how kind I'd been, a million thanks, and good night. End of story," said Fischer.

"I'll be damned," said Feinman. "That's quite a story, Mr. Fischer."

"It's God's truth," said Fischer. "Do you mean to tell me she held up that station while she was gone? That girl? My God, I can't believe it, but if you say so— No, I didn't notice where she went, the phone was alongside the station office and I was facing the other way. My God, I didn't think anything about it, why should I?" He spread his hands. "Look, you can look up my record. I've got a good job, I'm doing all right, I don't cheat on my wife, why should I all of a sudden go off the rails and start robbing gas stations? I was just sorry for the girl, trying to help her out." Now he was angry again. "My God, to think of her letting me in for a mess like this—me just trying to be nice and kind!"

Rodriguez laughed. "Well, that's quite an interesting racket she's invented." Fischer was quite obviously what he claimed to be, the ordinary honest citizen.

"Thank God you believe me. You do believe me? It's God's truth, I swear. But why in hell should the girl go to all this trouble, involving somebody else? If she wants to rob a gas station, why shouldn't she just go and do it?"

"Well," said Feinman, "that's just the pretty part of it. Very cute indeed. If she used her own car the attendant could give us a description of it and maybe even get the plate number, as happened last night. As a matter of fact, this same girl has apparently pulled four other jobs like that that we know of at other gas stations, and in at least two of them the attendants had spotted a man in the car. We'd taken him for an accomplice, but hearing this it's a safe bet that she put over the same story to different men, and what a cute little tale it is. There'll be quite a few respectable, honest men around who'd feel sorry for the poor girl stranded at night, go out of the way to do her a favor. And so if the attendant remembers anything about the car it won't be hers."

"Very ingenious," said Rodriguez, amused. "I don't suppose you can tell us much about her."

"I'd never seen her in my life before," said Fischer. "I'll be damned, I'd never have thought of that one. And it was dark. All I can say is, she was somewhere in the late twenties, around there. She had blond hair, sort of short and curly. She had on a red pantsuit. She was fairly good-looking, not a real eyeful, she hadn't much makeup on, she acted like a nice modest girl, a lady, kind of shy."

Rodriguez chortled. "Oh, a very nice act. Trust a female to think up something like that. This is a new one on us."

"Oh, another thing," said Fischer, "I remember she had a mole beside the corner of her eye. Her left eye. I noticed it in the streetlights when we were getting into the car. A big dark mole, it was. That's all I can tell you. My God, I'm glad you believe me."

"Well, if you're putting one over on us we know where to find you, don't we?" said Feinman. "You can go home, Mr. Fischer."

"Thank God. Well, at least it was an experience for me, a night in jail. But I swear to God, that's the last time I ever try to be a gentleman and help out a lady in distress!" The jailer handed him back his possessions, including the hundred and four dollars, and he used the phone to call a cab. "I'll never hear the last of this from my wife," he said, but he sounded almost cheerful.

"That's quite a neat little game," said Rodriguez. "Something new does come along now and then."

Feinman scratched his jaw. "She'd have left her car somewhere close by where she told him to drop her."

"Probably. But she'd have to size up the men carefully, pick the nice polite gents like Fischer who wouldn't try to get up to any funny business. I rather think she knew something about the general neighborhood."

"Seventy-seventh Street, Hollenbeck, and here?"

"Well, it's possible. People move around. We haven't got anything but a very general description. But now we've got the mole. We could ask Records to have a look at the distinguishing marks file."

Feinman shrugged. "A long chance. We can ask."

"Damn it," said Rodriguez, "if we knew where she picked up the other men—it might be a starting point. But we know where she picked up Fischer. It might be just worthwhile to prowl around that block and ask about a blonde with a mole."

They also wanted, being here, to have a look at the two bums who had showed up at the house on Raleigh Street. They went over to the other side of the jail and asked, and one of the jailers said, "Oh, them. The Traffic man said to hold onto them, they're wanted in a homicide."

"Was there any I.D. on them?"

"Nothing. One of them had five bucks on him and the other eighty-seven cents. I'll bring them up."

When he brought them into the interrogation room Feinman and Rodriguez eyed them with recognition. They were both the typical derelict winos who hung around the skid row of any big city. One was tall and one was short and thin. They might be any age over forty, but the life they'd led had aged them prematurely.

Rodriguez asked for their names and they gave them passively. Juan Munoz, Jacob Koontz. "What do you know about Chebinski?" asked Feinman.

"Never heard of him," said Koontz, who was the tall one.

"You've been camping out in that empty house on Raleigh Street, haven't you? You came back there last night."

"Oh, yeah."

"Well, somebody left Chebinski's body in the backyard there, after stabbing him."

"Oh," said Munoz, "was that his name? Yeah, that place was empty, it made a place to sleep. They don't let you sleep in parks and besides there ain't so many parks with the nice grass. We got in there a while back, it was a place to go."

"Kind of more private," said Koontz. "We didn't know that guy's name. We been panhandling downtown, he kind of joined up and we let him stay there."

"Till I find him robbin' me," said Munoz aggrievedly. "The damn bastard, I wake up and he's goin' through my jacket pockets. I'd only got about four dollars that day but we had a couple bottles left and that was for next day, and he was robbin' it."

"So what did you do about it?" asked Rodriguez.

"Why, I stuck my knife in him," said Munoz. "What else? He fell down and I got my money back."

"And then you found he was dead."

"That's right," said Koontz. "So we dragged him out to the backyard. We never went back there till last night, account we met up with some guys had a room somewhere down on Temple, we been there."

"But I left my jacket that place and a couple of blankets, we went back to get 'em and the damned fuzz grabbed us and threw us in the tank."

They wouldn't be strangers to the tank. Rodriguez and Feinman didn't talk to them long; there wasn't much reason to. They both saw enough of the ones like this, the ones at the bottom wandering around any big town. "It makes you wonder," said Feinman in the corridor, "about progress. Some people might as well still be living in caves." They booked them into the other side of the jail, went back to the office, and started the machinery on the warrants. Murder two and accessory to homicide.

"Doing what comes naturally," said Rodriguez. They had just sat down at their desks when the desk sergeant called.

"Oh, good, there's somebody in. I had a call a while ago from Chicago. Somebody there wants to talk to detectives about something on N.C.I.C. His name's Moran, a Sergeant Moran of Bunco."

"So let's see what he has on his mind," said Rodriguez. "Get me Chicago."

At Chicago Police Headquarters he was passed along here and there until he finally got connected to Moran, who had a deep bass voice and sounded like a fairly elderly man. "You spotted something on N.C.I.C. we may be interested in?"

"Oh, yeah, this con game. You put out the M.O. on it and of course I spotted it right away. The damndest con game I ever ran across, and believe me when you've worked Bunco for eighteen years you think you've seen them all. Her claiming to be the Vice-President's daughter."

"You know something about her?"

"There can't be two brash enough to pull that one. Only here it was the governor's daughter. You may not believe it but she took six marks for ten grand with that story. That was about four years back."

"Did you ever charge her?"

"Yeah, we picked up both of them." Moran laughed. "I tell you, there are so many damn fools around it scares you. You wonder about the human race. She's the governor's daughter, he deserted her mother, and all the rest of it. And if she hadn't run into a woman with enough sense to add two and two she might still be at it, but one of the marks just happened to remember that the governor we had then was only about forty himself, and unless he was getting married in his cradle he couldn't very well be the father of somebody about the same age."

"Oh, for God's sake."

"Yeah. She came in and told the tale to us, she had the sense to set up a date with the woman, pretend she's fallen for the scam, and we picked her up. Her right name, as far as we know, is Dempsey, Anita Dempsey, and the husband's James Dempsey. He had a record of various Bunco games here and in Massachusetts. They were running a Spiritualist church on the side. She only had one count, and you won't believe it but it was the old pigeon drop."

"I'd believe anything about human people," said Rodriguez. "I've been a cop a while too. What did they get?"

"Well, we got enough on him to charge him as accessory, he'd paid the bill at the answering service. They both got a one-to-three and served fourteen months, got out on parole. They jumped parole and vanished into the blue and we haven't heard of them since. I don't know if this is any use to you."

"Not much," said Rodriguez. "We haven't got a line on her at all. We knew she was an old hand. She's graduated into a higher social class, hasn't she, now the Vice-President's daughter. Of course there's the Spiritualist church. It's possible they're using their right names, and running that game too. Or the religious racket under some other church name. Anyway, thanks for the background." He told Feinman about that and Feinman abandoned the report he was typing on Koontz and sat back.

"It might be a place to look. The Spiritualist churches. They'll be listed in the phone book."

Rodriguez was already looking in the phone books. Countywide there were six Spiritualist churches listed, and none of the ministers, if that was what they were called, was named Dempsey. That said nothing. "But hell, Joe, I know just enough about it to know that that's an accredited church, they don't approve of all the frauds pulled off in their name. They'd be the first ones to come down on the spurious ones. The fly-by-nights would be more apt to call themselves by a fancier title. And we've only got a general description of the damned woman. She could be somewhere this minute pitching the tale to some mark."

"Well, in a way it's their own fault," said Feinman reasonably. "When they haven't got any better sense than to fall for the idiotic scam."

"We're supposed to be here to protect the public," said Rodriguez. "I sometimes think the public belongs in day care centers under adult supervision." Feinman laughed. Rodriguez lit another cigarette. "And nobody ever looked up that Greene."

"Oh, on Dunning. That sounded far out."

"You never know what people will do," said Rodriguez thoughtfully. "I was dragging my heels on it too, but just to be thorough we ought to look."

"So you go and look," said Feinman. "I've got to finish this damned report."

Neither Daisy nor Helen was in the other office, and everybody else was out on the legwork.

Earl Greene's address was on Perlita Street in Atwater. Rodriguez landed there after lunch. It was a shabby old duplex long unpainted. A fat woman opened the door to him and he asked for Greene. "Well, he's at work, acourse."

"Where?"

"He works at Ernie's Plumbing and Heating in Glendale. What do you want?"

"Thanks very much." Rodriguez found a public phone and looked up the address, Glendale Avenue. Ernie's Plumbing and Heating occupied an old building set back from the street with its own parking lot. He went in and asked for Greene. A thin girl at a desk in front was chewing gum and reading a paperback romance. "Oh, he's somewhere in back, you can go on through."

Rodriguez went through to a larger rear space comprising most of the rest of the building. There were two men there, one working on a hot water tank and one poring over a set of blueprints. "Mr. Greene?"

The man at the tank looked up. "That's me, what can I do for you?"

Rodriguez showed him the badge. "A few questions."

Greene was a man about fifty, big and stocky, with a fringe of hair around a bald head, a bad-tempered mouth. He scowled at the badge, standing up. "Well, what's it about?"

"You had a little trouble with the law recently," said Rodriguez. "Your son got killed in an accident, and you thought the cops and the judge were all wrong to blame him for it."

"You're damned right," said Greene. "They was always pickin' on Mike, just on account he smoked a little pot and liked to drink. That guy smacked into his motorcycle, he shoulda landed in jail. It was just on account he was drivin' a Caddy and wearin' a four-hundred-dollar suit the damned judge didn't even put a fine on him. And the God-damned cops sayin' it was Mike's fault too."

"You made a little fuss about it in court, tried to start a fight, and one of the cops put an armlock on you."

"So what about it?"

"So you threatened him," said Rodriguez. "You said you'd like to beat him up good. Did you try?"

"What the hell you mean?"

"I don't think you remembered the witnesses' names—"

"No, for God's sake, they was just names, why should I?"

"Do you remember the cop's name? The one who gave most of the evidence at the inquest?"

"It was Donny or Danny or something."

"And you knew what he looked like, and that he was working out of the Hollywood station. Did you hang around to spot him going off duty and follow him home one night?"

"Why the hell would I do that?" asked Greene roughly.

"To find out where he lived. So you could catch him to beat him up."

"Oh, for God's sake, I'd of beat him up all right that time, but I didn't do anything about it after." But his eyes were suddenly furtive and he looked away. "I'd have beat 'em all up, Mike dead and them sayin' it was all his fault. The Goddamned fuzz always sides with the rich people and so do the Goddamned judges." Rodriguez's interest in him quickened.

"Can you tell me where you were two weeks ago Sunday night?"

Greene licked his lips. After a moment he repeated, "Week ago Sunday night? Why?"

"Because that's when the cop got himself killed," said Rodriguez.

Greene was staring at the floor. "Killed," he said, "killed. Who killed him?"

"Well, it just could have been you, couldn't it? Where were you that night?"

Greene said resentfully, "Damn fuzz. I never killed nobody. I didn't kill him. Sure I was mad as hell at him that day, and all the rest of 'em, but I didn't do anything about it after. That judge, he fined me two hundred bucks, I had to borrow it, and I was mad about that but I wasn't about to stick my neck out and get in more trouble."

"Where were you that night?"

Greene licked his lips again. "I was at a friend of mine's pad. Up to about eleven, I guess I got home about eleven. We was just shooting the breeze, had a few beers. His name's Dave Spiegel, he lives on Fargo Street."

Rodriguez was rather liking Greene as a suspect now. He wasn't very bright, and Dunning's murder was just the kind of crude violence that one like Greene would be capable of, the very elementary plot. But the alibi would have to be checked out. "Where does he work?"

"He's, uh, out of a job right now," said Greene.

"All right, that's it for now," said Rodriguez casually. He went back to his car and looked at a map to locate Fargo Street. It wasn't far off, in the Silver Lake area. He found the address and it was an old apartment building. Spiegel was listed at the rear downstairs but nobody answered the bell. He drove back to the station and found the office empty; as he'd come past the desk the sergeant had told him that a new daylight heist had gone down and another burglary been reported. He sat down at his desk and called R. and I. downtown and asked for any package on Earl Greene. The policewoman called back in ten minutes. "We've got a package on him, sir. Shall I send it up?"

"Let's be sure we're talking about the same one," said Rodriguez. "What's the description?"

She read it off. Male Caucasian, five-eleven, a hundred and seventy, brown and blue, no marks, forty-eight as of two years ago. "That sounds like the boy. Is it much of a package?"

She said dryly, "You could say so. It goes back twenty years."

"Send it up," said Rodriguez.

It came in forty minutes later by uniformed messenger. As he read the Xeroxed pages, his eyebrows climbed and he muttered, *"Caray."* Greene had quite a package, going back twenty years. He'd first been charged with armed robbery, and had served a three-to-five in Folsom. The next count was burglary, and then assault, assault with intent, robbery with violence. He'd got out from his last stretch two years back; he'd done another three-to-five for burglary. The last line shot Rodriguez's brows up again. *See Spiegel, David.* He called R. and I. again and asked about Spiegel. There was a package on him too. He had done a stretch for burglary last and by the dates it was at the same time that Greene had been in. "Does it say anything about Earl Greene?"

"Yes, sir. Known associate, he was charged on the same count last time."

"Maravilloso," said Rodriguez. Could they have something here? Greene coming out with that alibi so quick—probably knowing that Spiegel would back him up. The stupid louts, never stopping to think that the cops had records, could figure that out too. But if Spiegel swore to the alibi, it would hold: the law didn't reckon the quality of oaths or who they came from. And Greene would probably have had the sense to get rid of Dunning's gun. Or would he? Would he indeed? When he was given to the armed robbery he might have looked on that gun as a gift from heaven and hung onto it. Or he might have handed it to Spiegel. Rodriguez wished fervently that they had got to Greene sooner. But it wouldn't do any harm to ask for the search warrants. If that gun should turn up in Greene's possession or Spiegel's, that would be very definite evidence indeed.

Somebody else would look and find out. Tomorrow was his day off.

Maddox read Rodriguez's report on Friday morning and also wished that they had looked at Greene sooner. The only reservation in his mind was that the ones like Greene and Spiegel were just naturally cop-shy and like the fellow in the Bible who fled when no man pursueth. Greene might simply have offered that alibi to get off the hook, he might not have had one damned thing to do with Dunning's murder, suggestive as he looked. But it certainly wouldn't do any harm to exe-cute those search warrants, which had come through this morning.

Bill Nolan and Dowling were in, and he took Nolan with him. They tried the house on Perlita Street first. The woman let them in reluc-tantly, but being married to Greene she'd be used to this kind of thing. They had a thorough look through the house and garage, and then they went over to Glendale and looked at Greene's car. They didn't find Dunning's .32 Colt. So they tried the Fargo Street apartment. Spiegel wasn't there but the manager let them in. The gun wasn't there either. At the moment Spiegel didn't have a car registered to him.

"I've got to finish that report sometime," said Nolan plaintively. They went back to the station, stopping for lunch on the way.

Maddox had just settled at his desk when Garcia called him. "I'm sorry to say we couldn't raise any prints on that paper bag. Just smudges. Sorry."

"Well, it can't be helped," said Maddox. Daisy wandered in and asked about John Ivor. "Oh, doing fine. It ties Sue down, nursing him, but she doesn't seem to mind."

"Watched over by that monster," said Daisy, smiling. "Quite a mon-ster."

"Isn't he?"

"I haven't seen you to talk to you since Helen and I got that obnox-ious little brat to back down and admit she lied."

"No!" said Maddox, diverted. Hearing about that, he laughed. "And I wonder what the Remlings are making of that. If the man's got any integrity at all, he ought to ask the *Times* to print a retraction and apologize publicly to Pollard."

"He won't do that," said Daisy. "He'll be feeling too much of a fool to admit publicly that a ten-year-old could fool him. Though she was convincing—quite a talent for lying, our Brenda. He'll just stop talking about it and let it lay."

"And possibly Brenda never will learn how to read." But Maddox was thinking about Mabel Rouse again, and when Daisy went back to

her office he started out on the legwork and went over to that apartment on Stanley. He could imagine Feinman swearing about that new
burglary.

Feinman wasn't working the burglary. At midnight last night a missing persons report had been called in, and the night watch had done all
the automatic things, checked with the morgue, the hospitals, accident
reports, without turning up anything useful. The husband had been
calling in by the hour, demanding action, demanding reports, and just
before noon Feinman had gone out to see him and get more details.
They didn't worry much about a missing adult for at least twenty-four
hours; people being people, they had vagaries and did unexpected
things. They had spats with husbands and wives, they got fed up with
the humdrum routine, they went off with a new girl friend or boyfriend. If they hadn't been involved in an accident, and it didn't seem
that Mrs. Marjorie Poole had been, most of the time they turned up
safe and sound, having had a little spree and feeling penitent.

The husband, Bruce Poole, was a forceful personality and kept bark-
ing out denials that anything of the kind could have happened. "Good
God, man, we're not riffraff like that! We live an orderly settled life!
We've been married for twenty years and never an argument between
us!" It would take another forceful personality to argue with him,
Feinman thought. "Marjorie's always home when I come home! I'm
out of my mind with worry, can't you see that?"

"If you'd just tell me—"

"Good God, I have told you! I told that officer I talked to last night!
I should have called the police long before, but I kept thinking she'd
call and explain, the car going out on her, somebody sick and asking for
help—but she'd have left a note—"

But he was also a practical man and businesslike; he was a chemist
with a big pharmaceutical company downtown. He gave Feinman details. His wife was forty-five, five-five, a hundred and thirty pounds,
blue eyes and frosted brown hair. She had her own car, a two-door
Chevy. He supplied the license number efficiently. "The first thing I
thought of when I found she wasn't home was something wrong with
Jim"—their sixteen-year-old son, off at summer camp at Lake Arrow-
head—"and I couldn't get through there or get hold of anybody who
knew anything until eight o'clock, and he's just fine—I didn't want to
worry him, I didn't tell him—and then I started calling hospitals—she

might have gone out shopping, or delivering Avon orders—she doesn't need to do that for extra money but she's done it for years, she enjoys getting out and meeting people—but she'd certainly have been home by five-thirty or six, when I'd be coming home." They also had an eighteen-year-old daughter who was visiting her aunt and uncle on a farm in Illinois. He had reached her that morning and she hadn't heard from her mother since last week.

At further questions he got annoyed. The police had a nerve insinuating that his wife was unstable or ever dreamed of picking up strange men. They were strict Episcopalians. She had probably been abducted by some violent criminal, raped and murdered.

Feinman didn't think it was anything as drastic as that, but it didn't sound as if Marjorie Poole was the kind to run off in a huff after a spat with her husband. He went back to the station and put out an A.P.B. on her car.

This time the door of the apartment on Stanley Avenue got answered. "Mrs. Rouse?" said Maddox.

"Yes?" She was a woman about forty, a nice-looking woman of middle height, a slim figure, with graying dark hair and friendly brown eyes. She certainly didn't look unstable in any way. She looked at the badge in surprise, no alarm. "Well, you'd better come in and tell me what it's about."

He went in to a comfortably furnished living room and she sat opposite him on the couch. He started to tell her about the baby. "Oh yes, I saw that on the TV news, a horrible thing, it was a mercy they got her back safely."

He told her about the paper bag the baby had been in when she was returned. "Well, isn't that the queerest thing," she said.

"You see, Mrs. Rouse, we found something on that bag. Your phone number was written on it. That's how we traced you."

"My phone number?" she said in blank astonishment. "Why, that's impossible, you've got to be joking."

"No, it was there. How did it get there?"

"I simply can't imagine. It sounds weird. My phone number—how very funny—" She broke off and then she said sharply, "Oh!"

"You've thought of something?"

"Well, yes, I have, but it sounds impossible too. Anybody who'd steal a baby must be out of their mind, and she doesn't look like one like that. But—"

"Who?" asked Maddox.

"Well, I just suddenly remembered. She did write my phone number down on her grocery bag, that day. She hadn't anything else to write on."

"Who?"

"Why, this customer who comes into the market. She told me her name that day too, but do you think I can remember it, it's gone right out of my mind—but she did write my number down on her grocery bag. She borrowed my pen."

"Why?"

"Well, it was a little funny but not really. You see, they keep the air conditioning so low at the market, and I'm afraid I'm rather a chilly person. I usually wear a cardigan at work. This woman comes in nearly every week, she usually pays with food stamps. She's just an ordinary-looking woman maybe a little older than I am. And that day, it was a couple of weeks back, she said I had on a pretty sweater, it was unusual. Well, it is. I knitted it myself. And I told her that and she said she liked to knit too, she'd like the pattern number so she could make one for her daughter. It is rather an unusual pattern, two colors. I said I still had the pattern at home, and she asked if she called me if I'd give her the pattern number. That's how I came to give her my phone number. And she gave me hers, and said if she forgot to call would I call her— that's when she told me her name. And I can't remember it. I did call her that night and gave her the pattern number."

"Have you still got her number?" asked Maddox anxiously.

"But good heavens, you don't think she's the one who stole the baby? Such an ordinary woman— Now what did I do with it— I know I gave her something to write it down on, a customer had left a receipt on the counter and she used that—" She stared into space for a moment and then said, "Now it just could be— I've been up at Big Bear for a week, on vacation, but I didn't take that cardigan, I took an older one in case the evenings were chilly. Let me look." She went into the bedroom, came back a couple of minutes later with a thick fuzzy wool cardigan knitted in shades of pale lavender and purple. It had patch pockets. She tried both and came up with a strip of tape from a cash register. On one side it bore a short list of prices, a total. On the other side in rather straggly writing was a name, Mrs. Karnas, and a phone number. "Karnas, that was it, I remember now. Goodness, do you think she stole the baby? She looks so ordinary—"

Maddox smiled at her. "This may be very helpful, Mrs. Rouse, we'll hope to find out."

"My heavens," she said. "I certainly hope you do. If she's crazy enough to steal a baby she ought to be tucked away."

Back at the station he got onto the phone company again and while he waited for the supervisor to call back he told Feinman about it and Feinman told him about Mrs. Poole. "I don't know, she doesn't sound like the sort of woman to take off in a huff. Maybe the A.P.B. will turn her up. But that's a funny one. A to B to C. It's funny how things happen, isn't it? Just by chance, the woman wanting that knitting pattern."

"Lucky chance," said Maddox, "if it means we've caught up to her."

The supervisor called back and gave him the name—Ann Karnas and the address, on McCadden Place. Feinman was curious enough to tag along. It was another old apartment house in that old part of central Hollywood. Karnas was listed in apartment twelve on the second floor. Maddox pushed the bell and after a moment the door opened and a woman looked at them. As Mrs. Rouse had said, she was a very ordinary-looking woman. She might be forty-five and comfortably plump, with untidy brown hair and no makeup. Maddox showed her the badge. "Police," she said. "What do you want?" She didn't look frightened.

"We have some evidence," said Maddox formally, "that the baby stolen from the hospital last Sunday was brought to this apartment. Quite good evidence. I suppose you heard about the baby on the news." She stared at them. "We'd like to ask you what you know about it."

After a moment of silence, when she put a hand to her mouth, she said unexpectedly, "Oh, my Lord. I didn't think it was such a smart idea but Jewel was set on it. And of course it did mean the extra money. From the social services thing, whatever they call it. Lordy, I hope you don't want to put Jewel in jail."

"Who's Jewel?" asked Feinman.

"My daughter. I suppose you've got to come in." She stepped back and they went in to an untidy but clean if shabby living room. There was a pile of clean laundry on the couch, scattered toys on the floor, and a playpen in one corner. In the playpen was a fat and healthy-looking baby wearing only a diaper. "Oh, Jewel, the cops have found out about it. I was afraid they would, but you were so set on it."

The girl who appeared in the bedroom door was eighteen or nineteen. She was a pretty girl with her mother's round face, curly brown hair, a rosebud mouth. She was wearing shorts and a T-shirt, and she had a luscious figure and good-looking legs. She looked at them, and her expression was disappointed. "I never thought they'd find out."

"Miss Karnas? Or Mrs.—"

"No, it's miss, I'm not married. That was just it." She smiled at the baby, who was playing with a stuffed toy. "Isn't he a darling? This is Randy. He's nineteen months and just a doll. I like babies."

"You took the baby?" asked Maddox.

"Well, you see, I lost mine," she said. "The second one. I was awful sorry, like I say I like babies, but I had a slip and lost it, that was in January. That wasn't Sam's baby, Sam's Randy's father, but he's in the Army and over in England. That one was Tommy's baby. I was sorry. But you see, the lady at the social place there knew I was expecting it in July and it meant I'd get more money when it came." She wrinkled her brow thoughtfully. "And I had this good idea, if I showed her a baby she'd think it was mine and send the extra money every month. She don't come here but the way it was when Randy came, I'd have to go to that place and tell her when the baby was born and all, and she'd see the baby and I'd get the extra money from the welfare."

"So," said Feinman, "you just went to the hospital and took a baby? Any baby?"

"Well, it was kind of easy. I thought it might be. It was the same hospital where Randy was born, and there's a lot of visitors on Sunday. I didn't have an appointment with the social lady until Tuesday but I thought it might be easier to get the baby on Sunday." She was explaining carefully. "And it was. I just went in about three-thirty and waited until the visitors started to leave. I'd put on one of the white dresses Mama used to wear when she worked at that restaurant. I just went into the nursery and picked up the baby in the first crib. I had a sweater with me and I wrapped that around it and I went down the stairs instead of taking the elevator. When I got home I see it was a girl, a real sweet baby. She didn't like the formula at first, same as I'd had for Randy, but finally she drank it. She was a real little doll and I took real good care of her, like I say I like babies. We got along just fine. And on Tuesday I took her to show the social lady. The social lady, she's usually pretty busy and I figured I could fool her easy, and I did. See, when you have a baby they give you a piece of paper, it says the doctor's name and the date and all like that. Well, I had Randy's, and I did it real careful. I just drew over the R to make it into a C so it was Candy and I changed the numbers, Randy was born in December and it said twelve five, the month and day, see, so I kind of smudged it and made it look like seven fifteen. And I left the doctor's name the same, and Sam's name as father, she wouldn't know about him being so far off and me not seeing him for a year. And she was real busy with some papers and she just copied it on one of those form things."

"So it was all very easy," said Maddox.

She smiled. "Yeah, it went fine. I thought it would, and it meant I'd get the extra money."

"But you took the baby back."

"Oh," she said wistfully, "I'd of loved to keep her, she was a darling, but it wouldn't of been right, her own mother'd want her. I just went up on the bus, I'd just give her a bath and fed her and she was sound asleep. I couldn't go in with a baby and just leave her, so I put her in the market bag. Nobody noticed me, it was about noon and there was only one lady at the desk. I just left her there and went out. I knew somebody'd find her. I'm sorry you found out about it because now I won't get the extra money."

"My God," said Feinman under his breath.

"Miss Karnas, you'll have to come with us. You're under arrest."

"Are you going to put me in jail?"

"I'm afraid so. There'll be a charge of abduction. Have you ever been arrested before?"

Her mother began to cry.

"Of course not, and I don't see why you got to put me in jail. I wasn't going to keep her and I took real good care of her."

"Yes, I know, you like taking care of babies."

"How long do I have to stay in jail?"

"That will depend on the judge. It might not be very long. How old are you?"

"Eighteen."

With no previous convictions, and the fact that the baby had had good care and been returned safely, she might even get probation. She said, "I'm sorry you found out. I'm going to miss Randy something awful."

"Oh, Jewel, you know I'll take just as good care of him as you would," sniffed her mother tearfully. "You don't have to worry about him."

"I know you will, Mama, but I'll miss him. Should I take anything to jail with me?" she asked Maddox.

"Er—well, cosmetics, a comb—they'll give you clothes."

"Well, I'll get my purse." She came back with it and she only began to cry when she kissed the baby good-bye. "Oh, Mama, take real good care of him, won't you? Can they come to see me in jail?"

"Certainly," said Maddox. "Every day—there are regular visiting hours."

"Oh, that's good," she said, slightly comforted.

Usually the squads got sent to trouble by the dispatchers, but sometimes the squad car men spotted trouble on their own. It was what they were there for. At 2:30 A.M. Johnny McCrea, cruising down Coalinga, saw something going on in an empty parking lot, a couple of men fighting, a man down, and he turned in there and got out. Two men were beating up a third, and when McCrea came up that one was down and one of the others was riffling his pockets. Muggers. McCrea jerked out his gun and told them to freeze. It wasn't often they caught up to the muggers. He put the cuffs on them, called an ambulance for the victim, and took the muggers into the jail.

There, it emerged that one of them had a gun on him. McCrea left it with the watch commander. The watch commander dropped it off at the lab when he went off shift.

Maddox had just got in on Sunday morning when Baker called him. "I don't know the ins and outs, you'll have to ask Traffic, they left this gun here. I don't know what anybody wants us to do with it, but I had a look at it and it's Dunning's gun. It's the right serial number."

CHAPTER NINE

Maddox and Rodriguez got down to the jail in double time. The two muggers were Juan and Arturo Martinez, and they looked very typical. They were brothers, one about twenty-five, one a couple of years younger. Both were fairly big. Between them they had had nineteen bucks in cash and about twenty marijuana cigarettes. They faced the detectives sullenly and answered questions reluctantly.

"Which one of you had the gun?" asked Maddox. That, of course, they knew.

"Me," said Arturo.

"Where'd you get it?"

"I found it, man, I just found it."

"Come on," said Rodriguez sharply, "where'd you get it?"

"I found it."

"Now let's forget the double-talk," said Maddox. "Where'd you get it?"

"I told you, man, I found it. Right in the street."

"Where?" asked Rodriguez skeptically.

Arturo shrugged. "It was in the street, on the sidewalk. It was outside a disco on the Strip. I'd took a chick there and when we come out I saw the gun laying there and I picked it up." They both spoke unaccented English.

"Let's forget the double-talk," said Maddox. "You took the gun off the man you jumped down on Romaine, didn't you?"

"I don't know what you're talkin' about, man."

"Two weeks ago tonight," said Rodriguez. "You were drifting around that area looking for somebody to mug, and you spotted him turning into that drive and jumped him. Why did you kill him?"

"We never killed nobody," said Juan. "You're talkin' the double-talk, man. Arturo found that gun just like he says."

"When?"

"I dunno which day it was," said Arturo vaguely, "maybe a couple of weeks ago. We never killed nobody, you're crazy."

"You jumped him and then you found out he was going to be a little something out of the ordinary for you to handle, he was big and tough and he started to put up quite a fight, and he brought out the gun."

"Who you talkin' about?"

"And you lost your heads and knocked him down against his car and then you shot him."

"You're just crazy, man, we never did nothing like that." They were both looking alarmed now. "Who you sayin' we killed?"

"The cop," said Rodriguez. "Of course you didn't know he was a cop, did you? Down on Romaine. When he pulled the gun you lost your heads, you knocked him down against the car and then you shot him."

"You just crazy, man, we never done nothing like that." But they were both looking scared now; they would know how cops felt about cops getting killed. "Where you say, Romaine, we don't even know where that is." It was feeble bluster. "We never killed nobody, no place."

"But you run together, don't you, mugging the citizens in the street. Does either of you have a job?"

They admitted they didn't. They had given the same address, Poinsettia Boulevard. "So how do you pay the rent and buy the groceries?"

"Mama, she gets the welfare," said Juan. "You can't pin no murder on us."

"Have you been arrested before?"

"Yeah."

"Done any time?"

"We been in the county jail sometimes. We never done no murder, that's crazy. Why'd we want to kill a cop?"

"You didn't know he was a cop," repeated Rodriguez. "He was in plain clothes. You saw him getting out of his car and jumped him. Two weeks ago tonight."

They went on saying no and Maddox said, "All right, so tell us where you were two weeks ago tonight, who you were with."

"How the hell you expect anybody to remember that far back, for God's sake? We was just around, someplace. I dunno where we was."

"But you were together?"

"I dunno," said Juan, "some nights Arturo he'll be with some chick and some nights I'll be with a chick. We never shot nobody."

Maddox and Rodriguez went on prodding at them and didn't get beyond that, and finally handed them back to the jailer.

"But I like that pair," said Rodriguez. "I like them the hell of a lot, Ivor. I like them because there are two of them."

"Yes," said Maddox. "It always seemed a little queer that Dunning would be taken off so easily, not a mark on him, just the fractured skull. He'd have given a good account of himself, anybody attacking him. But a pair— We can read it. That pair are just the run of the mill muggers, they live hand to mouth, Mama on the welfare, they'll do a little selling of the pot on the side, wander the streets looking for the easy victims to mug— Small-timers, but they ended up committing murder without intending it. Romaine's pretty dark along that block, you said that yourself. They just happened to be drifting along there when Dunning drove home. They jumped him when he got out of the car, and if you want an educated guess—"

"Oh yes," said Rodriguez, "he used the judo on them. That surprised the hell out of them, they wouldn't be used to a victim putting up any kind of efficient defense. That explains why Dunning's hands weren't marked up, he reacted automatically with the judo. He got loose from them and pulled the gun, and they panicked, do you think?"

"We'll never know exactly how it went, and there are different possibilities. Say Dunning was holding the gun on them and stepped back and tripped over something—they saw the chance to put him down and went for him together and he was off balance and fell against the car. They wouldn't have known he'd fractured his skull, they were in a panic then—and also mad at the victim for fighting back— We know the type, César. They've never done murder before, but it's just the type that ends up doing the stupid senseless murder. They grabbed the gun and shot him."

"They didn't take his billfold, why?"

"Small-timers," repeated Maddox. "Don't we know the type. They were spooked and scared."

"Why didn't they just run?" Rodriguez was having momentary doubts. "You'd think it would have been the natural thing for them to do."

Maddox reflected. "You might think so, but it could be they were scared the shot had been heard. And the two of them could handle him. They weren't thinking, all that kind don't think, live from minute to minute. They bundled him into the car and drove off just to get out of the immediate neighborhood. They'd have a car somewhere, or would they? We'll find out. Say they did. I still like it the hell of a lot better than Fernandez or Greene, because there were two of them. They ended up in that market lot, and by then they just wanted out of the whole thing. Barnsdall Park was right on top of them, the market closed, and that's a big lot, they were a good way from the street. No crowds around that time of night."

Rodriguez smoothed his moustache. "They dragged the body up there, not far, and made tracks."

"I like it," said Maddox. "It's exactly the senseless violence a pair like that would pull, César. God knows how many muggings they've been responsible for, they're no strangers to violence. And the gun is solid evidence. Arturo finding it in the street, for God's sake. But of course they weren't expecting to be picked up, to have us coming down on them, and they had to say something."

"When you come down to it," said Rodriguez, "the gun's all we've got on them, and the imagination to read the story."

"And we'll see whether the D.A.'s office thinks it's enough," said Maddox grimly. "Have the hell of a lot closer look at them."

They started to do that energetically, and it took the rest of the day. There was an old VW registered to Arturo, and it was located about noon by a squad, the plate number out on the air. It was parked in a lot a couple of blocks up from where the Traffic man had pounced on them. "So they had transportation," said Maddox, "and we can read more of the story. When they'd hightailed it away from Romaine, in Dunning's car, they drove around some, discussing what to do next, and then they picked up the VW and one of them trailed the other up to that market lot."

They roped D'Arcy and Nolan in and spent the rest of the day building it. They saw Mama and assorted younger Martinezes, at the sleazy apartment on Poinsettia. Mama had a string of arrests for prostitution. She said her husband had gone off somewhere a few years back. They found the names of the various girls Juan and Arturo went with and talked to them. They were all typical too. Only one of them had a job, at a cafeteria, and two of the others had arrest records for shoplifting. None of the girls they talked to remembered going to a disco on Sunset with Arturo and seeing him pick up a gun in the street. None of these people had any liking for the cops, and it was like pulling teeth to get them to answer questions, but the whole thing was satisfactory if from a negative viewpoint. People like these drifted where the wind listeth, and were vague about dates and times. Nobody exactly remembered where they had been two weeks ago, where the Martinez brothers had been. That had been a likely place for them to have been any night, looking for the possible victims. But the chief importance was the gun.

By the end of the day they were ready to go for it, but whether the D.A.'s office would go for it was something else. If the charge was voluntary manslaughter the case just might go to a hearing, not a jury, and at least they'd serve some time in for it. Tomorrow Maddox would spend some time in the tedious discussion at the D.A.'s office.

Feinman was cussing again about the burglary ring; they had pulled another job at a hardware store last night and he and Dowling had been looking at the evidence, such as it was. "The only really surprising thing about it," he said, "is that no halfway smart burglar ever thought of that M.O. before that I remember. Pulling the circuit breakers to knock out the power. Of course, most new buildings have the circuit breakers inside." He was more interested in the Martinez brothers, as they all were. With no real evidence on the only two suspects it had looked as if they'd never get anybody for Don Dunning, and it was gratifying to think that they now might.

It had been a long day and a busy day, out on the legwork, in the heat, but it had been a satisfactory day. Maddox was tired when he got home to the old house on Starview Terrace, and told Sue all about it over a drink before dinner. "Oh, and George came in. He's looking better. His wife's at a sanatarium out in the Valley, so at least he doesn't have to worry about her getting picked up drunk."

"That's good," said Sue. She looked down at John Ivor, who had just finished nursing and was placidly asleep. "You can understand it in a way. An only child. You know, Ivor, I'd like a girl too. We ought to have at least two."

"Whoa," said Maddox, grinning at her. "We can think about that later." And then Margaret called them to dinner.

On Monday morning, with D'Arcy off, Maddox and Rodriguez had a long session with one of the deputy D.A.s downtown. They kicked it around. They had handed over all the reports on Dunning, and gave him what they had on the Martinez brothers; the paperwork on that still had to be done.

"The gun's the solid evidence," said the deputy D.A. "And they haven't any rational explanation of how they came by it." He sighed. He was a youngish man, and still finding out about the appalling stupidity of some members of the human race. "You'd think a kid of two would make up a better story, finding it in the street, for God's sake. Now if they'd said frankly they'd stolen it from a victim, or bought it from a stranger in the street, there might have been some small doubt about it, the possibility that they might not have stolen it from Dunning."

"Do you think it's enough to bring a charge?" asked Maddox.

"Well, we don't like to waste the court's time when it looks like a thin case." He ran his hands through his hair. "But considering the fact that they can't explain how they came by the gun, I think it's enough for a voluntary manslaughter charge. I can see all that happening just the way you deduced it. It's a damn shame about Dunning, I understand he was a very good man."

"The best," said Rodriguez. "The kind we don't like to lose. It'll be some satisfaction to see somebody pay a little for it."

"That is so," said the deputy D.A. equably. "I'll start the machinery on it and get the warrants made up."

Rather strangely the A.P.B. hadn't turned up Marjorie Poole's car. When he had some time to himself after writing the report on the latest burglary, Feinman wondered a little about it. By all he'd got from the husband the woman was a stable and ordinary wife and mother, living a routine life, and it was odd, her suddenly taking off somewhere. But it wasn't likely she would have been abducted in broad daylight. The husband kept calling in, and they got tired of him. "But you know, Ivor," said Feinman on Tuesday morning, "we ought to try to backtrack her, find out where she was on Thursday afternoon. If something has happened to her—"

Maddox said, "Hell, look at the time, I've got to cover that damned inquest on Chebinski. Waste of time on a routine matter."

The men left in the office wasted a little more time that morning, unavoidably, when the Robards came in to thank them for rescuing Alice and arresting Lopez. They were a nice couple, plain and countrified, and they were anxious to take Alice home but worried that she'd have to come back and testify at that awful man's trial. D'Arcy smiled at them and said, "Not likely. She's under age, she can give a deposition, and he's admitted the abduction and rape. The law has some quirks. The Feds—the FBI has priority on him for the bank robbery, he'll be tried on that first, and the charge for what he did to Alice will be a federal count too, he'll face a second trial for that. He'll probably go up for a good long stretch."

"Well, thank the Lord for that," said Robard. "We're just so thankful she's going to be all right. He could have killed her. But we just can't get over this Mrs. Ratcliff, you know. I never put much stock in this psychic stuff—it was my wife saw a story in some magazine, how she'd found missing people before, and was bound to write to her. And we can't get over it, her knowing just where Alice was. It's sort of like magic. Well, like the preacher at home says, God works in mysterious ways. We're just so thankful she's safe."

Rodriguez was thinking about that blonde again. That was a very cute little idea she'd had, on those heists. As it had happened, on the other one here the station attendant hadn't been able to describe the car. He wondered if any of the others had. He went down to Seventy-seventh Streeth division on Tuesday and talked to a Lieutenant Ryan, who was fascinated by Sydney Fischer's story.

"Such a simple little idea," he said. "And of course it explains the discrepancy. You know we had two like that in our territory. On the first one the station attendant was ready to swear on a stack of Bibles that the car was a Caddy, a late-model four-door, he couldn't say about the color except that it was dark. And we didn't pay him much attention because the idea of somebody, a girl, in a late-model Caddy ripping off a gas station for a hundred bucks just didn't jibe. On the second one, the attendant said it was a little car, maybe a foreigner, something like a Datsun or Toyota. That seemed funny but they could both have been mistaken. People don't use their eyes. Now you uncover her M.O., we can see they were both right. That is the damnedest thing, Rodriguez."

"Trust a woman to think of it," said Rodriguez cynically. "And there was another one in Hollenbeck. Just going by what Fischer says, we can make a stab at pinpointing the area where she picked up the other men. Fischer says she wasn't in the car a minute before she was talking about calling her sister, asking him to stop at the station so she could phone. So she'd have found the nice kind gent with the Caddy some-where right around that station, and the other fellow near the other one."

Ryan nodded agreement. "You're thinking that if we ask around we might locate them and hear the same story. But it's a long shot that the other men could give a better description. It was dark, she wasn't with them long."

"That's so," said Rodriguez. "But they might have noticed some-thing. I'm wondering whether she's familiar with the neighborhoods."

"Pretty far apart," said Ryan dubiously. "The two stations here are within a couple of blocks of each other but—"

"Maybe she was working around here, living around here, and then moved up to Hollywood."

"Reaching," said Ryan. "I'll tell you one thing it says to me. That is, her own car is a distinctive one of some kind, one that might stand out in a crowd. And that's the reason she thought of this little trick."

"Now that hadn't occurred to me, but you could be right."

"And no way to get a line on her," said Ryan. "That mole. Did anything show up in the distinguishing marks file?"

"*Nada,*" said Rodriguez. "It's not a very distinguishing mark, like a scar or a tattoo. I think I'll have a look around the area where she picked Fischer up in case anybody remembers her, but of course it's a long chance."

"I doubt if anybody'll ever pick her up," said Ryan pessimistically.

"Well, you never know," said Rodriguez. "Sometimes we get the breaks."

At two o'clock that afternoon Mrs. Ella Perkins came home from the market. She had just turned into the driveway when she noticed that her neighbor Mrs. Kettinger had just arrived home too and was turning into the other drive. The driveways adjoined. "Hi, there," she called. "Did you have a good time?"

"Oh yes, it was fine." Mrs. Kettinger took a suitcase out of the trunk. "I wish we could have stayed longer, four days isn't much, but I couldn't take any longer off the job and neither could Jean."

"I've never been to Mexico," said Mrs. Perkins. "Acapulco, it sounds romantic. Was the hotel nice?"

"Oh yes, but awfully expensive. I hope Dwight's been getting along all right."

"I haven't see him, but you know how he is, probably had his nose buried in books all the time you've been gone." They both laughed.

"Well, I left him enough TV dinners to last him." Mrs. Kettinger started for the house with her suitcase. Mrs. Perkins carried in the first of her two grocery bags and began to put things away in the freezer.

She hadn't put away more than four packages when she heard a terrible high raucous scream, and it seemed to come from next door. Perplexed and startled, she went to the back door and looked out. The scream came again, high and wavering. Then Mrs. Kettinger came lurching out her back door, her face an awful mask of open mouth and staring eyes. She half fell down the back steps, and she screamed again and saw Mrs. Perkins and screamed at her, "Call police—quick—all the blood, all the blood—don't go in there—call the police—" and she fainted in the middle of the drive and sprawled prone.

Terrified, Mrs. Perkins ran to the phone and called the police, and then she went to see what she could do for Mrs. Kettinger.

The police car came about five minutes later, and Mrs. Kettinger was still unconscious. "I don't know what the matter is," said Mrs. Perkins. The officer was young and nice-looking. He went in the back door over there and about two minutes later he came out again and he was looking rather pale. He talked on the radio in the police car, and then he came to help with Mrs. Kettinger. She came to only halfway and they got her into the Perkins' house and he told them both to stay there. Another police car came. After a while another car came, an unmarked one, and three men got out of it and went in next door. Mrs. Kettinger was moaning softly.

"Great God Almighty!" said D'Arcy.

And they had all seen the violence and the blood, but this one was pretty bad. The woman, or the various parts of what had been a woman, were in the living room. She had been decapitated. The head had been placed tidily in the seat of a chair. She had been undressed, and the clothes were folded and stacked neatly in another chair. The legs were lying side by side across the room, the arms in the opposite corner. The torso itself was on its back in the exact center of the room. There was blood everywhere, on the carpet and the furniture, and it wasn't fresh blood, dried and brown.

Maddox, Feinman, and D'Arcy stared at the body parts and felt sick. The Traffic man said behind them, "I didn't touch anything. He was sitting there just like that when I came in, sort of grinning at me. I just got out in a hurry and called in."

"I don't blame you," said Maddox. "Go and call up the lab, will you?"

The boy or young man sitting on the couch might be eighteen or nineteen. He was tall and thin and his face was pasty white as if he didn't get much exercise and spent a lot of time indoors. He was smiling cheerfully at them. They didn't move toward him, to disturb the scene. "What's your name?" asked D'Arcy.

"Dwight Kettinger."

"Do you live here?"

"Yes."

"Do you know what happened here?"

"Yes, I did it," he said in a self-satisfied voice. "It's just like Thorne, you can see, or Crippen. Or Patrick Mahon. I always thought that Mahon was better than the others. And I'd have liked it to be like Haigh, only I didn't know where to get the acid to dissolve the body."

"Oh, my God," said one of the Traffic men sickly.

"I planned it out very very carefully," said Dwight Kettinger. "I'll show you." He got up from the couch and went to the little desk in the corner. He picked up a piece of paper, typewriter size and unfolded, and came and handed it to Maddox. "You can see how thorough I was, I thought of everything."

D'Arcy looked over Maddox's shoulder to read what was typed there, in neat expert typing. It was a list, a curious and macabre list, a reminder of actions to be carried out.

"1. Call on phone and tell Mother wants to order perfume. Ask to come in afternoon.
2. Open door and let in.
3. Ask to sit down.
4. Ask if like lemonade.
5. Bring lemonade.
6. Get rope from drawer, go behind and tie to chair.
7. Put gag in mouth.
8. Begin torture.
9. When finished torture cut off head.
10. Cut off legs.
11. Cut off arms."

D'Arcy was breathing heavily over Maddox's shoulder. Maddox handed the sheet to Feinman. Nobody said anything.

"You know," said Dwight Kettinger, "when Mahon was cutting up that girl he put her head in the fireplace to burn it and her eyes opened from the fire even if she was dead. I'd have liked to try that but of course it's summer and there isn't anything to start a fire with. We have fires in the fireplace in winter but not now. I thought about cutting her open like Jack the Ripper, but I was sort of tired, it was hard sawing through the bones." He had arranged the tools he had used in a precise neat line on the coffee table, five kitchen knives and a heavy saw. "That's what Mother uses the saw for, to cut up wood for the fireplace in winter. I think I did it all very well, I'm quite pleased with how it turned out. Just like Mahon or Thorne. Only of course Thorne buried the pieces of that girl. I didn't want to do that, I wanted to keep looking at her."

At last Feinman found his voice and said simply, "God."

"Do you know who she is?" asked Maddox.

Kettinger laughed. "That's a stupid question. It's Mrs. Poole. Of course I knew her. I thought of other people, you know. There's Mrs. Perkins next door, only her husband would have been there, and I thought about Mother, I suppose she'd have been the easiest. But it was really because she'd be away that I had the chance to do it. She went to Mexico with Aunt Jean. And so I thought it would be easiest with Mrs. Poole. To get her to come. Because Mother orders things from her all the while, Avon things, and she knows us. That tells you just what I did. I think it was very clever. I phoned her and said Mother wanted to order some perfume, and she didn't know Mother was in Mexico. And she came."

"When?" asked Feinman.

"Oh, Saturday afternoon," he replied promptly. "And I asked her in and told her to sit down and Mother'd be right there, and I brought her some lemonade. And I went up behind her with the rope and tied her to the chair—it was one of the straight dining room chairs. And I'm a lot stronger than I look. She tried to fight me but I tied her up good and tight—and I put a washcloth in her mouth—I had it all ready, and tied more rope around her head so she couldn't get it out. I'm very pleased it all went just the way I'd planned it. Of course she wasn't expecting anything like that, she didn't know I'm an expert. An expert in crime. I always admired Haigh and Thorne and Crippen, but

I think I've always liked Mahon the best, there was just something about Mahon that was different. I guess you could say he's a hero of mine." He uttered a strange high-pitched laugh.

Maddox found his voice and said, "Better cuff him and take him in."

One of the Traffic men produced a set of cuffs. "Where?" he asked, sounding nervous.

"The psychiatric ward at Cedars-Sinai. He won't stay there. I'll call Norwalk and they'll come to get him."

"I just wish we had a set of leg irons in the squad," said the Traffic man.

Feinman and D'Arcy went over him. The only things on him were a handkerchief and a book of matches. Maybe he'd used the matches in the course of the torture; the doctors would tell them. Dwight regarded all that with a polite smile; he was quite cooperative.

"I know you've got to do all this," he said cheerfully. "It all has to happen the right way. And then my name will be in all the books. The books about all the real crimes that really happened. I'll be just as famous as Mahon. I wish I could have got some acid though, because some ways Haigh was just as good as Mahon. You know, the acid dissolved everything but Mrs. Durand-Deacon's gallstones, that must have been interesting to see." He went out to the squad looking quite happy.

When he was gone everybody drew a long breath. "Good God in heaven," said D'Arcy quietly. "Those were all killers, weren't they, the names he was talking about?"

"The classic cases," said Maddox. "The ones who cut up the bodies. It doesn't matter what label the head doctors will pin on him, schizophrenia or whatever."

The lab van pulled up in front and Maddox went to open the front door. Baker and Garcia came up the walk with the big lab bag, the heavy camera. "I understand you want the full treatment on something," said Baker.

"You are so right," said Feinman, "though it's nothing that will ever come to trial."

The lab men came in and Baker said, "Great God Almighty, what happened here?"

The detectives left them to the job and went next door to see if they could talk to the mother. She was a woman in her early forties, tall and full-figured, and she was lying on the couch in the Perkins' living room with her eyes shut. "I think she ought to have a doctor," said Mrs. Perkins anxiously. "I don't know what's happened but it must be something awful, the way she's been. I thought at first it might be Dwight, that he'd got hurt some way while she was away—"

"Do you know him, Mrs. Perkins?"

"Well, just as the kid next door. He's supposed to be awfully bright, what they call a high IQ, he's reading and studying all the time. But then I saw him go away in the police car. Did something happen to him? Does he need a doctor too?"

"Definitely," said Maddox.

Mrs. Kettinger opened her eyes and Feinman said, "Mrs. Kettinger. We won't bother you with questions if you don't feel up to it. Later will do." She might be in shock; maybe they'd better call an ambulance.

She said in a weak voice, "If I hadn't been a fool. I thought— nonsense. Just because—a loner—adolescents, they have quirks. That teacher—saying about counseling—I thought that was silly."

"Mrs. Kettinger, where is his father?"

"He's dead. He was killed in an accident—five years ago. Please, I don't feel like talking."

"Is there anyone we can call for you, to stay with you, any relative?"

"My sister—Jean. Mrs. Richard Elliott. It's Pasadena."

Maddox used the Perkins' phone to do that. Before the sister arrived, a younger woman all business and asking no questions, D'Arcy had discovered Marjorie Poole's car in the Kettinger garage.

"He moved it later, she'd have parked in the street."

They left the lab still taking pictures. When they were finished they would call the morgue-wagon, and they could all wish the doctors joy in piecing together that corpse and figuring out exactly what had happened to the woman.

Maddox wondered if Mrs. Kettinger would ever go back to live in that house again. It was a nice little house, a California bungalow on a quiet street, much like the Perkins' house next door.

Back at the office he called the psychiatric facility in Norwalk and talked to a Dr. Cohen, explained the circumstances. "Yes, we'd better fetch him in as soon as possible," said Cohen genially. "By what you say he'll probably be quiet as a lamb for a while, these things go in cycles, whatever you want to call it. I'm blessed if I know why or what triggers it, sergeant. We like to think we know quite a bit about the human mind, but sometimes I wonder if we really know one damned thing for certain. Of course we'll have an intensive look at him, run tests, but what it boils down to is that he'll end up in Atascadero permanently."

"I should certainly hope so," said Maddox. It would be a while before he forgot the sight of that living room.

"Did you hear about the cut-up corpse?" Brougham asked Donaldson when he came in late.

"The desk sergeant was telling me about it. God, what a thing. The nuts seem to be all over the place these days."

"And a nut of the worst kind, I gather, what I heard from Joe—the kind nobody looks at twice until all of a sudden he goes berserk and kills somebody. I'm just as glad I didn't have to look at it."

They got a call to a hit-run but it wasn't much of anything, the woman not seriously hurt, just the report to write on it and no useful witnesses. Then about nine-ten they got a call to a heist and Stacey went out on it.

It was a liquor store on Sunset, and it turned out to be something a little unusual. Just as Stacey pulled up in the loading zone an ambulance was taking off. The Traffic man was Byrd, and he said, "He was in the middle of pulling the heist when he had a stroke or heart attack or something, and fell down unconscious."

"Well, I'll be damned," said Stacey. "That's a peculiar one." The witnesses were the owner and a customer, a girl. When Stacey heard the description he was more interested.

"He was maybe fifty-five and sort of fat. He had a kind of pudgy face, real pale, he wasn't tan, and he had on a cap," said the owner. "Imagine a guy that age pulling a holdup! There's his gun there, he dropped it when he fell down." Stacey edged it into an evidence bag; it was an old Smith and Wesson .32 automatic. "I was just about to hand over the money from the register when, by God, he makes a funny noise and just keels over." The offbeat fat heister, thought Stacey. He got their names and asked them to come in tomorrow to make the formal statements, but he was more interested in the heister, and he went over to the emergency wing at Cedars-Sinai and asked about him, explained the circumstances to one of the doctors.

The doctor was interested too. "That's a damned funny one. Well, he could be worse. It was a heart attack, we've just got him stabilized in the last five minutes. He's not going anywhere for a while and it'll probably be at least a couple of days before you can talk to him. We'll let you know when you can arrest him formally."

"Was there any I.D. on him?"

"Plenty," said the doctor. He handed over a billfold. The heister's name was Bernard Heinz and by his driver's license he was fifty-four, and lived at an address on Yucca Street. In the billfold also was his Social Security card, a bank credit card, a credit card from Montgomery Ward, and in the inner pocket fourteen dollars. When they'd undressed him they had emptied his pockets, and the doctor handed over the contents to Stacey: fifty-eight cents in change, a handkerchief, a half full pack of Pall Mall filter cigarettes, and a disposable lighter. Stacey didn't ask to see him; he was in the intensive care unit. He found the address on Yucca; it was an old frame house, but it was all dark and nobody answered the bell. He was curious enough about their offbeat heister to try the house next door, and talked to an elderly man named Cooper.

"Why, sure we know the Heinzes, they've lived here for years. That's terrible, Bernie having a heart attack like that. Isn't Mrs. Heinz home?"

"She doesn't seem to be."

"That's bad. She ought to hear about it. Tell you what, we'll keep a lookout for her and break the news when she gets home, see she gets to the hospital all right."

"Do you know what car he drives?"

"Sure, it's kind of a beat-up old Chevy, dark gray." It was probably parked down there somewhere, they'd have a look for it. "Say, I'm sorry as hell to hear about Bernie. He's a very nice guy, steady, dependable kind, you know. He's a bookkeeper at a Crocker Bank downtown." And that made Stacey all the more curious about the offbeat heister. He went back to the office and started typing the report on it.

There would be some paperwork on the cut-up corpse, and it had been a bad job yesterday breaking the news to the husband. He didn't look like the type to give way, and maybe if she had just died he wouldn't have, but the dismemberment had reached him; he had collapsed and they'd had to call an ambulance. Feinman knew about the daughter in Illinois, the son at summer camp; they had found the Illinois phone number and called. The aunt and uncle would come right out with the girl, stay until Poole was feeling better.

Rodriguez had just got back from lunch and was sitting ruminating about the blonde with the mole when the witnesses on the heist job last night came in to make statements. He had read Stacey's report on the fat heister and was idly curious about him. He happened to be alone in the office. He offered the witnesses chairs and prepared to take notes. Having an eye for the females, he just noticed that the girl was a knockout in a quiet way, black-haired with very white skin, a good figure, a rather small girl not more than five-two. The man was paunchy and middle-aged. As he got out his notebook he noticed that she was eyeing the man with a distinctly unfriendly look. "May I have your names, please?"

"Kitty O'Flynn. That is, Katharine. And if I'd know this fella was coming here at the same time I'd have put it off." There was more than a hint of a lilting brogue in her voice. "The unfeeling one he is."

"Now really, miss," said the man, "you can see the way I felt. That damned robber putting the gun on me!"

"That's as it may be," she said. She had a deep contralto voice. "No human feeling you showed when the poor fella fell down."

Rodriguez saw suddenly that her eyes were a pure silver gray with very long black lashes. She looked back at him directly. "The way it was, I'd gone in to pick up a bottle of whiskey for Tim." Rodriguez suddenly felt a little light-headed for no good reason.

"Er," he said, "you haven't been here long, have you, Miss O'Flynn? Is it, miss?"

"It is," she said. "Six months. For after Aunt Catriona died there wasn't any family left, and my two brothers Tim and Pat here for five years. I've a job at a shop in the Crossroads of the World, and I'd stayed down to do some shopping after work. And it's Tim's birthday today, and I went to the liquor store to buy him a bottle of whiskey, I'd already got him the necktie."

"Er—you live with your brothers?"

"I wouldn't be invading another woman's house, dearly as I love Pat's wife. Tim and I have an apartment together."

"My name's Al Loy," said the man in a loud voice. "And I don't want any funny cracks about it. It's a perfectly good name, isn't it? But my brother-in-law, he's a metallurgist and he's always making cracks about alloys."

Suddenly Kitty O'Flynn gave Rodriguez a mischievous wide smile

and revealed a devastating dimple at the corner of her mouth. Rodriguez uttered a meaningless sound. He felt as if he'd been hit over the
head with a blunt instrument. "Now that is a queer name altogether, I
didn't catch it last night." She sobered. "I'd just time to pick up the
whiskey before the last bus came by. This fella here was just wrapping
it for me when the other one came in and held him up. And then he
had the heart attack, poor fella."

"How did you know it was a heart attack?"

"Ah, he looked just the same as Aunt Catriona when she had hers.
And if you'll believe me, this *omadhoun* here, he just stands there and
laughs!"

"The damned robber, just a no-good criminal, I was happy to see
him fall down in a fit, why shouldn't I be?"

"And I says to him, the man might be dying, I says, for the love of
God won't you call an ambulance, and he just stands there. So I pulled
the man's shirt loose, and I says, have you no human compassion in you
at all, I says, and still he won't call. The heartless fella he is, and it was
me called the ambulance and the police." She regarded Loy with a
darkly disapproving look. "So the fella's a thief, he's still a human man
and I hope I'm a good enough Christian to go to anybody in need of
help. You're just like those fellas in the Bible who passed by on the
other side, Mr. Loy."

"Now look, miss, you chewed me out enough last night." Loy was
annoyed. "I'd of called an ambulance sooner or later."

"And maybe too late to save the man's life. There are things I don't
like about this country and that's one. People turning their backs on
each other, not offering help, not wanting to be friendly."

"Well." Rodriguez tried to pull himself together but something
queer was happening to him, he wasn't sure what. "Then you just
waited for the police and the ambulance."

"And a little nuisance it was but it couldn't be helped. For of course
I missed the last bus, and if you think I was going to ask this scoundrel
here for a ride home you're wrong. After the ambulance took the fella
off the police asked questions and then the detective came and asked
some more, and told us to come in here to sign a statement." Suddenly
she showed Rodriguez the dimple again and he felt definitely dizzy. He
dropped his pen. "So I had to call Tim from a public phone, and first
he was thanking God, him thinking I'd been kidnapped by gangsters
on the way home, and then he let go his temper at me, a terrible

temper he's got but it runs in the family. But when I explained it to him he saw I couldn't have helped myself, it was just an accident I was there at the time." She gave Loy another dark look. "A lucky accident for the robber, I'd say."

Rodriguez heard himself say feebly and irrelevantly, "His name's Heinz. The robber. He's in intensive care but they think he'll recover."

"Is that so now?" She was interested. "And just maybe a brush with death will make him see the error of his ways and he'll straighten up and take to honest work."

"That'll be the day," said Loy. "These no-goodniks running around."

Kitty O'Flynn said severely, "Now we know with God all things are possible."

Rodriguez never knew how he got the statements typed up. But he memorized her address—Ashcroft Avenue—and her phone number. There was a queer pang in his heart when she left the office. When Maddox came in five minutes later he was staring at the wall wearing a dreamy smile. For the first time since he was fifteen César Rodriguez had fallen suddenly and violently in love.

"Damn it," said Maddox, "I've got to get a statement from Mrs. Kettinger sooner or later. What the hell's hit you? You look as if your brain's addled."

"Is that so now?" said Rodriguez absently.

CHAPTER TEN

It was Thursday afternoon before they could talk to Mrs. Kettinger, and D'Arcy and Feinman saw her at the Elliott house in Pasadena. It was Maddox's day off. She couldn't tell them much; the psychiatrists would have more to say, but they had to get a statement from her for the record. Dwight had always been a loner, she said, never made good friends at school, spent most of his time reading. She hadn't thought much about it, he was supposed to be very bright. She'd known of his interest in the true crime, hadn't thought much about that either; a lot of people liked to read about that. She seemed queerly calm, and as they were leaving the sister said, "I got our doctor to prescribe some tranquilizers for her. I was always afraid that boy would go off his head some way, there's always been something not right about him, not natural. But I never thought it would be such a horrible thing as this. His father was a bit queer too, I always thought, but he seemed to suit Georgia."

Once they'd filed the final report on it, it would be out of their hands, transferred to the doctors and the court. That day and on Friday they got an unexpected spate of business showing up, nothing important to work but things that would take up time and make paperwork. A dead body turned up in an alley off Harold Way, the body of a young man with absolutely nothing in his pockets, and nothing obvious to say how he had died. The lab man took his prints; maybe somebody had him on file, and the doctors would say whether it had been an overdose. There was a daylight robbery at an independent pharmacy on Vine; by what the owner said, a couple of teenage punks with knives. It was the anonymous thing, he couldn't give a decent description. On Friday morning, three new burglaries were reported, and Feinman was disenchanted all over again with the stupid citizens. Neither the house nor the two apartments had had anything like good security, the flimsy locks, the sliding glass door so easily jimmied, and at one apartment the burglar had got some valuable jewelry and a lot of antique coins. "You'd think people who have anything of value would take some steps to safeguard them," he said exasperatedly to Dowling. "She thought that was a good hiding place for the coins, under the towels in the linen closet—my God, the first place a pro would look!"

Dowling just grunted around his briar pipe. "Human nature," he said.

It was going through the motions, because that probably had been a pro, but Feinman put the jewelry on the hot list for all the pawnbrokers, and sent the lab out to look for prints.

Late on Friday afternoon another suicide turned up, a teenage girl coming home from a beach party to find her mother dead. She called the police before she fainted, and later was able to give them her father's address, so D'Arcy and Feinman did a little overtime and talked to him. He was a worried-looking man about forty, a clerk at a men's store. "She was the one who wanted the divorce," he told them. "She was the kind, as soon as she got something she didn't want it anymore. She'd take up some new interest and then drop it, went from one thing to another. And she had as good a life as anybody else, I suppose, but she was never satisfied, envious of other people. I can't say this is a real surprise to me, but I'm sorry Linda had to find her like that." The woman had slashed her wrists.

Two more heists went down that night. On Saturday morning the hospital called and said that somebody could talk to Bernard Heinz, and Rodriguez went over to see him. He was lying flat and still in the narrow hospital bed in a three-bed room; he'd been transferred from intensive care yesterday. There wasn't any sign of the wife, though it was during visiting hours. The nurse had pulled the curtains around the bed so there was an illusion of privacy. Heinz looked at the badge Rodriguez showed him and moved his head weakly. "I've been expecting you, of course. I suppose I'm under arrest."

"Technically, yes, but you can't be moved out of here for a while." Kitty had felt sorry for this man and Rodriguez's tone was gentle. "Where did you get the gun, Mr. Heinz?"

"Oh, I had it. I bought it about ten years ago when the crime rate began to get so bad. I don't really know much about guns. They checked to see I didn't have a police record," and the ghost of a smile passed across his mouth briefly. "That's funny, I hadn't remembered that until just now."

"Mr. Heinz," said Rodriguez, "we've found out that you have a good job, you've never been in any trouble before, you have a very clean record. Why did you start pulling the armed robberies?"

Heinz shut his eyes and was silent for a moment, and then he said in a tired voice, "It was Lucille. My wife. I don't understand it at all, you know. I know that some people are like that but it was like knowing that some people are drug addicts or alcoholics, it wasn't anything to do with us, do you see? She's always been a good wife, a good mother. We've got two children, Arnold and Gloria, and up to the time they both left home Lucille had enough to keep her occupied. Keeping the house, and meals to plan. Then Arnold got married and then Gloria, and I know Lucille missed them. If they'd stayed right around here it might have been different, but they didn't. The girl Arnold married, he met her at UCLA, she was from Oregon, and her father's got a big CPA business, he offered Arnie a job. It wasn't charity, Arnie's always been good at figures like me," and the ghost of the smile showed again. "He's got a degree in accounting and business management. They were married here and then moved up to Portland, and Arnie's doing fine, he likes it there and it's a good job, he's all set. They've got two children now, a boy and girl, but we don't see them very often, they don't get down here once a year. You've got to let children go their own way, and I'm glad they're happy and doing well." Rodriguez was letting him take his own time. He moved restlessly. "And Gloria, she got married last year in February. She met Ed through the brother of a friend of hers, and Ed's a very nice guy. He's in a good job too, he's an electronic expert, sort of a troubleshooter for his company. They make all sorts of electronic equipment that's used in hospitals and offices. They send him all over repairing them. But the company's based in Chicago and so Gloria moved back there when they were married. They're both good children and they write letters but they're busy and happy and they don't write so often. If they'd stayed here I think Lucille would have been all right, they'd be coming to see us. But you see how it was, Lucille hadn't enough to do, that was it. She's always been a busy person, she never was one for reading or watching TV, and I suppose she got bored and unhappy. And we have friends, certainly, but we've always been quiet people, don't gad around much. At least Lucille never used to. It was a woman she met at a neighbor's down the street, a Mrs. Lentz, that got her going to the card rooms."

"Oh," said Rodriguez. "Down in Gardena."

"I don't know much about that sort of thing," said Heinz. "I never cared much for cards myself, and I know a lot of those things are supposed to be illegal, roulette and blackjack, but some of those places have them anyway. It was just as if all of a sudden she'd taken to drink, and she's lost some terrible amounts of money. I couldn't understand it, I tried to talk to her, show her we didn't have that kind of money, but then she'd win something and think she'd go on winning, but in the end she always lost more than she won."

"Naturally," said Rodriguez.

"We've got the house paid for but everything's expensive now, and she began to run up bills. She used the housekeeping money for gambling, she didn't pay any of the ordinary bills. We had the power cut off and the phone until I scraped up enough. And my salary at the bank's all right, but it couldn't cover all that. It was like a nightmare. I didn't know what to do. I think it's worse than the drink, somebody addicted to the gambling. She just didn't seem to realize what she was doing. She had access to our joint account, and several times she took everything out. She spent all our savings, and the bills coming in and not getting paid. I didn't know where to turn, I was at my wit's end. You see, if they found out at the bank it wouldn't look good. But more than that, she got to owing money to these people and some of them threatened to garnishee my wages, take everything I had."

"You were in a spot," said Rodriguez.

"I've always been an honest man," said Heinz simply. "I never did a crooked thing in my life before. But I just didn't know where to turn, I was desperate. I couldn't stop her, I couldn't keep her locked up, could I? Finally I thought about the holdups. And I was terribly ashamed of myself, and terribly scared too, doing them, but it was the only way I could see to get some money. And now it's all over." He looked ready to cry. "They say I'm going to be all right, but of course you'll arrest me and I'll go to prison, a terrible disgrace for Arnie and Gloria, and what will happen to Lucille God knows."

"Don't you think your children will understand, Mr. Heinz?"

"I don't know," he said wretchedly. "If it had been anything else but dishonesty—a crime—I don't know. But there's no help for it, I did all those holdups and I'll have to pay for it."

Rodriguez felt sorry for him. In some ways he was right, the compulsive gambler was worse to cope with than the alcoholic. Heinz could probably sign a statement. Rodriguez talked to a doctor. He'd probably be ready for release in ten days or two weeks, and then he'd spend a while in jail waiting for trial. Considering his good record he might get off lightly, a one-to-three. And maybe the shock of having her husband in prison would bring Lucille Heinz to her senses, but Rodriguez wouldn't take any bets on it. The compulsive gamblers didn't get cured overnight, or cure themselves.

On Sunday they had another suicide, an elderly man gassing himself in a fit of depression, and that made more paperwork. The only relatives were back in New Jersey and had to be called. Then another body came to light and they all did some swearing about it because it looked like posing some intensive work. The husband had found her when he came home from playing golf about four o'clock. It was an apartment house on Los Feliz and their names were David and Martha Grimes. She was in their apartment, beaten over the head with something, and no weapon visible. The husband was shaken but coherent.

"Of course no one had any reason to murder her—and you ask me to look and see if anything's missing, and nothing is, everything just as usual—" That of course was after the lab men had finished dusting for prints, and Maddox and D'Arcy were doing more overtime. "She was just as usual when I left."

"Was she expecting anybody, do you know?"

"I don't think so—of course it's the beginning of the month and the tenants have been dropping by to pay the rent, Martha was the manageress here as I told you." He was retired; they were both elderly; she had been sixty-nine. "All of them had already been by, I think, except Mrs. Lovelace, and she's often late. That's Mrs. Bernice Lovelace on the second floor."

Maddox grumbled, "I'm damned if I'll do any more overtime tonight, we can talk to the tenants tomorrow. The lab may turn up something."

D'Arcy agreed. "I had a sort of tentative date too, damn it, but Doris is easygoing and didn't mind."

Maddox cocked his head at him. "The last time I heard it was somebody called Rita."

"Oh well," said D'Arcy vaguely. "She's gone to Argentina to visit her sister." On the way home Maddox reflected that it was a pity about D'Arcy. He wasn't really a chaser like Rodriguez, he ought to be settled down with some nice girl, but he had a deep and dark phobia about his very peculiar first name, had them all trained never to use it. And whenever the latest girl found out what it was inevitably she teased him about it and he dropped her. People, thought Maddox, came all shapes and sizes.

On Monday they were out and about doing the legwork. Most of the tenants at that place worked and had to be chased down. The delinquent Mrs. Lovelace was at home, a garishly made-up woman about sixty, and she said she hadn't left her apartment all day, hadn't seen Mrs. Grimes. Another woman had been in bed with a cold. None of the tenants had, according to them, seen anything of Mrs. Grimes on Sunday. They had all spent Sunday at home, except for a couple who had gone to a wedding. The lab was still processing the latents they had picked up in the apartment.

Maddox and Rodriguez got back to the office near the end of shift, and Rodriguez said, "At least there's nothing to write a report on." He stared absently at the desk blotter.

"You're acting a little vague lately," said Maddox. "Anything wrong?"

"Why should anything be wrong? I'm still thinking," said Rodriguez abstractedly, "of having a look around there where the blonde picked up Fischer, somebody might recognize a description."

"The legwork for nothing," said Maddox. "Damn it, there's something right at the back of my mind trying to get through, and I'm damned if I can think what it is."

"I expect it'll come to you," said Rodriguez.

On Tuesday morning Garcia called and said, "This Grimes thing. There were a lot of prints in that apartment, but they all belonged to both of the Grimes."

"Hell," said Maddox. "That's a big help. It couldn't have been the husband, he's alibied up to three-thirty and she was probably killed somewhere around noon by the look of the corpse."

"Sorry," said Garcia. "We can't make bricks without straw."

The deputy D.A. they'd talked to about the Martinez brothers called and gave Maddox an interim report. They were due for arraignment sometime next week, but probably the hearing wouldn't come up for some time; the courts were backlogged as usual.

Grimes had given them the names of friends and acquaintances, and they would all have to be interviewed and questioned. Any of them might have some information, not realizing it was valuable as pointing to the killer. If the place had been ransacked they would know better where they were, the ordinary violent burglar—though burglars were seldom violent unless they were high on something—batting the woman over the head when she tried to put up a fight. As it was, it was just up in the air. And there was still the faint bell ringing in Maddox's head about something, but what it was wouldn't come to him. He spent the whole day looking up the friends and acquaintances with D'Arcy and Rodriguez, to talk to, and came back to the station to compare notes. Nobody had come across anything useful. Nobody had apparently seen Mrs. Grimes lately but her husband, and apparently she'd had no difference of opinion with anybody.

As it happened, Rodriguez lived in an apartment on Los Feliz, another one. Sometimes he cooked for himself, but it was easier to go out. He stopped at a restaurant for dinner, and at eight o'clock was contemplating the phone, feeling absurdly adolescent and nervous. Finally he dialed and the warm contralto voice answered him.

"Oh, Miss O'Flynn. This is Detective Rodriguez. I just thought you might like to know what we found out about Mr. Heinz, you were interested."

"Indeed, and what have you found out?"

He told her at some length. "Now there's a terrible shame, isn't it?" she said. "The poor fella, he wasn't really a criminal at all, and I'm glad I was there maybe to save his life."

"I just thought you might be interested," said Rodriguez feebly.

"Yes, I am, and thank you for telling me."

At the moment he couldn't quite get up the nerve to ask her for a date.

There were still reports to do on Grimes, they hadn't talked to all the acquaintances yet, but on Wednesday morning Rodriguez left that to the rest of them and went down to the vicinity of that parking lot near Fischer's furniture store and surveyed the block. It was a rather typical block of business. Besides the furniture store there was a coffee shop, a small gift shop, a variety store, a hardware store, a women's dress shop, a paperback bookstore, a pharmacy on the corner. The furniture store took up most of the block. Across the street was a big Chrysler agency, a used car lot at one side, an appliance store, a theater advertising porno films, an optometrist's office, an art supply store. He contemplated a day's work, talking to everybody at those places, probably all for nothing, but you had to start somewhere. He started with the pharmacy, asking about the blonde, and drew a blank. He really didn't have a good enough description. He proceeded on to the gift shop. By eleven-thirty he had crossed the street and was walking into the Chrysler agency. A hopeful salesman came up and said, "What can I do for you, sir?"

"I'd like to ask—" Rodriguez began, and then the words died on his lips, because he had just seen the blonde. She was twelve feet away from him, sitting in a little cubicle at a high desk, with a sign over it, *cashier*. She was a fairly good-looking blonde about thirty, and she had her left profile to him and the mole was clearly visible, like a beauty spot.

"I'll be damned," said Rodriguez to himself in surprise. And then, "Can you tell me your cashier's name?"

The salesman was also surprised. He said, "Why, Mrs. Abbott. Eleanor Abbott. But why—"

"Has she worked here long?"

"Why, about two months, but why—"

Rodriguez went over there and pulled out the badge. He showed it to her and said, "Mrs. Abbott? Police. You're coming downtown to answer some questions."

"For God's sake, what about?"

"About some armed robberies," said Rodriguez. She stared at the badge, at him, and then she came out with a very rude word. Rodriguez put her in his car and drove her back to the station, and she was silent all the way.

He ushered her into the detective office ahead of him. Maddox was there alone. "See what I've found," said Rodriguez.

Maddox looked at the blonde and began to laugh. "Beginner's luck?"

"Or fate," said Rodriguez. They took her down to an interrogation room and meticulously Rodriguez told her about not answering questions without an attorney present. She just shrugged, and got a cigarette out of her bag. He lighted it for her.

"Mrs. Abbott, it's very probable that those station attendants will be able to identify you. And possibly Mr. Fischer will too—he was your latest cat's paw. Would you like to tell us something about it?"

She took a drag on the cigarette, and said, "Oh hell. I don't know how you spotted me."

"Mr. Fischer noticed the mole," said Rodriguez.

"I knew I should have had that doctor take it off."

"It was quite an ingenious little idea," said Maddox, "in its own way. How did you come to think of it?"

She shrugged again. "Seeing I've lost the throw I might as well tell you. I was in a bind when I first thought of ripping somebody off. I've never done anything like that before, you'll find that out. I was just going to get the divorce, and the lawyer was dunning me. My late no-good husband had stripped the bank account. I was still living down on Crenshaw, I was at the other agency then, in Gardena, and I thought about it, and I got the idea because of my car. I've got a Jaguar sports coupe, it's old as the hills and I'm about the tenth owner, but it's a car you'd notice. That's why I got the idea."

"And very nice," said Rodriguez. "It worked just fine."

"Yeah," she said. "I got caught up on some bills, when Ed walked out he stripped me and I owed rent. Then Mr. Butler asked me to come up here, he owns both agencies and the other cashier had quit. So I moved up here a couple of months ago." She supplied an address. "The rent was higher up here, damn it, and then the TV went out on me, and so I did a couple of other jobs. I never thought there was any way the cops could find out about it, I've never done anything wrong before, I haven't got a record."

"Where did you get the gun?" asked Maddox.

"Ed left it when he walked out. At first I was going to pawn it, and then I had the better idea. At least it seemed like a better idea at the time," and she looked rueful.

Rodriguez laughed. "Would you be willing to sign a statement, Mrs. Abbott?"

"Well, I suppose I've got to be a game loser. Why not?"

Rodriguez typed the statement and she signed it. He arrested her formally and took her over to book her into jail. "You're allowed a phone call, you know. You can call your lawyer."

"Yes, I know. I don't like that guy so good, and I don't know any other lawyers. I think I'd better call my brother Frank, he'll get me a decent lawyer, and I suppose there'll be bail."

Rodriguez went back to the office to put through the machinery on the warrant. Maddox was rereading a report on Martha Grimes. Rodriguez reached for his phone. Maddox's phone rang and he picked it up and said his name. And twenty seconds later he sat bolt upright and said in a loud voice, "My God! My God, I knew there was something— I'll talk to you later." He put the phone down.

Rodriguez eyed him curiously. "What was that?"

"Deputy D.A.," said Maddox. He was staring at the opposite wall. "As soon as he said something about the cut-up corpse the bell rang and it came to me."

"What?"

"Lovelace," said Maddox. "Mrs. Bernice Lovelace. Talk about the classic cases. I remember seeing in the paper a couple of years ago that she was out."

"Out?"

"Of Tehachapi. It must be twenty-five years back, she'd have done the full time. It was a front-page case at the time. I've run across it in the true crime collections. She must have done quite a stretch."

"For what?" asked Rodriguez.

"She murdered her husband," said Maddox, "because she'd got hold of another fellow with more money. No reason she shouldn't have divorced him, but instead she banged him over the head with a hammer and cut up the corpse and buried it in the backyard. The other man didn't even know she was married."

"For the love of God," said Rodriguez mildly.

"Only of course he was missed, his sister got suspicious, and we went looking and found him. The papers called her the Veiled Lady because she wore a veil all through the trial."

"My God," said Rodriguez, "are you thinking she could be the one on Grimes?"

"Well, it's like getting olives out of a bottle, César. The first one's always the hardest. I wonder what she's living on. But I think we take a closer look at her."

"Let's go and have lunch first."

They found her at home and asked questions, but she just simpered at them through the mask of makeup and denied that she'd seen Mrs. Grimes that day. Maddox called out the lab and asked for the full treatment, and Mrs. Lovelace told them it was an invasion of privacy.

The lab took its time as it generally did, but on Friday morning Baker called Maddox and said, "Jackpot. The hammer in Lovelace's kitchen still had some blood on it, and it's Mrs. Grimes's type, A. Lovelace's prints were on it."

"Thank you so much," said Maddox. Before they went to pick her up he was curious enough to call Welfare and Rehab, and eventually got hold of her former parole officer, one Steve Farrow. She had spent twenty-four years in; that far back the courts hadn't been so lenient. Farrow said, "So what do you want to know about her?"

"What the hell is she living on? That's a nice apartment."

Farrow laughed. "Oh, she inherited a nice little bundle from the other man." He was cynically amused. "Evidently the guy was besotted about her, never thought she was guilty. He paid her defense lawyer. He died just before she was released and left her everything he had."

"My God," said Maddox. "The vagaries of human nature."

"Why are you asking?"

"Well, it looks as if she may have done it again," said Maddox. "You'll be hearing."

They brought her in for further questioning and spelled it out to her what the laboratory evidence was. She fidgeted with her heavy gold bracelets, but she wasn't simpering any longer. "You killed her," said Maddox, "didn't you? You went to her apartment and hit her over the head with the hammer. Why?"

She looked at them defiantly. "Always asking for the rent, saying I was late paying it. My investments haven't been doing so well lately. I was thinking of moving to a cheaper apartment. And when I explained to her that I couldn't pay for a few days, she was inexcusably rude and I'm afraid I lost my temper. That's all."

D'Arcy said, "Short and sweet. You'll be going to jail, Mrs. Lovelace, and after another trial you'll probably be going back to Tehachapi."

She said in an expressionless voice, "Well, it's a little lonely being alone after you've been used to other people around. I can't say I really mind."

That night Stoner was cruising his regular beat about ten o'clock. He was down on Virgil. This was all business here, and of course everything closed up at that hour, the public parking lots empty, so he noticed the car parked in a loading zone right outside a big appliance store. He slowed and crept past, looking, and saw lights inside the store.

Burglars? he thought, and then dismissed the idea. The car was right in front in plain sight, a four-door Ford, and there was a U-Haul trailer attached to it. Probably the legitimate owner was just moving some merchandise. But he wasn't sure that those lights weren't flashlights instead of regular lights, and it might be just as well to check. He copied down the Ford's plate number and was just about to get out of the squad when he got an urgent call to a heist up on Vermont. That took priority, so he lit out on that. But at the end of shift at midnight he had a word with the watch commander and left the plate number with him. "You might pass it on to the detectives, in case that was a burglary."

"Will do," said the watch commander. He left it with the night watch, and Brougham left it on Feinman's desk with a note.

Saturday was Feinman's day off and he didn't see that until Sunday morning, and after he'd talked to Dowling and read the latest report he said, "Well, by God, don't tell me we're going to get a break on that at last." That had been a burglary all right on Friday night, the owner had called in yesterday morning. "By the grace of God the Traffic man spotting the car in front—it was that damned ring again—" He shot the plate number up to Sacramento.

When Communications called back five minutes later, Maddox had come over to talk about Mrs. Lovelace. Feinman interrupted him to answer the phone, took down the information, and scratched his head. "Now why the hell does this ring a bell in my mind? Wayne Cross. But that had to be the car the ring was using, and thank God we've got a line on them at last."

"Wayne Cross?" said Maddox sharply. "What about him? The burglary ring?" Feinman explained.

Maddox said, "My God in heaven. It can't be. It mustn't be."

"Do you know the name? It just rang a faint bell with me—"

And Maddox said tautly, "He's a Traffic man on the graveyard shift." They looked at each other. "Let's go and see if he's home."

And Maddox had completely overlooked the fact that Cross's apartment was on Kingswell Avenue, two blocks from Barnsdall Park. It hadn't seemed remotely important.

He was home, and he looked at them there in the open doorway, and Maddox thought since the other time he'd seen him Cross had lost weight and looked sick. "What was your car doing outside that place where a burglary was going on, on Friday night?" asked Maddox without preliminaries.

Cross backed into the living room, and his voice sounded dead. "It's all over. It's all over, thank God. However it gets over. Whatever happens. I'll tell you all about it. I was going to get out, tell them I'd had enough, and wanted out, but I was afraid if I did that right away they'd suspect it was me—on Don. Everybody's been talking about Don, of course."

"Oh, Christ," said Maddox. "Oh, no."

"I'll tell you all about it," said Cross. "I've been in hell. He was my best friend. I don't know how the hell, why the hell we got into it, it was crazy. But it snowballed." He started to tell them about it, sitting on the couch with his big hands clasped loosely between his knees. And they'd never thought it could be anything this bad.

"It was Tom Hearne," he said in that dull dead voice. "He'd just got married, they put a down payment on a house and he needed a lawn mower. He didn't have enough credit. He was mad at the guy for turning him down. Tom and I are pretty good friends, he was riding swing then. He said he'd pay the guy when he could, all those places are insured, it seemed like kind of a joke. He couldn't put the lawn mower in the squad, so I met him there and took it, and he picked it up next day. He pulled that one right on the job, while he was riding his beat, broke into that place. And while we were there I saw a calculator I could use, I took that. And it was all so easy, it still seemed kind of a joke. And Tom told Jeff Tanner, they were at the Academy together, and he came in. It just snowballed, I don't know why or how, it was a crazy damn fool thing to do." Maddox and Feinman were listening appalled. Three of their own, three men from this force with its high proud standards. "It all went so smooth," said Cross. "It didn't seem exactly wrong, kind of a hobby. All the same we knew it was wrong. Tom found a fence, he talked to some street informants and found one. But you only get about a third of the value, you know. And then we had the idea about the swap meets, we'd get more there. They're on weekends, and both Tom and Jeff were riding day watch then. We used to pull the jobs on swing watch hours. Jeff was off on Saturday, he moved some of the stuff at the swap meets then. We picked up all sorts of stuff. We used to stash everything at my apartment or Jeff's until we could move it. And then we got those typewriters at the office-supply store. I'd been transferred to the graveyard shift. And Jeff wanted to see his girl that day, so I said I'd cover the swap meet that weekend. It was three weeks ago today." His voice was still dead. "I ask you, how the hell could I have expected to see Don there? How the hell? It was a crazy place for him to be. And if anybody asked, I was supposed to have the typewriters for sale because my uncle was closing out his store, but I couldn't say that to Don, he knew I don't have an uncle. It wasn't anything he could miss, it wouldn't look queer to anybody else but of course Don knew right off there was something wrong about it, me sitting there with five brand-new typewriters and a pile of calculators to sell. Of course it looked funny, it looked wrong. He didn't say anything but hello, but there was a queer look on his face. He just looked at me and at the stuff. And I knew he wouldn't say anything to anybody— until he'd seen me and asked how come. I knew he'd come to see me and ask. And I couldn't think of one damn thing to say to him, I couldn't make up any halfway plausible story. It was like I was kind of numb. He'd have liked to have heard a story he could believe—we were friends. But I just couldn't think of anything. I knew he'd come. I just packed up everything and left, and later I told Jeff and Tom I hadn't had a bite on anything.

"Don came that night, about eight-thirty. I couldn't think of anything to say, to do, and I told him everything." And they could imagine Dunning's reaction. "I was feeling desperate and all of a sudden it was all staring me in the face. My whole career gone, and I begged him—I begged him to give us all a chance—we'd quit doing the jobs and somehow repay everybody for what we'd taken. I begged him—but he was like a rock. He wasn't a man to excuse anybody for being dishonest, he saw things in black and white. And I keep seeing his eyes—there was such awful contempt in his eyes. He said we weren't fit to wear the uniform. And he'd blow the whistle on us, I knew—I followed him out to the landing, I was still begging him to give us a chance. And he was right at the top of the stairs, and he turned to say something else, I reached to get his arm, keep him from leaving—and he stepped back and tripped and fell all the way down the stairs on his back and knocked himself out."

"Christ," said Maddox again.

"I went down after him, that lobby's all cement, he was dead out. And I had to do something. I wasn't thinking straight—but he'd blow the whistle, he'd ruin us all—and I found where he'd parked his car and I dragged him out there—it's a quiet block, nobody around—and put him in it. And I knew he'd have the gun on him, and I found it and I shot him. My best friend. I just went driving around, but I had to do something with him. I had to show up for briefing for the midnight shift. I drove out to the Strip somewhere and I threw Don's gun out into the street." So Arturo Martinez had been telling the truth after all. "I put him up there in the park, and I left his car in that lot and walked home. I don't know how I got through the shift," said Cross. "If we'd been running two-man cars I never would have—anybody could tell—something was wrong with me. I don't know how. And I was afraid if I told Jeff and Tom I wanted out they'd know I'd had something to do with Don. And now it's all over and I don't care. I'm glad it's over, the whole stinking bloody mess." He put his face in his hands.

"You know what you've done, don't you?" said Maddox icily. "This is a top force, we've got the top reputation in the country. You've let down every man on this department. The papers will have a field day with it, the crooked cops, the cops gone to the bad. Every man on this department will be getting less respect and trust for quite a while, all on account of three cops who went wrong."

"I know that," said Cross in a muffled voice. "I know. I'm glad it's over." He stood up submissively. "I'm ready to go."

It would make the headlines, and a lot of people would be happy to see the cops on the defensive, hauled up in court. There were things to be done and they did them dutifully, but without much interest. The Martinez brothers were released and the warrants withdrawn. Warrants were issued for those three and they were booked into jail and dismissed dishonorably from the force. There were interviews with the Chief in all the papers.

The usual run of cases came along to work, and they went at the work with less enthusiasm than usual.

That Wednesday morning Rodriguez was glumly typing a report when Kitty O'Flynn came into the office. "Ah, you're here then."

Rodriguez looked up in gratified surprise. She sat down in the chair beside his desk. "I just thought I'd tell you, I went to see the man in the hospital. Poor Mr. Heinz. He's a nice enough fella. We had quite a talk, and do you know he tells me his wife was raised a good Catholic.

I've been wondering now if maybe Father Casey at St. Mary's could help the poor woman get over her foolishness. I'll ask him to see her."

Rodriguez said skeptically, "Well, I can't say I've got much time for the church."

"You ought to then," said Kitty severely. "It never does any harm to pray about a thing and times it does a lot of good."

"Well, maybe you're right," said Rodriguez humbly. "Maybe you'd let me take you out to dinner and we could talk about it."

She considered him and then showed him the dimple. "Well, I daresay that would do no harm either."

Maddox was still feeling at odds with the world when he got home. At least, as usual in August, the weather had cooled off a little. He went in the back door, kissed Margaret, and made himself a drink.

In the living room John Ivor was in the playpen staring dreamily up at the ceiling, with the brindle bulk of Tama vigilantly near.

Sue regarded him wisely and said, "It'll die out of the papers eventually, darling. It's just a thing we have to take in stride. It really doesn't matter what labels people wear, they all come good, bad, and indifferent."

Maddox began to feel a little better. "When you come to think of it, a cop of all people should know that."

"Relax and roll with the punch," said Sue. "It's all we can do."

"Women always think they know all the answers."

"Well, mostly we do," said Sue simply.

Maddox laughed. But looking at her fondly, at the baby, he began to feel a lot better. And presently Margaret called them to dinner.